SABRINA

AND THE

LADY

BOOK I OF THE COMUS

DUOLOGY

SONYA LAWSON

Names, characters, businesses, places, events and
incidents are either the products of the author's
imagination or used in a fictitious
manner. Any resemblance to actual persons, living or
dead, or actual events is purely coincidental.

TABLE OF CONTENTS

Epilogue

A NOTE TO READERS

This book involves references to and instances of
violence, domestic violence, and sexual assault.

DEDICATION

To the friends who've shared laughter and tears, ideas and emotions, hard times and wild nights. Love you all.

PROLOGUE

She ran as the branches snapped backward, whipping around to stay out of her way. She pushed forward blindly, tears streaming down her face while she pumped her legs hard, running full tilt toward nothing in particular. Every so often she thought she heard them coming up behind her, stomping soldiers bent on her recapture. All she knew for certain was she was clear of the Palace and would never return. Never. It was the only way to keep herself and everyone else safe.

All her senses were heightened, pushed to the limit by the magic that poured out of her without intention or direction. Trees were upending, whole trunks shoved aside at impossible angles to make room for her. The ground rumbled beneath her feet. She vaguely registered the sound of screams when a large sinkhole opened up directly behind her. A group of guards had been right on her heels, but now there was blank air and the fading sounds of men falling into a deep, dark pit.

She thought about none of this on a conscious level. She was deep in flight mode and her magic seemed to work through her, fighting as she scrambled. There was no rhyme or reason beyond escape, survival; getting away as quickly as possible. Her magic seemed to know only that. Everything in front of her bowed inward, scurried backwards, twisted and turned to get out of her way. Everything behind her closed ranks, created steep hills, thrust jagged rock out of the earth, released creeping vine to burst forward at hyper speed to tangle and twist and impede any who would attempt to follow. There was no plan, no thought or organization, just the drive forward, far and away, and the desire to stop what came from behind at any cost.

As much as the earth wished to meet her, wanted to help her in all ways, it could not control her limbs for her. She was stumbling over her own feet, and eventually, she went down hard, her chin crashing and scraping against the forest floor. She took half a second to suck in air, grit through the pain, and then sprang up as fast as she could, helped by an upward swelling of the ground, a gentle lift of soil bringing her to her feet. She started off running again and this time was a little more steady, a little more mindful of the path directly in front of her, how one foot planted while the other leaped forward, propelling her farther and farther away from all the horror and pain and hurt that she left in The Palace.

Big, wrenching sobs clogged her throat. Tears streamed down her face, but she couldn't voice them. If she started, she knew it would have no end, it would go on and on, carrying years of pain into the night air.

After what felt like hours of running blindly she began to slow. She heard no one behind her, but she was on her guard still. Magic was noiseless after all, and she needed to keep an eye out even if her ears told her she was alone. She walked now, briskly but without the stumbling frantic pace from her initial escape.

When she became aware of her surroundings, she found herself deep in the Wilde Wood, which meant she had somehow ended up far beyond Summer Forest, which surrounded the Palace. She walked toward a birch, tall and mighty, and touched its bark. It had been so damn long since she had touched anything of the earth. He had kept it all from her, afraid of what would happen. When she stroked the bark, the tree seemed to shiver, and it began to glow faintly before it burst forth with a mass of red leaves that immediately fell to dance in the wind around her, unable to hold their tentative place on the winter-slicked branches. She backed away from the tree, now afraid to touch anything for fear of causing pain or chaos to the land.

Too much going on in her head, her heart. Too much to sort through. She needed a plan, but she had nothing. Nowhere to go that she could easily reach. No one was near to help. Even if they were with her in this place, or she could miraculously find The Falls where her family now hid, being around her was a danger in this moment because of her uncontrolled magic and the forces that stalked her from the Palace. She missed her old home, she missed the Palace from before, she missed her family and her Queen and her ideals of love now horrifically dashed. She had missed her magic, and now it frightened her because she knew not how to rein it in at this moment. So much to do, to think, to remember, to fear, to hate. Too much. All too much. She finally gave it voice, scrunching her tear-stained face and releasing a scream so fierce and desolate, so filled with magic and loss and pain, that when she caught her breath afterward, she saw her wail had literally ripped a hole in the night air.

Another forest poked through, wild in its own right but smelling of strange soil, utter stillness, and, oddly, a hint of humanity. She approached the split with wonder. She knew of no one who had ever torn through the veil of the realms with only a scream, no spell craft or intention. But it was just what she needed. A spell was traceable — formal magic scented the air, lingering long after casting and making it easy to follow. Her magic in that moment seeped everywhere, pouring out of her in a continual stream without a definitive ending point or anchor. Comus could not trace this type of magic, mostly because it was something new and unknown. Wouldn't even consider the possibility of this wild, unwieldy magic because it was something far beyond his own power and therefore inconceivable to one such as him. No one in Comus' power could come close to figuring this out, either. None of his lackeys had even the hint of that type of power because Comus liked to always be unquestionably the best and most powerful in any room.

Gin could do it. Maybe Mother. They could possibly find her again. They would be the only ones she would want to find her, as defeated and disgraced and dangerous as she was. It was her out, her way to save herself and the rest of Fae. After making up her mind, she slipped through the tear in her reality.

From the other realm, surrounded by new trees and earth and air, she watched the hole in the night heal itself without her intention. Knowing she was in the human world, untouchable by hate or love, apart from all she knew for good and bad, she felt adrift, but also relieved. She did not know this place or the people who inhabited it, yet it did not matter. She was safely away from Comus and utterly alone for the first time in years, her only companion the dense, cold, untouched forest. She breathed a sigh before laying on the leaf-strewn ground and introducing herself to this other earth.

PART 1: SABRINA RISES

Sabrina fair,

Listen where thou art sitting

Under the glassy, cool, translucent wave,

In twisted braids of lilies knitting

The loose train of thy amber-dropping hair;

Listen for dear honor's sake,

Goddess of the silver lake,

Listen and save.

John Milton, *Comus*, 1634

CHAPTER I

Most in Wilde had no need to navigate the deep, dark

curves of Ludlow Lane this late at night. It was all

dense forests and dark trees with only a few patches

of open fields, a deer stand here and there, and one

lonely house nestled deep in the woods. This house

— cottage and nursery to be more precise — was the

sole reason Sabrina was out in the night. She didn't

mind. It was early spring, so while night still came on

quickly and a chill lingered in the air, there was also

a promise hanging there, like you could smell the

leaves ready to escape their winter prison and sway

proudly on the now bare branches. Taking a deep

breath of that brisk but promising night air, Sabrina
plowed forward, the headlights of her old Cavalier
gliding through the inky pools of shadows that
stretched across the lane as the country miles ticked
by. She sang along loudly to old Mavericks tunes
blasting from her speaker, filling the night with
engine whines and throaty twangs about lonely and
foolish hearts.

Wilde, the seat of Castle County, was a
small town at the base of a coal-mined mountain in
the foothills of Kentucky's slice of Appalachia. Some
may say people are the same everywhere, which is
somewhat but not exactly true. Small town folks are
like any humans — both good and bad in turn. But a
type of isolationism is sometimes bred in such spots,
and Wilde is no exception. While it grew, it never
boomed like other towns or counties around it. If
developers tried to come in and do too much, they ran
into trouble, whether that was legal trouble from the
city council or illegal trouble from neighbors taking
the initiatives to warn people away none too kindly.

Still, individuals in the town, though wary of
strangers, were mostly regular folks. Sabrina was
considered odd by those in Wilde who knew her, but
in reality there were few that still claimed to know

her. She had been raised here, these were people Sabrina had known her whole life. Hell, she spent thirteen years with many of them in the same classroom, going to dances and band practices and running the high school yearbook staff. That didn't matter much now, though, because many saw Sabrina as someone high-and-mighty, as they would say, even without proof of this. She had just committed the cardinal small-town sin, which made her a bit of an outsider in a place she had been born and raised.

Sabrina had left when most had stayed. Those from Wilde who went to college after high school usually went to one of the small private religious colleges nearby or studied at the local community college. She had thought about staying, had gotten scholarships to local schools and assumed she would stay where she was, living with her Gran in their old farmhouse and hanging out with her high school friends for the rest of her life. She had felt a certain level of comfort in the knowledge the people she cared for, the place she had always known, would stay the same. She had lost her parents when she was seven. They'd both died in a car crash on I75 after having a quick weekend getaway in Lexington. Her father never talked of his family. Her mother was an only child, raised by her single mother in Wilde. You might think that would be taboo in a small town, but people everywhere understand sex and need. Gran raised Sabrina's mother on the small farm she had inherited.

When her mother and father died, she moved in with her Gran. They were the only family each had, and they clung to each other in their grief and loneliness. It wasn't a dreary life for them, though it held pain and loss. Gran loved to laugh — big belly laughs spurred on by good stories or strange events. The two had a life filled with big and small joys. It was a relatively happy childhood for Sabrina, tinged by an overarching sadness based in grief she could never quite shake. She learned early that life gave you both and you had to take the good where you found it as you worked through the bad. Gran loved to say "We laugh so we ain't always crying," and it was dark, but true as far as Sabrina could see.

This meant she was content as a teenager, and none-too-eager to see that change. She and Gran weren't rich, far from it, in fact, and to go to college at all was a big deal. She needed all the financial aid and scholarships she could get, but the private colleges around her weren't too keen on giving someone that had no home church or religious upbringing a large chunk of money. She thought she would have to work full time, take out loans, and do what she could to get a degree in some field that didn't hold her interest but offered a comfortable living, like radiology tech or nursing. Both vital professions, sure, but neither really appealed outside of the paycheck. However, late in her senior year, she got a better offer from the University of Louisville. Their financial aid package meant she could work less during the school year, take time to explore what she wished, and be free to choose what she wanted to study for four years.

U of L was not exceptionally far away, just a few hours by car, but a few hours can seem like eternity when you're young. It was also in the middle of a big city — the biggest city in the entire state of Kentucky as a matter of fact. It was well outside of what she knew, and she had considered passing on their scholarship. Gran knocked sense into her though, quite literally.

As Sabrina sat at their small kitchen table and whined about the travel to and from, the size of the city, the size of the campus, and any and all other things she could think of as a reason to not go, Gran walked up behind her and gave her a sharp smack in the back of the head. It didn't hurt, not really, but it was definitely unexpected from a woman who had only ever hugged and kissed her granddaughter.

Sabrina, shocked, turned wide eyes on Gran, who stood behind her with her arms crossed and hip jutted. "Look here, little miss. Those are just excuses to not do something that would do you a world of good. You need more than this house, this town. You have a chance. Get gone and be happy in the going. You'll come back, to stay or to visit we can't say, but either way you'll be better for having left."

Sabrina huffed, Gran tsked and turned away, but Sabrina did think on it more and decided she was brave enough to take that leap. Her Gran packed her up, carted her off, and dropped her in Louisville with a wave, a smile, and a few tears.

University life was new and different, and for a while she wanted to stay firmly planted in her old life by getting rides to and from Wilde every weekend. That first month she was there she was so homesick for the small town she had always known, she cried often. Rides out to the foothills were scarce though, and soon her sadness was replaced with everyday worries and new friends and learning and books. The books are what really kept her in place. When she had visited U of L late her senior year, she had been awed by the library. From the interior view of campus, the outside wasn't much to speak of — a brick and concrete block that rose out of the quad and seemed to loom a bit. However, at any point during the day, as soon as you went through the shaded doors, all you saw was light. The front of the building was all windows, from floor to multi-leveled ceiling, and sunlight poured in across stacks and study tables and suspension staircases that led up, up, up into a maze of books.

Sabrina had always been a reader, a lover of books from a young age. She found solace in books when she was grieving the death of her parents, knowledge about the world outside of her small town, comfort in both old and new stories told to her like a secret whispered in her head. Books were important to her, and here was a beautiful home for so many books. She quickly applied for work study in the library and was lucky enough to get chosen. She worked there all four years of undergrad and majored in English, a department housed in Bingham Humanities Building, at the peak of the shadow of her beautiful workplace and second home — Ekstrom Library.

She loved working in the library, loved her English classes, and kept on going. She had no desire to be an academic, no big dreams of professorship for her future, but she liked classes. She enjoyed learning and could get lost in research mode easily. She stayed on at U of L and got her MA in English Studies, working first at the writing center then as an instructor, teaching First Year Writing courses to Freshman. She liked the work of writing, research, and teaching. It was mellow and thoughtful and engaging all at once. She may have even stayed longer in school, gone on to a PhD program, if her Gran had stayed well. But at the very end of her MA, Gran found out she had cancer. Sabrina moved back home after graduation, took a job teaching writing at the same community college where so many she'd known went for classes, and cared for her Gran.

Gran fought hard to stick around, but she couldn't hold on in the end. She died less than a year after her diagnosis and Sabrina was left alone. Forced to sell the home and most things in it to pay Gran's medical bills, Sabrina had enough left to stick a small single-wide trailer on a plot of land her family owned since her great-grandfather moved down the mountain. It was out in the wilds of Wilde, away from everything, and Sabrina's mindset at the time appreciated the isolation. After time spent grieving and going through the motions, she looked up to find she not only had no family left, but her so-called friends had left her behind as well, and there was little for her in Wilde beyond teaching, visits to the graveyard, and daily walks through the small copse of trees that fringed the land where her trailer sat.

Luckily, those trees brought her to Nina, and Nina was the reason she was happily driving down a dark and winding road at 8:30 on a Friday night in April.

CHAPTER 2

Sabrina met Nina about two years ago, back when mourning still hung heavy around her. She wanted to buy a new tree to plant on her land to leave her own mark on the small wood passed down through her family. Raised on a farm by her Gran, who gardened and grew both food and pleasure, she knew enough to know she did not know enough about trees to just randomly go buy something and stick it in the ground. Sabrina was no arborist (though she did know that fancy word) and she rarely planted. Since Gran's passing, she managed to grow one tomato plant because she wanted to remember the taste of sunshine her Gran gave her through those ripe red globes.

It worked fine, but she ended up with too many, and she didn't have the will to care for the plant properly, so it drooped and tomatoes fell to the ground, rotting where they lay beside the concrete blocks serving as makeshift stairs at the back door to her trailer. Because she wanted something to last, something that would always connect her to her family, she needed to do better. Better started with getting some expert advice.

After a Google search (which is a good place to start on most things, even if it is never the end point) and a Facebook discussion with an old high school classmate who ran a construction crew that worked on a lot of houses and outdoor spaces out in the county, she landed on Nina's Nursery. The nursery itself had little online presence — an out dated, one-page website with a phone number and address that looked like it was created using the most generic template available and a Yelp page with minimal, though great, reviews was all Sabrina could find. She called and did not expect what came from that first conversation. The hello she got after a few rings was husky yet melodious, the throaty voice of a woman that had a presence to her words, even when it was a short, clipped greeting.

"Hi…um, is this Nina's Nursery?"

"Yes." Silence. Waiting. Sabrina hesitated a beat when she heard nothing more, but plowed ahead.

"Yeah, okay. I'm, uh, looking to buy and plant a tree. Could you help with that?"

"What type of tree do you wish to acquire?" the voice asked, now showing at least some interest in the conversation.

"I don't really know. I know nothing about trees. I just want to add something to my land?" she answered with an uptick of her voice, a vocal habit she had that came out when she was hesitant about an issue or answer. It made some statements sound like questions.

"How much land will the tree have?" the woman, who she imagined to be Nina, asked. It was an odd question. Sabrina thought she meant how much space would the tree have to grow, but it sounded a little off. More like the woman wanted to know how much land the tree would come to claim for itself, like the tree would own part of Sabrina's lot as it began to grow.

"Well, a bit. I have a small grouping of trees already. They're close together, but not too close. Like, I'd say, maybe three feet apart or so? But it's not planned or regular distance between each or anything. Three feet is, like, average? Altogether, it takes up about an acre of land before it bleeds into a field that's not mine. I'm not good at judging distances or whatever and I've never taken an actual measuring tape to the woods. Can't be sure. Anyway, I wanted to add something to those trees. Maybe along the inner edge? My kitchen window faces out the front of my trailer and I'd be able to watch the tree grow from there. I walk around out in the trees. I like their height and sturdiness, so I want something that will match that and grow quickly. I just want something that feels right next to what is already there. Like a part of it even if it isn't original, you know?"

After Sabrina stopped her rambling about the trees and feelings, there was a beat of silence where she thought she had lost the arborist, or the woman was confused by her tree tirade. Then she heard a soft sigh of appreciation. It was a gentle hum, something Sabrina herself did when she was caught up in a book or a movie and liked what just happened. It was a bit of savoring Sabrina didn't expect in this conversation.

"You feel trees, so you must take the time to feel what will do well there. I cannot help you do this without more information from you and the land. I can come walk with you and give suggestions, then you can come to my nursery and we can walk more. Find the tree that fits with you and the others. Where do you live?"

Sabrina gave her the address without thinking. She usually didn't like people coming out to her place. In fact, she hadn't had anyone in her trailer since the workers had come to set it up and connect everything. Part of that was grief and loneliness, but part was also that she liked her own space. She was an introvert at heart. The idea of walking with this whiskey-voiced woman didn't seem quite so bad, though. Sabrina said okay when Nina declared she would be at her place at 8 the next morning, even though that was a little too early for her.

Still, bleary eyed and thinking about the coffee brewing in her trailer, she waved from her porch as a giant white dual-wheeled GMC Sierra drove up her gravel drive.

The woman who hopped down from the cab was not what Sabrina expected. She was petite, tiny even. She likely hit just at 5', but her frame was in perfect, lovely proportion to form a miniature hourglass figure. Her thick chestnut hair bounced around her head in a disheveled halo, the type of hair that you could tell she did nothing with but looked like sun-shot brown silk regardless. It was the same with her clothes. She wore work clothes, but they appeared to be just … more on her. Grubby jeans, a plain white tee, and a faded flannel looked like high fashion draped on her body. The thick Columbia hiking boots she wore didn't look clunky on her small frame. They added to her look, which projected effortless, disheveled beauty from head to toe. The sun shone right in her eyes, but somehow, they were still wide open without sunglasses or shade, and the sparkle in her large hazel irises matched the sweet smile she gave as she stared right at Sabrina.

Sabrina felt shitty in that instant. Here she was, a black faded U of L sweatshirt and yoga pants stretched across a body a little rounder and plumper than the social ideal, dingy Reeboks on her feet and crusties still in the corners of her squinting blue eyes. She touched her hair, thinking the dirty blond locks wrapped in a messy bun somewhere near the crown of her head were strictly disheveled without the effortless beauty part added. When Nina got closer, however, her eyes brightened and her smile widened even more, and she reached out a hand as a small offering. In that instant, Sabrina felt calm. She was at ease and forgot any comparison brewing in her head when she confronted the openness and warmth that was Nina.

"Oh, Sabrina. It is lovely to meet you in such a glorious place. Thank you for allowing me here, on this land." As far as greetings, Sabrina found it was a little odd, but nice.

She took Nina's hand as she'd failed to do so when first offered and they stood there for a moment, clasped together. It wasn't a handshake, it was a hand holding. It also wasn't awkward, which was surprising for Sabrina. She spent a good part of her life feeling awkward. It was somehow comforting. Both seemed to think so because a long minute passed before Sabrina let go with a little laugh and said, "You are very welcome. And nice to meet you, too. Would you like to come in for coffee or go walk or walk then coffee or, you know, whatever?"

Nina laughed, a throaty and full burst of mirth at the rushed offers Sabrina was happy to make. "Let us walk first," she answered, "then we shall talk over warm drinks." She looped her arm with Sabrina's, tucking close to her side like they were about to share some whispered secret while circling a parlor in a BBC period drama, and led her down her own porch. They walked like that, arm-in-arm, feeling the woods, making occasional comments, and learning of each other as they strolled.

During that walk, what would be the first of many together, Sabrina noticed Nina's tendency to tilt her head and squint a bit when listening to her. She looked the same when she stared at some of the trees, almost like she was giving them equal attention, as if she listened to Sabrina and the woods and the little plot of land when she picked the place the new tree would go.

At one point, the pair reached a large, damaged elm. Nina frowned at it and Sabrina began to ramble. "It was hit by lightning years ago. You can still see the singe marks high up. It looks gnarly and bad, but it's strong. It survived. It's grown. If there's more I can do for it, let me know."

"Oh, no. Leave it be," Nina said, walking up to the trunk, laying her hand on it in a soft caress. "It has seen enough, this one. Proven it will fight to survive and grow. It deserves to be left in peace. Given space to thrive or flourish depending on its own."

"Like most people," Sabrina muttered, maybe a little bitter.

Nina turned her way, studying her face again, a serious expression on her own. "Yes. That is true. People do need space. Need peace. But both people and trees also need care and connection. We creatures of the earth are all the same, in the end. We survive or thrive, depending on what we are given or what is taken."

Sabrina locked eyes with Nina and felt drawn to her. It wasn't romantic or lustful. It was a sense of kinship, a feeling that, although she did not know this woman, what she heard her say, what she felt from her, denoted something important. Sabrina was lonely, lacked human connection, but was afraid to reach for it. Nina sensed that, maybe even felt the same, if the feeling behind her words were any indication. Sabrina may have imagined it, but she hoped not. When she allowed Nina to take her arm again and continue their stroll, she hoped something was planted there between them. Something like a garden, a thing to be cultivated so it could bloom.

* * *

Of course, Nina helped pick the perfect tree, a lovely cottonwood that flourished. However, planting that tree was not the end for Sabrina and Nina as a pair. They soon started hanging out regularly, falling into a friendship that was easy and natural. Nina's grace and warmth helped soothe Sabrina's lingering grief, and Sabrina's humor and rambling excitement about things seemed to bring Nina enjoyment. They weren't exactly opposites, but they were different enough they smoothed each other out like good friends do, gave differing perspectives on life and all the things in it in a way that made living a bit more interesting for each. Adult friendships could often be awkward and hard to maintain, but they seemed to fit together in a way that worked for them. Love was there, mellow yet strong, the kind you find only with good friends over years. It just developed quickly for Sabrina and Nina.

All this made Sabrina happy to come out at Nina's call on a Friday night. The plan: eat pizza Sabrina picked up in town, drink wine Nina had stored away, and laugh or cry, depending on the topics of conversation and what rabbit hole they meandered down. As most often happened when the two connected, all this would last well into the night.

The two-lane highway that led from the local pizza place/gas station combo to Nina's place could be treacherous, but Sabrina knew the roads of Wilde well. She navigated the sharp curves with a little too much speed, as most who grew up in the country did. Hell, she'd learned to drive by the time she was nine, and she had been weaned on these windy county roads long before she got her license at sixteen. It was second nature to her. She rounded the curves and crested steep hills while crooning along (a bit off-key) to "O What a Thrill," letting the mandolin and fiddle seep in and calm her, even as the lyrics made her a little sad, thinking about all that more she was starting to want in her life.

Sabrina slowed and cautiously turned off at the bottom of a steep hill onto a hidden drive. The sign reading "Nina's Nursery" was concealed, more than a business sign should be. In the darkness ahead, she saw the clear outlines of Nina's massive greenhouse structure. It dominated the top of the hill, a glass castle shimmering in hues of blue and green from sunup to sundown. Sabrina loved the warmth of the greenhouse. That was the point of all greenhouses, really, but Nina's seemed to burst with more life somehow. The greenhouse felt like part of Nina, not just her business, and that may be why few people came out here or even knew of the place.

Nina was oddly selective with customers coming and going. She sold a lot to farm stands dotting the countryside, in the multi-county farmer's market that was held twice a month rain or shine at a large local fairground, and by word-of-mouth business that allowed her to pick and choose who came and who she delivered supplies to when they might need them. Sabrina didn't understand business at all, and this made little sense to her, but Nina seemed comfortable and never complained about money or her work, so she figured Nina knew what she was doing.

One of the reasons she likely didn't encourage too many customers was around the back of the massive greenhouse structure. If you followed a narrow gravel lane around the left side of the greenhouse and down a ways into a little hollow at the base of her hill, you found her home. It was pure Nina: a small cottage that was cute, petite perfection, just like its owner. Also like its owner, the cottage was all comfort and warmth, at least for Sabrina. The front porch, home to wicker rocking chairs with soft cushions and a white wooden porch swing that always had a quilt thrown across its back, faced the small drive and offered a beautiful view of the shining greenhouse on the hill. The house itself, seemingly built from varied gray-toned stone, was a simple, square. Single-story structure that held only what Nina needed, a single bedroom, a bathroom, a living room, and an eat-in kitchen. It was the definition of quaint, a real-life version of the Thomas Kinkade prints every Kentucky woman of a certain age had hanging in their house.

Sabrina, used to the cute, paid little attention as she flung her car door open after parking next to Nina's huge truck. Her keys jangled in her hand, and she smiled at the feel of the large glass keychain there. It made her smile often, the gift Nina made for her, a glass vial filled with the last of her Gran's dandelion wine. It even had a tiny, shimmery dandelion that floated in it. The gift made her think of

Gran and Nina both, two women who made her happy. She bent into her car, stuffing the keys in her ever-present backpack and grabbing both it and the warm pizza from her passenger seat, when she heard the screen door slam shut.

"Good evening, Sabrina," Nina yelled her way. It was an idiosyncrasy Sabrina noticed early on — Nina was very formal in her speech.

Sabrina chuckled to herself as she rose from the car with her hands full, nudged the door shut with the jut of a hip, and gave Nina a head nod with a lolling "Sup?" in return.

Nina was all smiles and jokes. "I knew it must be you. I could distinctly hear what you consider singing for the past five minutes. Are you listening to The Mavericks once again? Does anyone other than yourself listen to them?"

"Hey, now. They were a favorite for some people for a very brief time in the 90s. Show some respect."

"Ah, yes. How could I have forgotten? Forgive me," Nina stated in mock humility, giving a stiff, perfect bow.

Sabrina put on her best fake British accent to snootily reply. "Yes. Do correct yourself. I will

tolerate no such disrespect in the future! As Queen, I
do not allow such tomfoolery in my presence."

Nina chuckled. "What Queen Sabrina
demands shall come to pass. I can think of far worse
rulers than you, my friend, but would still not wish to
incur your mighty wrath. Come now, let us eat pizza
and drink wine." She opened the door for Sabrina and
followed her inside.

She deposited the pizza on the table,
plopped herself down hard in a chair while slinging
the backpack to the floor, and sprawled for a second.
"Ugh. It was a rough day today, friend," she told
Nina.

"How so?" Nina asked, pausing by her with
concern etched across her face.

"Oh, just end-of-semester things. The usual.
Students asking for extensions and extra credit.
Division heads and Deans asking for us to work for
free on committees and projects over the summer.
Basic and predictable annoyances that are still extra
annoying sometimes." Sabrina waved it off.

"The people of that institution take
advantage of you. I fear you do too much."

"And you don't? You work every day in
your nursery."

"That does not feel like work to me, Sabrina. It is part of who I am."

"So is what I do, in a way. Not really, though. More like a forty/sixty split if I'm being honest. I love to teach. I love to learn. I hate when people try to take advantage, which is often. I hate the system and how it exploits and fails people; me and students. Also often."

"I wish more for you."

"Of course you do, lady. You love me," Sabrina said with a grin, getting up to help Nina, who was now gathering dishes for their meal. She grabbed stemless wine glasses from a cabinet while Nina pulled old cloth napkins from a drawer. They moved around each other in the kitchen easily, dancers in a choreographed number they performed many, many nights over the past two years.

"That is truth, my Sabrina," Nina said, flashing a smile as she piled napkins and plates on the table. "However, it is also a general truth that your position in that place affords you little power and you are often used abysmally. It is unfair to you, as it is unfair to all like you."

"It is what it is. For now, at least. Can't change the system. Maybe one day I'll win the lottery and leave that place behind." Sabrina flung open the pizza box, taking a gooey slice from within and not even putting it on her plate. It went directly into her mouth. She savored for a moment and paused between bites to add "Though, I'd have to actually start playing the lottery for that to happen."

"A game unplayed is never won," Nina quipped between bites of her own slice.

"Oh, thanks for those wise words. How about you spend money on lottery tickets and just split your winnings with me if you hit it big?"

"I think not. No risk, no reward."

"And the platitudes continue."

"I am full of such wisdom."

"Gotcha, lady. Guess I'll have to earn my millions on my own. Then I can leave behind this life of drudgery and live in luxury for the rest of my days. Until then, though, I can be happy knowing I don't have to serve on committees this summer or teach summer classes and I'm a handful of papers away from having final grades done. There is light at the end of the tunnel."

Nina filled the glasses with wine, lifted her own and said, "Cheers to you, then, my friend. May your grading be swift and your summer season be beautiful."

Sabrina grinned and nodded, thinking that would be nice. It buoyed her spirit, as did the pizza and company overall. She changed the subject, asking Nina how her nursery was going. It was not a sad evening where the two worked together through pains, past and present. It was jokes and sarcasm with some sitcom viewing thrown in for good measure. It was a laugh-filled night, which was good. Much crying and worry would come later, so it was a good thing they let happiness rule that evening.

CHAPTER 3

It was less than a day after she left Nina's cottage and Sabrina was pulling back into that hidden gravel drive. She came bearing gifts, though. She'd picked up two white mocha lattes at the coffee stand in town to surprise Nina, though her friend's was decaf. An early afternoon coffee break and another quick visit was what she needed. Sabrina spent hours grading final papers from her students. When she finished the last batch and posted grades early, she felt that familiar lifting of weight the end of a semester brings for any instructor. It was an ease of stress, even if fleeting, so she wanted to celebrate. Sabrina decided she'd treat herself and her friend a little before she went off to do adult things like buy groceries and clean her car and run other dull Saturday afternoon errands around Wilde.

Sabrina knew Nina had likely been working for hours at this point too, so she stopped in front of the greenhouse instead of driving around to the cottage. She balanced the two cups one atop the other and reached for the entrance door when the sound of multiple voices finally registered over her own soft humming. Not wanting to disturb her friend if she was with customers, Sabrina figured she'd prop the door a bit to check real quick. If it seemed Nina would be long, she'd wait in her car. On that thought, Sabrina looked around and marked there weren't any other cars besides her own in the small gravel lot. More curious, she leaned in to listen and sneak a peek.

The first thing that had her hackles up was the tone. It sounded like multiple people who were all edging towards annoyance, maybe even anger. What she saw through the crack in the door didn't help. Nina was standing with her back to the entrance, hands on hips, leaning in toward three people that seemed to loom over her. In the middle stood a tall man, dark skinned with close cropped black hair and beard. All Sabrina could think when she saw his face was that he looked regal. It was partially his face, achingly beautiful but seemingly untouchable, that made him look like long-lost West African royalty landed in the middle of Kentucky. He also had a sneer on his lips that told her he thought a whole lot of himself and a stiff, attentive posture that fit better with soldiers she had known in her life. He was looking down on Nina, both literally and figuratively, and disapproval was written all over him.

To his right was another man, shorter but by no means short or small. He had a wide smile and looked like he would laugh at any moment, but Sabrina felt like it was forced laughter, a way to cut the tension caused by the harsh tones Nina and the middle man were exchanging back-and-forth glances. He stood less stiff, but still at a ready stance, willing to step in if need be. He was beautiful too, in a more open way. He had a bit of a Mediterranean vibe, like a Greek man ready to offer jokes, a laugh, and all the ouzo you could stomach.

The third figure, standing to the left but distinctly apart from the two men, was vaguely Asian, androgynous, and covered in an old-time friar's robe. It was a voluminous coat, roped off haphazardly, with bell sleeves and a cowl that highlighted the sleek, elegant neck and close-shaved head of the person, which was all Sabrina could see of figure. They looked thoughtful, pensive even, and seemed to be staying out of the conversation while focusing intently on Nina's words and body language. They were also gorgeous, like Nina and the two men in front of her. Thick brows and high cheekbones framed a face beautiful yet serious (unlike the man on the right) but not stern (unlike the guy in the center). Sabrina took all these visuals in quickly then tuned in to what was being said.

"You know—" Middle Man said, tsking a bit at Nina, who cut him off quickly.

"Yes, I do know. I know as no one else knows. You are the one that does not know. You come here not knowing what awaits all of us if I go back and fail."

"You? Fail? Psst. Not happening," Right Man said, dismissing what sounded like real fear from Nina. Middle Man gave an annoyed sound at this and raised a hand to silence the man. He stepped closer to Nina, although he seemed to be addressing the robed person to his left.

"Borjigin, I tire of this as you must. Explain to her what we have seen and heard. Make her understand, as we do. She must come with us. Now."

"Mo…" the robed person said slowly, shaking their head, because they seemed to be the only other person who saw what Sabrina could see in Nina's locked stance. She was going nowhere.

"You think to force me back? You think you hold that power?" Nina scoffed at the Middle Man, a little recklessly in Sabrina's opinion, but she liked the fight in her friend. They both might need that.

"Oh, Little One, you have been long in this land, amusing yourself with your plants. You have forgotten. Not all things bend to your will so easily. There are those who are a match for you."

"Mosi. We have not sparred in many long years. You are the one who has forgotten who and what I am."

"Now, now, do I have to stand between you two like…" the man to the right said, strolling forward casually but cautiously.

"Do not interrupt, Sergius. Little One needs a reminder, and I gladly offer one here and now," Middle Man bit out. Suddenly, in a blink, a long golden spear popped into his right hand and a bright shield appeared, covering his left hand and side. Sabrina had no idea how that happened, but she wasn't going to let Nina face some weird man with odd, old weapons alone.

She dropped the lattes and stepped firmly into the greenhouse. All four figures in front of her froze as she pulled herself up to her full height and loudly asked, "What the fuck is going on here?"

The robed figure blinked rapidly, Middle Man's face registered surprise that quickly turned to a narrowed stare, and the Right Man gave her an appraising head-to-toe. Nina looked both stricken to see her friend charging to her defense and ready to vomit as she mouthed her friend's name. No words escaped, just a whoosh of empty air. Sabrina faltered, because all that from Nina was disconcerting. The Middle Man turned to the Right Man and, with gritted teeth, clipped, "Take care of this."

"Oh, I'll take care of her," Right Man drawled, stepping forward with a cocky smile.

In a flash Nina was beside her, holding her hand. She whispered, "Please forgive me Sabrina. And try to understand." Nina dropped to a crouch, plunged her hands in the pebbles that made up the greenhouse walkway and muttered in some language

Sabrina had never heard in her life. Suddenly, the cocky man headed toward them was pushed back by a literal wave of earth that swelled up from the ground beneath his feet. At the same time, the plants growing in the nearest section curled outward, forming a living wall as dense as an untouched jungle. It came chest-height to Middle Man, who began to hack away with his spear. It was fruitless though. More plants filled in any empty spaces left by the whack of his weapon.

The robed figure shouted sternly, clearly fed up with the antics of the others. "This has gone too far! Mo, put away your weapons. Serge, stand down immediately. Nin, stop manipulating the plants. Call back the earth. Let us all talk in peace. No force. No harm. Your human can even stay."

At that last bit — the human bit — Sabrina's body jolted and she looked wide-eyed at her best friend. Nina was sad, defeated, and seemed very, very tired all of a sudden, visibly deflating after all that bluster and bravado.

"Human?" Sabrina whispered.

"Yes, Sabrina. Human. Unlike me, or the others now in my greenhouse."

With that shock to her system her brain stopped firing for a second. Sabrina's legs felt wobbly and gave out. She fell with no grace, as per usual for her, and heard Nina's sharp cry of alarm right before her head connected with the corner of a plant rack and the world fell into blackness.

CHAPTER 4

Sabrina slowly woke to a pounding head and a room full of people she didn't know. Sprawled rather unattractively on the couch, she tried to back up quickly.

"Oh, no. You are safe, dear. I swear upon that. You are safe," the robed figure from the greenhouse said as they reached for her. They had kind eyes, a soft voice. It was meant to sooth. She imagined it would if she actually knew this person. As it was, she was in general freak-out mode and would not be calmed.

"Sabrina. Please." Nina begged from the floor by the couch. Her friend sat there, stone still and hesitant, but beside her, offering protection or support. Maybe both.

"What the fuck is going on here?" she repeated. It wasn't shouted with bravado this time. It was said on a hush, more to herself than to any particular person in the room.

"Sabrina?" Nina asked, lifting her hand up to brush away some of her messy hair from her bewildered face. Sabrina flinched, avoiding her hand. Her head hurt too much at the moment, but she could see her reaction saddened her friend, who hung her head down and fought back tears.

"Look, I don't know what's happening here, or why, exactly, I woke up with a headache on Nina's couch. But you need to give me answers. Right now." She said this first glaring in turn at every stranger in that room. Then, facing Nina, she softened her voice. "Nina. Lady. You okay?" she asked as she reached a hand out to her.

"You pulled away from me," Nina stated, taking her hand.

"My head hurts, babe. I didn't want you to touch it." Sabrina smiled weakly. "We're good. At least, I think we are. As long as I get some answers about what the hell all this nonsense is about."

The robed figure snickered, then reached out for Sabrina, stopping short of touching her. They waited, a question in their eyes, and indicated they needed to check her head with a slight nod. Sabrina, still scowling, hesitantly nodded and they proceeded to lift a bandage from her head.

"The swelling has subsided," the figure muttered, like they noted it casually to themselves and not to the room at large. Their voice strengthened and their eyes focused on her. "First, as for the headache, you fell onto the corner of a table in the greenhouse. I was able to stop the bleeding quickly and give you some medicinals. If you allow them to sit longer, rest more, your headache will soon fade and the injury will heal completely."

"Okay. That answers one question. Now, for the rest. Who even are you? Why were you fighting with Nina? And what did all that human business before mean?"

Nina gave a heavy sigh, stood, and began formal introductions. "Sabrina, these are members of my family. The man at the kitchen table is Mosi, or Mo. He is my eldest brother." Mo gave a swift nod and a soft grunt that could be construed as a hello. Pointing behind her, she went on, "This is Sergius, or Serge. Also an older brother." Sabrina took in the smirk from lush lips and scoffed as he purred, "A pleasure, my lady." She touched the arm of the robed figure and softly said, "This is Borjigin, or Gin. They are my cousin, my former teacher, and a much-trusted friend." They smiled back at Nina and offered a small bow to Sabrina. Then, reaching out a hand, clasped Sabrina's in their grip.

"An honor and a joy to meet you, Sabrina of Nin, daughter of Cheryl and Michael."

"What now? My name is Sabrina Powell. Where did Sabrina of Nin come from?"

"Ah, yes. Thank my little sister for that one. It was swift, and without your consent, but it beats waking up alone with a headache and no knowledge of anything that happened before. Or of 'Nina.'" Oddly, Serge put her friend's name in air quotes.

"Nin? No Nina, but Nin?" she asked, turning to her friend.

"Yes, Sabrina. Nina is the name I use here, in this realm. It helped me blend in better. It is far more average, and forgettable, than Nin, Princess of the Green, daughter of Inanna and Fannon."

"Princess?" Sabrina asked, becoming more incredulous by the minute.

"Yep. Our Little One was made Princess of the Green decades ago. At least 80 human years," Serge stated, a clear trace of pride in his words.

"Eighty years?" Sabrina whispered. It was like all she could do was repeat phrases in the form of questions. It was too much for her to question on her own. None of it made sense, and her head hurt, and Nina, no, NIN, looked so worried.

"You are not helping, Serge," Nina/Nin gritted through her teeth.

"Sabrina?" the one called Gin gently asked, waiting until they snagged Sabrina's gaze with their own. "Do you trust Nina?"

"Yes," she answered, without hesitation.

"Do you care for her?"

"Of course," she said, annoyed someone would question such a thing. Nina — Nin — whatever. Whoever. That was weird, definitely. If she was honest, it was also a little hurtful. Regardless, that woman was her sister, no matter her name.

"Then let her explain. She will tell you all, but it may take time. For now, Nin, give her answers to the most pressing questions."

"Yes. Of course I will. The most basic answer to all of this is that I, and my family, are all Fae."

"Fae. Like fairies? Or elves? But, you know, *Lord of the Rings* elves, not cookie elves. Obviously. You're small, Nina, but I mean…" She gestured up and down with her hand pointed at the now standing and slightly looming Mo, who cocked his head to the side in confusion.

"Yes," Nina/Nin said with a nod. "Like those elves, not Keebler elves. However, we do not call ourselves that. We are also not of your world. Our realm is adjacent to the human lands, but apart from them. What some physicists might call another dimension, only accessible through the most powerful of magics."

"Magic?"

"Yes. We are magical beings, some more magical than others. Some with certain gifts that make them powerful."

At this Sabrina started laughing. Despite the pain in her head, it bubbled up, causing her to throw her head back. It wasn't a mirthful laugh, but hard and brittle and disbelieving. "Nina, honey. Did you hit your head? Or is this some elaborate prank? Am I being Punk'd right now?"

"It is no joke," Mosi stated, crossing his arms and looking exceedingly annoyed with Sabrina.

"Magic isn't real. I mean, I wish it was. If I could have my dishes wash themselves, that would be awesome. But, sadly, it's not going to happen."

Nin sighed and looked down at her hands. "There are many reasons why I wish it were not so, that what we are to tell you was some fever dream. But the dream has been my time here, with you. The reality is, I am Fae."

"Sabrina, do you remember what happened before your fall in the greenhouse?" Gin interjected.

"Yeah. It was weird," Sabrina admitted. "He pulled a spear and shield out from somewhere I couldn't see. Then there was that stuff with the ground and plants." She stopped there, thinking. A rational explanation of what she saw had to be there, but nothing sprang to mind in that moment. She thought it had to be her head injury. Or her memory was fuzzy. Or her eyes played tricks on her. Those things couldn't be magic.

"Not enough?" Serge prodded. "Okay. Demonstrations are in order. We all have different types of magic, different specialties, if you will. We will show you. Want to start off, Mo?"

The darkly lovely man gave a sharp nod of assent, willing but also grudging. "I have metal magics, meaning an affinity toward the use and manipulation of metal." With that, he waved a hand vaguely in Sabrina's direction. The silver necklace she wore — a small clover charm given to her by her Gran when she was a teenager — lifted from her chest, waving slightly in the air as it hung suspended. She started, grabbed her chain, and clutched it tight in her fist, moving herself further back into the sofa in defense.

She scuttled further in when Serge strolled over, hand outstretched as if to calm. "Sshhhh. Sabrina. Sssshhhh. You are fine. You are well. We will never hurt you. You are Nin's and, through that bond, we are yours. Peace. Peace. Peace." The words washed over her in a wave, bathing her in soft sensations. Sabrina loved words, always had, but had never felt a physical caress from them. Now she did, and she found her body responding, pulling itself out of the couch, leaning toward the handsome man inching closer to her.

"That is enough of a demonstration, Serge," Gin muttered, and Sabrina felt the loss of the words. The sensation fell away, but it was only after it was gone that she even noticed the effect at all, and she looked up at the man who had done that to her.

He shrugged sheepishly. "I have word magics, which means I'm more effective at using language to do things. It does affect some more than others. It seems you have an affinity for words, fair Sabrina. I will keep that in mind and be more careful in the future. I promise." It wasn't much of an apology, but she somehow felt he was being sincere.

She was now sitting less defensively on the couch, and Gin sat gingerly beside her, giving her a wide smile. "Sadly, my magics are less obvious. I can heal, as you have seen, but that is mostly learned. I am a scholar, an expert in magical theory and history. I also teach."

"Sabrina is a teacher and a scholar as well," Nina added.

"Lovely," Gin said with a smile. "But, my demonstration. It is nothing special, by that I mean it is not tied to any special form of magic. It is a spell all master early in their lives. It can, however, be a beauty to behold. Especially if you have never seen it." With that, Gin opened their palm face up, directly in front of Nina's face. A spark flickered there, a flash one second that formed a small orb of light tucked safely in the palm of Gin's hand. "Everyone needs light now and then, no?" they said softly, and Sabrina wondered at the tiny mass shimmering in their hand. Gin closed their fist, and the ball disappeared, leaving Sabrina blinking.

"Sister," Mo said, looking toward Nina.

She looked at her friend, pain and sorrow in her face, and it made Sabrina ache for her. "It is fine, Nina. I mean Nin. Sorry, that'll take some time. I'll try though. Show me what you have."

"I will show you Nin," she whispered, and flicked her wrist in the direction of the windowsill. The small hen and chicks succulent potted there surged and grew, quickly spilling outside the pot and stretching across the window, up the casing, filling the glass. In seconds the entire window was covered by the purplish-green plant.

Sabrina stared at the window for several beats. She was a rational person. A teacher and scholar concerned with truth and proof and knowledge. Earlier that day she would have scoffed at the idea of magic existing. It was a nice idea, confined to stories. Or so she always thought. Confronted with these people, these actions, she couldn't deny. It was magic, but how could she reconcile that?

"It is but new knowledge, Sabrina," Gin added, seemingly attuned to her thoughts somehow. "All new knowledge expands the way we live in our worlds. It is a large leap, I know, but a familiar leap for you, I think."

"Yep. Hard to take in, but still true, Gin. Okay. Say I believe you now, Nin. I have many reasons to after all that. There's so much else I don't know. Like, are there Fae everywhere, all around, and we just never realize?"

Nin offered a swift and straightforward reply. "We mostly stay in our realm. There are thin areas, pockets where we can slip through and find entry easily, but most lose their grip on magic the longer they stay in the human realm, so they return to Fae after only brief visits. Humans also have stumbled into our world before. Humans can be in our realm, but they are affected by the magic of Fae in odd ways unless connected to it through other means, and they waste away or go back through the thin spots to return home. Some have told tales, but humans in general don't believe in us any longer."

"Is there a thin spot here in Wilde?"

Nin shrugged. "Not exactly. Thinner, maybe, but it is a spot that requires great focus and talent to penetrate. Only I, and now Gin, have done it in this spot in your realm."

"So…" Sabrina dragged out, getting her bearings. "You are Fae, like a magic elf. But not exactly. These are your brothers and cousin. They came for a family get-together or something? And why were y'all arguing?"

"Fae is in danger," Mo rumbled.

"Yes. Quite," Serge rallied, "but no need to be so ominous, Mosi. Allow Nin to continue in her own way."

"Thank you, brother. Yes. There are…things, dangerous things, happening right now in Fae. Our politics are sticky at the best of times, just as they are here, but a series of events have caused chaos in our realm. We are traditionally ruled by a queen. The Mae Queen was the reigning monarch. Held that position for eons and was the oldest living Fae. However, she disappeared decades ago. A powerful and malicious Fae filled the hole left in her absence. He and I have a particular history." At the catch in her voice, Sabrina reached out and squeezed her head, sensing the pain there. Nin breathed deep, squeezed back, and continued. "I am here in hiding. Have been for a decade at this point, keeping away from humans so they will not eventually notice my agelessness while staying far from home in an effort to stop him from getting everything he wants."

"And what he wants includes you?" Sabrina asked hesitantly.

"Our Nin is Princess of the Green. That means she is very, very powerful indeed. It is a title earned through magic, not birth. She is one of the most magically powerful Fae living now," Serge added. "It also means she is next in line for the throne. If the Mae Queen does not return, Nin should be the one to take the crown."

Mo moved to hover over the two friends. "We come to take Nin back. She must fight, as horrors in our realm have recently escalated."

"I fled for good reason, Mo. Things are more complicated than you like to admit," Nin asserted.

"Yes, yes, yes. All of this bears much discussion and consideration," Gin piped in, "but, sadly, we do not have much time to achieve these ends. Yet break we must. Sabrina needs a measure of rest still, and our tea is getting cold. Is this a good place to stop, Sabrina? Other questions will be answered, but can they wait?"

She gave a short nod and slapped a quick high five on Gin's outstretched hand, which made Mo and Gin very confused. Nin and Serge laughed.

Gin smiled, staring at their hand with a bit of fond confusion, then turned happily back to Nin. "All settled for now. Let us have tea. Could we possibly also partake in the sweets I saw when in your kitchen?"

Nin said yes and rose to help Gin navigate her kitchen. She paused then eased slowly back down on the couch. She scooted close to Sabrina "Are you fine?" she asked hesitantly.

"Not exactly. This is all a bit much. But we are fine," she assured.

"Are we truly?"

"To be honest, I can't say what I'm annoyed by or worried about or upset over at the moment. But I also understand why I was never told any of this. It's a weird spot to be in for both of us. I still love you though, lady. That won't change. Even if you're not just some human with a wicked green thumb."

Nin stared for a moment, her lips pursed in thought. Then she gave Sabrina a quick but fierce hug and told her to lay back for more rest. Sabrina doubted she would be resting much, now or anytime in the future. Her entire worldview had been upended, and there was little she understood about what that meant. However, she understood her friend, as she watched Nin quietly move about her kitchen. Understood she was the same as before, just a little more than she imagined. Wasn't that the way with people in general, though? All were masses of wonders and contradictions, just waiting for the ones they loved to get to know each new component and accept it in turn.

CHAPTER 5

Whatever the pungent rub Gin had placed on her head was, it did its work well, and now she just had the dull throb of her world being turned upside down to deal with. But, hey, she thought, at least the physical pain was gone. The psychological upending would just take some time to sort through. She eyed Nin (that new name would also take some getting used to) as she sipped her tea with her feet up on the couch.

Nin was at the table, sitting ramrod straight, slightly turned away from everyone else. She was distant physically, but Sabrina could also tell she was holding herself apart from everyone in another way. She and Sabrina had always been open to each other, in talking and in body language — a touch of the hand or shoulder, generous and long hugs, turned toward one another in a way that invited sharing and care. Now, there was a physical distance and she wasn't totally sure of what caused it. Sabrina had to admit she was a bit hesitant.

She couldn't help it. She just found out her best friend in this world was not actually of this world. She was some powerful elf-Fae whatever, and royalty to boot. She had magic Sabrina had seen and felt. She was more than the helpful, caring Nina with a deft hand at plants and making her feel comfortable. Sarina didn't forget she was also that, though. She was still the fast and fierce friend she had come to know. She loved Nin and would care for her always. Her loyalty ran deep and strong. She just needed to tilt the axis of her world back upright with all this new information.

Nin, however, felt the pull away on some level. Sabrina couldn't tell if Nin was giving her space to come to terms or because she was hurt, and that made Sabrina feel a stab of sadness, for herself and her friend and what might now be different between them. She'd try to set all that right soon, when the person hovering at her side let her take a step off the couch.

Gin lifted off the gauze at the side of her head and pressed a warm wash rag to what had apparently once been a pretty nasty wound. "All healed," they said with an easy smile. Gin gently wiped off the excess rub on her head that smelled faintly of sage and a number of unknown spices like some weird concoction someone would put on a fried turkey. "I'll just get most of this off for you. You can wash the rest from your hair later. You'll have a small welt here, maybe some redness, for the next day. After that, there should be no sign of injury."

"How did you do this?" Sabrina asked, vaguely circling a finger around her head.

Gin gave a tight smile "I learned long ago to use natural materials and Fae concoctions to quickly heal those who were ill."

"Can you cure anything?" Sabrina asked, with a bit of a pang, traveling back to those last few months of Gran's life with a new wish in her heart.

"My magic cannot go too far. Some diseases, even in Fae, are incurable. Some wounds are too heavy or magical to heal. I have lost people I have tried to help. I have lost those I loved, even one more adept at healing than I." At this there was a pause, a deep breath that marked an old pain Sabrina felt in her own heart. They continued, "It is not a perfect art, but I do my best. I can see the direction of your thoughts. You have lost someone recently. You wonder if my magical bag could have helped? Sadly, wounds are all that can be cured for humans as of now. The Fae do not have enough knowledge of your diseases and causes to intervene, and we have no real reason to do so. Maybe one day, but it is not so as of now."

Sabrina nodded, muttering, "Silly to think so."

"No. It is not silly to think of those you loved and wonder what more can or could have been done for them. Loving is never silly. I can see you love deeply and fiercely." Gin turned their head to Nin and sighed. "She needed that love, and as someone who cares very much for our Nin, I am glad you gave that to her." Turning back to Sabrina, with a more hesitant smile, they added, "I hope that you, as Nin's own, will be open to my friendship. It would be a blessing to have your loyalty."

Sabrina was flattered by this. A magical being, very powerful by all accounts, wanted to be her friend? She wasn't intimidated by them, though. Gin was a calming presence she appreciated more and more as this endless day wore on. She also suspected their friendship and loyalty would be a great thing. Something sparked questions at that moment.

"You said that before. Or at least someone had. That I was Nin's. Or was 'of Nin.' Or something. What do you mean by that?"

"Gin means you are now bound to Nin formally. She has taken you as hers."

Sabrina startled at the proximity of that deep, rumbling remark and belatedly noticed Mo had moved from the kitchen table and was now seated on the bench beside the couch where she reclined. It was unnerving she hadn't noticed this change. Moments ago, he had been firmly planted at the table, stoic and silent. It was also unnerving to have him this close. She could feel his disapproval like a physical thing. It pulsed from him through his scrutinizing stare.

She also couldn't deny his beauty was unnerving. It was a masculine beauty, but it was undeniable. His skin looked smooth and hard, a dark marble that practically gleamed. Those intense eyes glimmered like the pools of shadows that crept across the deep country roads at night. His hair was short to his head and his face, but still there, a dark shade that broke up and somehow helped define that smooth skin. His lips, full and lovely even in a hard line, sat below a strong nose that flared every now and then.

Sabrina didn't know him well enough to be sure if it was annoyance or anger or something else that caused the flaring, but something in her perked up at the thought of one day learning much more about him. That was odd. Sabrina was usually awed and intimidated by beautiful men, not intrigued. She would shy away, not wishing to know more. She caught herself leaning a little closer and thinking a little harder on him than she would like to admit to herself openly. Mosi presented a stark and tough beauty, intimidating in many ways, but Sabrina imagined it would be glorious and open if he laughed. It was difficult to actually envision that laughter with his hard eyes on her, but she found herself imagining the glory of it nonetheless.

The other brother, who was haphazardly lounged across Nin's glider, sipping tea and munching on cookies, decided it was also time to engage with her again, and chimed in too. "Yes. Little sister made you hers, so you are stuck with her, and by extension, us. Welcome to the family." He chuckled outright when Mo glowered at his words, and Sabrina could tell he did that often. His beauty was also arresting, but more open and inviting. Likely an invitation that many took and he accepted with a laugh and a smile. He came off as cocky and assured in his sexual appeal. Admittedly, he had every reason to be. He was the epitome of a good-time, a walking example of a wild ride. Where Mo was poised beauty, Serge was strutting handsomeness. His olive skin glowed, his arched lips smirked seductively, his sharp nose slashed through a perfectly symmetrical face topped with golden-brown eyes that shined with equal parts sex and mischief. All that glory was framed by glorious waves of dark, luxurious hair. The kind of hair you imagined running your fingers through, but the kind you also thought many, many others had likely run their fingers through, too. Serge was good-time Charlie made flesh, and Sabrina figured he would be a damn good time, as long as you didn't wish for more than that.

Both men, though beautiful in very different ways, were Nin's brothers, so she had to remind herself all that beauty was a non-starter. Sabrina didn't mix lust and friendship, and Nin was more important than any good time Serge had on offer, or whatever brooding heat made her feel drawn to Mo.

"That doesn't answer my question. Not really. How, exactly, am I hers?"

"I bound you to me through a spell. Simple, but effective and lasting," Nin stated dully, before getting up and joining the rest of the group in the living room. She sat crossed-legged in the middle of the floor, staring right at Sabrina but staying away from her to give her physical space. "It is a Fae edict, one of our most ancient and one that is never changing: no human can know of us unless they are bound to a specific Fae. If I had not vowed to take you as mine, Gin would have healed you, and Serge would have cleared you. Meaning you would not have remembered anything: your injury, the scene in the greenhouse, the Fae, or me. It would have been like the last two years were a haze to you, with me removed. It was selfish to do without your clear consent, and I will not blame you for your anger, as it is deserved. I could not imagine you out of my life. I

just found your friendship, and I… I still need it."
That last bit she said with a hung head, as if she were
shamed by what she had done or the fact that she
needed Sabrina.

"Oh, hon," she said, tears now popping in
her eyes. "It's hard to imagine something that would
wipe you from me. You're strong in here." Sabrina
thumped her chest when Nin looked up at her. "In a
perfect world, would I have liked a convo first? Yes.
Did you do what you had to do in the moment so we
could keep each other? Also yes. Can't be too mad
about it because I probably would've done the same.
Now we move forward and deal with any fallout.
Which gets me back to my initial question, which
again, hasn't been answered. What does it mean,
really?"

"We just told you what it means," Mo said
in a huff.

"Mo, she has no frame of reference for us.
She is a thinker, Nin's Sabrina. It is obvious," Gin
said through a smile.

Sabrina felt the need to defend herself. "In
general, I ask a lot of questions. Often. This whole
situation is different, though. I have no idea what is
happening or how your world works or what magic

entails or any number of things. So I'll be asking many, many, many questions throughout all of this." She eyed Mo, then cut away with a haughty sniff. Two could play his games. "Best get used to it now."

"Fire and bravery. Saw it before in the greenhouse. Still there. I like it," Serge purred.

"Now is not the time, Serge," Nin said in a voice that implied she'd repeated that phrase so many times in her life she'd lost count.

"Back to the issue of magic and meaning," Gin inserted before the old sibling back-and-forth ramped up. "The binding is rather simple, but strong. When Nin said the specific words, while holding a part of you and having a bit of your blood — all of which was because of your fall — it literally bound your fate in Fae with Nin's fate in Fae. It is not an issue here, in the human realm. Not even an issue if Nin returns to Fae and you stay here in the human realm, with the sole exception that other Fae who encounter you here must consider you as they would Nin and treat you accordingly. However, if you ever go to Fae, you will be extended magical protection, a shield of sorts, that is part of Nin's Fae life force offered over freely to you in the act of binding. It means you have some immunity from everyday Fae

magics that often negatively affect the average
human and are less open to physical damage done by
magic. It also gives you enough life force to make
Fae's environment non-toxic for you, something that
unbound humans in Fae have serious issue with
overall."

"Okay. It gives me some protection from
Fae here and a lot of protection if I ever go to Fae.
That's it?"

Nin added more. "You may feel my feelings
more acutely when we are in close proximity. And I
yours. Our connection is a physical and metaphysical
thing in some respects now. There are legal and
customary things about it within Fae, but those are
not important to you. You will not be going to Fae."

"We're not bringing her with us? How sad,"
Serge pouted.

"There is no going to Fae, for Sabrina or
me," Nin snapped. "Was it not clear earlier? I. Am.
Not. Returning. If I am not returning, Sabrina
obviously will also not be going. Even if I did return,
she would stay here. It is far too dangerous for her
right now."

"Nin…" Mo hissed.

"Okay." Gin jumped from their seat and clapped their hands together. "Sabrina is tired. She must bathe. She needs rest, and some time in a comforting place. Maybe someone one-on-one to answer any questions she might be afraid to ask Nin. My proposition: I take Sabrina to her home. She takes care of herself, I help, and I teach her whatever she wishes to know, or at least what can be taught before tomorrow morning. You three: behave and have an actual discussion. That means you," Gin pointed a wagging finger in Mo's face, "agree to calm down, stop scowling, listen to what your sister has to say with an open mind and treat her like a logical and responsible adult." He then turned that finger on Nin, "And you will agree to hear out your brother, let him tell you what has happened since you left and why it has forced us to come for you. Take in what he says and think through it rationally. Do not dismiss it out of hand."

Both Mo and Nin looked chastened and grumbled an agreement. It was a miracle to behold, or would be if Sabrina was not a teacher herself. Good students continued to listen to good teachers, even after they left their classrooms. It was a bond not all had and was special when it occurred. Sabrina could tell Gin was a good teacher, and Mo and Nin had been good, thoughtful pupils. Serge, though, maybe not so much. He still lounged with a smile playing across his face.

"You," Gin directed at him with a wave of the hand, "could use some of your own magics to help ease this instead of just seeing how it goes. Smooth ruffled feathers, Serge. That is your specialty. See that talks continue."

Serge nodded in agreement, but still smiled a bit too much for Sabrina to think he would take that completely to heart.

"Well?" Gin asked, turning to her finally. "May I accompany you home?"

"Sure. Why not? I need a long, hot shower and a very stiff drink. Tea won't cut it tonight."

With Mo and Nin sulking a bit and Serge still smiling too much, Sabrina left with Gin. She felt fine to walk and drive, though her thoughts still made her head heavy. Gin had promised to answer her questions, which was what she was after more than a shower and a drink. Still, she looked forward to the hit of hot water and cool bourbon before they played twenty questions.

CHAPTER 6

"So…this is it. Home sweet home and all that," Sabrina muttered as she threw her car keys onto the small table by the door. Gin first slipped their head into the door, wide-eyed and assessing.

"Fascinating," they said. "This is called a trailer? How exactly is it different from a house?"

"Trailers are called trailers because they are literally moved around behind big trucks, like any other hitched trailer. They also have wheels. Unlike Nin's place, this was not built on sight, but created somewhere else, moved here via truck, then hooked up to all utility lines. Also, unlike Nin's place, the trailer itself depreciates in value every year it is here, so…yay."

"But you can move it where you will, at any time?"

"Actually, no. You really can't. Once it is set up on blocks, like this one here, and connected, it begins to settle. Theoretically, it can be moved, but the reality is that if you try to move it once it settles into one spot, you risk destroying the whole thing. This trailer will be here until it falls apart or is hauled away to some dump."

"You sound unhappy about all of this. Why?"

"A trailer is a fine home for someone who cannot afford to buy or build a house. I don't want to seem snotty or ungrateful because I do have my own place, which is more than many have here in rural Kentucky. I just thought I would have more at this point. After my Gran passed, this was what I could afford with the little money left to me. My teaching job doesn't pay much and I do what I can."

"It seems a fine home to me, Sabrina. I am honored you agreed to let me accompany you here and that you would share your space with me."

Sabrina blushed at the small bow Gin offered with this, shook her head, and walked into the kitchen to grab something to drink. "Would you like some water?" she asked, raising a glass to Gin with a nod.

"Yes. Thank you."

"Please, have a seat." Sabrina smiled at them nervously, gesturing toward the small sofa along the wall opposite of the front door. She brought Gin their water, setting it down gently on the chipped coffee table in front of them. Then she began to fidget, something she did often and at the best of times, but also a tell-tale sign the awkwardness of a given situation ratcheted up her anxiety. "Here you go. Please, feel free to make yourself at home. I need to take a shower, so I hope you don't think it's too rude of me to leave you alone for a bit."

"No, no, no. Please, do what needs to be done. A shower will help make you feel better, and likely clear your head." With an absent look around the open but cramped living room/dining room/kitchen area, Gin waved her along. "I will be fine here."

Sabrina shrugged and hurried through the kitchen toward her bedroom at the back of the trailer.

She might have felt bad about leaving Gin, who was clearly a little out of their element, alone in her home. It was definitely not the thing a welcoming young lady should do as a good hostess. Those Southern manners ran deep. However, she was exhausted, mentally and physically, and desperately needed to get the odd scent of Gin's medicinals off of her. Not to mention, she found a few streaks of blood along her neck earlier, and that was just creepy. She quickly grabbed a change of clothes and closed herself into the tight bathroom. The hot water worked wonders, and soon that small space filled with lovely steam. She wanted to take time to luxuriate in it. Just stepping under the hot spray felt like a complete release. She did allow herself a few minutes of blank staring at the wall as water cascaded down and around her. She imagined it washing away not just her blood and the herbal blend that Gin plastered on her, but also her worry and her stress and her apprehension about all that she had learned today.

Of course, her shower water couldn't do that. It may feel like magic on some levels, but she had in fact learned that day that real magic existed in this world, and another, and her water definitely could not do what she had seen Nin and her family do in the greenhouse and her cottage. She heaved a sigh, grabbed her shampoo, and started scrubbing. She could at least wash away the physical evidence of the morning's events, and that was the first step she needed to take to get her head on straight.

When she stepped out of the shower, the soft soap smell of her plain Ivory clinging to her scrubbed and pink-tinted skin, she heard the faint sound of familiar music. Gin found her records. She knew this because her pressing of James Brown Live at the Apollo Theater was thumping through the trailer. She quickly toweled dry, dressed, and pushed a headband through her wet hair then went out to find Gin swaying slightly beside the record player as "Lost Someone" blared from the speakers. When they noticed Sabrina, they swayed her way, offering a hand, and Sabrina gave them a soft grin.

For a few seconds they swayed while facing one another, locked hands to elbows. Sabrina closed her eyes and let Brown take her a little further away, helping relax her even more after that nice shower had washed away some of her grime.

"What is this?" Gin asked, now bobbing their head to the music. "I know it is music, of course. But what exactly is this music? It's so hearty. It has weight. It's…hard to say. But I feel it."

"That's R&B music. More specifically, soul music."

"Fitting," Gin laughed. Opening their eyes, they moved closer to Sabrina and guided her to the couch. "You look livelier. Fresher. You do still need rest, for now, but let us sit and talk, you and I." Sabrina settled and looked to Gin to begin, because, honestly, she didn't really know where to start. "Tell me about your Nina, our Nin," Gin asked.

That request was easy. Sabrina related how they met, how she felt with Nin, how they bonded over pasts that were sad and dark, how she loved Nin's kindness and quiet, her soft humor and solid ear. The hilarious times they had as well as the tears each had shed with the other. Gin let her ramble, as she often did, and nodded every so often, showing they were listening and thoughtfully not interrupting or interjecting.

When Sabrina stopped for a moment, she thought of all she had just said, then became a little upset. "Nina. Nin. Nin was hurt by my reaction to, you know, all the things today. I saw it. I did a little to ease that, but probably not enough. It was all a little much, you know? Hard to believe at first, hard to take in even when I did believe after those demonstrations. I could have done more, probably, but…I just don't know. I've got guilt and hurt and confusion all rattling around inside."

"Nin knows what you were thrust into today. She was saddened by all of it. Do not put that on yourself. She cares for you deeply. She would never have bound you otherwise. More than that, the way she spoke of you and the way she cared for you when you were injured showed me her love for you. Now, I know you care for her just as deeply. I suspected it before, the way you charged into the greenhouse ready to fight for your friend without thought of your safety. That was very brave and loyal. All you said now, and the way you said it, helps me see there was love and laughter there as well. It is heartening. I now believe I can trust you with whatever information I can give to help you better understand what Nin is facing in Fae."

"I need to know more about that for sure. What is she facing, exactly, and is there a way I can help?"

"Whether or not you can help remains to be seen, sadly, but I can tell you a little more about the current issues in Fae. It may help you better understand her — and likely Mo and Serge and myself as well." Gin wiggled a little more into the sofa and looked away from Sabrina for a breath. She thought they would completely pull away from her, put up distance while telling secrets of their own world, but that didn't happen. They turned back soon enough, and Sabrina saw a glisten in their eyes. It would be a sad tale, so she braced.

"There is much to Fae and its beauty and its history I would love to tell you now, but there is no time to talk only of the good. But know that there is much good. There is, however, also much bad. Normally, Fae is ruled by a queen. The Mae Queen, specifically. She has been our monarch for millennia. She is older than all, very powerful, and none have living memory of a time before her rule. She is just and fair, as far as rulers can be, and does all to protect her realm and the beings in it — noble and lesser Fae alike." Sabrina moved to ask a question, but Gin brought up a hand. "I know you will have questions. Please, let me get through some more information before you ask. I will answer all I can, I promise you this. You must first listen."

Sabrina nodded and leaned back into the arm of the sofa, squarely facing Gin to give them her full attention.

"Thank you. Again, Mae Queen is our official ruler. However, she has not actually ruled in a few decades. She disappeared. No one knows where. No one knows why. One day, she was just gone. Fae politics are complex, but the very simple explanation of how it had always worked is that, while the Mae Queen ruled, The Fae Council, a group of five to six powerful and respected Fae, gave advice and helped her in her rule. When she left, the Council began to rule in her stead. Many on the Council said it was simply until Mae Queen was found. However, one man not on the Council was displeased with this and used the power vacuum and confusion to his advantage. Comus, a noble Fae from an old bloodline, wanted more."

Sabrina started at the name, an odd one and something so familiar to her from her past studies that it was weird to hear in this context, but she let it go and continued to listen intently to Gin's story.

"Comus wanted more of everything, but power was the ultimate draw. He quietly maneuvered towards this goal for many, many years without anyone taking any real notice of his machinations. Long before the Mae Queen's disappearance, he lured Nin into a relationship. He was very loving and charming when he wished and it got him what he desired. He was also manipulative and used his time with Nin to groom her. See, our Nin is powerful in magic. In fact, she is likely only matched by the Mae Queen herself. Both can call on Earth magics, an exceptionally rare gift among even our kind. She was trained for a while by the Mae Queen herself, taught secrets of that magic craft I do not even know. She was made Princess after her training, a serious and powerful title in our realm that meant she took a Council seat at a much younger age than any other Fae before her. Comus used his looks and charms and magics to woo her, get her in his clutches, and when the Mae Queen vanished, to position her as a figurehead he could potentially control."

"Now, our Nin may have loved, and love can make us all blind in many ways, but she was never stupid. She did not agree to much of what Comus wanted her to do. That, I think, is when the abuse began." Sabrina blinked hard at this and Gin breathed deep for a moment. "Around that time, Comus discovered two very powerful magical artifacts, a chalice and a wand." Here Sabrina started, sitting ramrod straight, connections and impossibilities screaming through her mind. She took a beat to push those aside so she could concentrate more closely on Gin's words.

"With these relics of ancient and powerful magic, he was able to stage a surprising and bloody coup, overtake the Palace, and lock away our Nin for a time. He believed with more abuse, more control, he could bend her to his will. He set up a puppet Council and declared himself Prince of Fae. Those loyal to the missing Mae Queen were rooted out and killed or forced into hiding. Nin's family tried, again and again, to free her, but Comus' power, now entrenched within the magical barriers and wards that protected the Palace, was too much to successfully overthrow without more knowledge and more planning. Then, one day, we heard rumors Nin had not only escaped, but that she had completely vanished from Fae. At first, we knew this to be true and not just a cover for something more nefarious, because Comus' wrath was a breathing thing throughout our land as he hunted for her. He searched high and low, but to no avail. Still, we fretted for our beloved Nin.

"Eventually, she managed to get a message to me so we knew she was safe and in hiding because Comus planned to bind himself to her in a way that would allow him access to her magics. If he did that, he would be the most powerful Fae anyone had ever seen, and even if the Mae Queen returned, she would be no match for him. Nin fled, to save herself and Fae, hoping hiding would be enough until the Mae Queen was recovered and order was restored. However, things have changed, and we have come to bring Nin back to fight against Comus."

Sabrina was reeling, trying to take all of that in. It saddened her, for sure. While she never personally experienced political intrigue, it can't be fun to live through a coup and such uncertainty, especially when you've had the same leader for thousands and thousands of years. She had also never experienced physical abuse from a partner, but emotional abuse was something she had been through, and assault was familiar in one form or another to all women, sadly. All of it made her heart hurt for her friend and for Fae in general.

Yet, the most amazing thing about all of this was the story was just so damn familiar. It was John Milton's *Comus* playing out in Fae in real time. She was fairly certain of it, but she needed to know a little more to confirm it in her mind. Before she got into more specific questions about the real-to-Fae Comus, though, she needed answers to some more basic questions. More general knowledge would help her determine if the connections firing in her head were accurate or not. She knew so little of Fae and its people and magic in general, she had to start with that foundation before she started rambling on about John Milton's masque.

"Questions now?" she asked.

They nodded and waited for her lead.

"Okay. Let's start with basic knowledge. How big is Fae? Is it Earth size or America size or what?"

"Much smaller than in population. Tens of thousand beings, noble and lesser Fae, in total. In land, about the size of the continental US, or as far as I know of it. However, space between realms is tricky and not foot-for-foot. This is why Fae throughout time have popped up in various lands across the human realm. Like ships passing along a trade route, both Fae and your realm match up in certain spots but never at the same time or in connection with the same area. Nin just happened to land in this space because that is the area where Fae and your world met when and where she crossed over. I was able to come through in her greenhouse at that time because I traced her message to this location and waited for the right time to break through the barrier here. Time and magic function the same exact way in each realm, although the vast majority of magic originates in Fae and must be brought here through an artifact or an individual."

"All right. That answered a few other questions in one, so good looking out." She smiled back at Gin. "More practical issues. How are we talking right now? You clearly understand what I say, and I understand you perfectly. You don't even have an accent. How did you learn English?"

"I didn't. It's a spell of understanding. I'm actually speaking in Faeish right now, you just hear English. And vice versa. It's a basic spell one casts on themselves. It would work the same if you spoke French or Mandarin. Would also work the same if cast on you and you went to a different land with a different language."

"That's pretty awesome. Could I learn that spell? And, in general, could I learn magic, like through studying?"

Gin frowned at her and shook their head. "No. Not if you are without magic in yourself, and I feel no magic in you, Sabrina. I am sorry. If you have traces of magic, which is standard for Fae but extremely rare for humans, you could grow and learn."

"Magic is contingent. Different types of magic exist, and a being is usually adept at only one to any real extent. Doesn't mean a spellcrafter cannot use water magics, or that Nin cannot also use healing spells. Rather, we all have our basic skills enhanced by particular affinities and talents, and there are many types of affinities. All elements, earth, wind, fire, and water, have their own magics, as do all things related to these elements."

"For example, Nin has earth magics, her mother, Inanna, has fire magics, and Mo has metal magics. Language is its own type of magic, and Serge has a hand in that, though spellcrafting is not his calling. He can create feelings with words. There are theories regarding how particular magics may or may not be familial, but Nin's family shows that it can often be tangential at best. Although, each of the three siblings had a different father, which adds an additional genetic variable."

"Yeah, I kinda noticed all of you look, um, noticeably different. Families are like that sometimes, though," Sabrina added with a shrug.

"Fae is a matriarchal culture, and one that does not always value monogamy, at least for the long term. When you live thousands of years, it is hard to stay with just one person. It does happen occasionally, and that is a particular magic in and of itself, but for the most part, it can get dull over many, many decades with the same person. Their fathers are no longer living, but all three siblings were raised and remain strongly connected with their mother. I am an actual cousin, on their mother's side. My mother, rest her, was the elder sister to their mother."

"Gotcha. Now, of immediate concern is the three of you came here to convince Nin to return with you, and in so doing, hopefully save Fae." Gin nodded at this. "Can you tell me what's suddenly so very important?"

Gin hesitated for a moment, finally replying after the weighty pause. "Without leave from the Council I cannot tell you all, as it is a matter of strategy and security. What I can tell you is that we have come to believe Comus has already acquired great power without Nin, and if that is the case, the only person beyond the Mae Queen who could potentially match him would be our Nin. His power grows, so we must sadly ask her to give a great deal, risk all of herself, in order to save Fae from Comus. It is not fair, and I bleed for my lovely Nin, but it is the only course forward we can see."

"I need to know more about Comus," she stated, a look of hurt and anger warring on her face.

"There is little more I can tell. Nin could reveal more to you if you ask."

Sabrina shook her head. She didn't want to force those answers on Nin, at least not right now.

"Well then, he is exceptionally handsome, as most noble Fae are. He is the son of two famous Fae who made themselves known even in your human tales, Circe and Bacchus, though Bacchus was no god as the stories here tell of him. For humans long ago, if they were not cleared, the Fae did appear as gods or powerful witches. The magic, you know. It's one of the reasons the edict for clearing was created. There were too many Fae popping into the human realm, using magic to reach more people, and getting tales told about their exploits. It was embarrassing and dangerous. Fae live long, but we are not immortal, and if humans knew of us, well, the more likely it was we would be hunted down. Your realm does not have the best track record with anything that is seen as different, you know. But back to Comus. Handsome, smart, of a noble line, though orphaned at a young age. He is charming when he needs to be, and intelligent. Very adept at spellcraft, which is language-based magic. It's not as powerful as Earth magic, but very powerful nonetheless. He is also ruthless in his pursuit of power, callous to those he perceives as weaker than himself, which includes most Fae beings, and narcissistic to an extreme. He cares about himself alone and will do anything to ensure he gets what he wants. What he seems to want most right now, and what he may be poised to grasp, is Fae in his total control."

Sabrina finally let out her thoughts, though she was hesitant in her knowledge. "Do you know any John Milton?" she asked Gin.

"No. Is he well known here?"

"Was. Is. Sort of still, anyway. He was a very famous, well-known writer in England in the 1600s. He's known today mostly for his poetry, particularly an epic poem he wrote titled *Paradise Lost*. One of his lesser known works is a masque, a type of court play, titled *Comus*." Gin started at the name, head tilted in rapt attention. Sabrina took that as encouragement and continued on. "In this play, the title character comes across a Lady in the woods, takes her to his hedonistic Palace, and tries to make her drink from an enchanted chalice while he also uses the magic of a wand to control her and others in the Palace." Gin gasps at this, but she is in the zone, so she continues. "In the play, Comus is the son of Circe and Bacchus. The Lady is unnamed, but her two brothers search for her when she is taken, and they have a smart guide to help them in their search. And, in the end, there is another woman, a goddess, named Sabrina, who comes in to help save the Lady. This sounds weird, I know. I barely believe it myself even as I list all these connections, but I think, somehow, this old human play has to be tied to what is happening in Fae right now. There's just too much to be coincidence."

Gin shot up from their seat and began to pace, muttering to themselves. They then spun to Sabrina, ideas shining in their eyes. "There are seers in Fae, of course, but that is a gift few have. True prophecy is even more rare, but not unheard of, and exceedingly important when they are found. This play may just be a Fae prophecy in disguise. I will need to read it."

"Yes. Yes. You need to read this and tell me that all these connections and coincidences are not all in my head." With that, Sabrina strolled into the spare bedroom off the living room and motioned for Gin to follow. She plopped down on the carpet in front of one of the five large bookcases that crowded the small space.

"Your library," Gin said, pleasure lacing their voice.

"I wouldn't call it a library. It's my office, really, where I do my grading and writing and whatnot. I do have a lot of books. Maybe too many according to some."

"Those some would be wrong" Gin stated gravely, "There is no such thing as too many books."

"For sure" Sabrina beamed, turning back to a shelf and reaching for the worn, purple copy of the *Norton Critical Edition - Milton's Selected Poetry and Prose*. She handed it to Gin, who flipped through carefully, handling the book with care.

"You've written in it." It wasn't a judgement, more an observation, but Sabrina felt the need to explain herself, one scholar/reader/teacher to another.

"Books should be written in. You want to hold them, think through them, write down ideas and underline quotes and laugh in the margins. Reading should be interactive in many ways. But that one has many, many notes because I used it to help write my thesis for my M.A., which is also why I have a little more knowledge about Milton's more obscure play than most."

"I see. You studied this writer and became an expert. What else do you have?"

Sabrina pulled down more books by and about Milton. She found an old folder of printed journal articles specifically on Comus in the filing cabinet in her desk. The two scholars sat, Gin absorbed by her stories as she explained more specifics of the play, more ideas about the play from other scholars, more arguments people made about meaning and allusion and detail for hundreds of years as they thought about and produced this play.

Gin stared at Sabrina with wide eyes and when she gave a pause to let them ask questions, they blurted, "This changes everything. Sabrina, this is years of study. I need to read through all of this, understand it as much as possible, but I do not have the time to do so. Comus is poised to strike at the heart of Fae, take it completely. This may well be the key to stopping him. We need you, Sabrina. To help Fae. To help Nin fight Comus."

Sabrina was shocked by Gin's decisive statement. She hadn't thought about the implications of her discovery, the very tangible outcome it could have for her and everyone else. She was dumbfounded and uncertain. It was just a play, wasn't it? Even if it held some tips or tricks or secrets of some kind, it seemed like others that knew Fae and magic better would be far more useful than her. She didn't know anything that would actually help bring down a real-life tyrant, right? That seemed unlikely.

She rose shakily and headed to her kitchen. Gin followed behind, looking both curious and anxious. Sabrina pulled a bottle of Woodford Reserve from the cabinet above her stove, the good stuff she saved for dire need. "I thought I needed this earlier, but now it's absolutely necessary." She got two glasses, filled each with a generous pour, and slugged hers down swiftly, not even stopping to savor the sweet mash taste. She needed the jolt of liquid fire down her throat. She shivered, dropped the cup down on her counter and poured herself another. "Drink up, Gin. We'll likely both need fortification before this is all over and done with." Gin hesitated but joined Sabrina as she lifted the second drink to her lips. They both tipped back, downing the amber liquid and adding fire to their bellies.

CHAPTER 7

Sabrina needed to decompress more, even after those quick shots of bourbon. She ordered some pizza, posted up on the couch, and introduced Gin to YouTube. They watched old James Brown performances for a while and Gin was riveted, asking question after question about music and culture and technology, although she suspected they were just filling time to put her more at ease after her reaction to their declaration in her office. With a belly full of pizza, a bit of a buzz, and the warmth of her favorite throw blanket surrounding her, Sabrina could no longer stifle her yawns. The one she let loose was long and loud, and Gin gave her a concerned look before shooing her off to bed. They said the couch was just fine with them, Gin didn't sleep much in general apparently, and took the extra pillow and blanket from Sabrina's linen cabinet before wishing her a good night.

Sabrina had a lot on her mind, and a sleepless night would not be unusual for her when she was thinking hard on a problem or issue, but that was not the case then. Luckily, she was out not long after her head hit the pillow, drifting quickly into an easy sleep. That sleep didn't last too long, however. In the dead of night, a loud banging on her front door startled her awake.

Groggy and not fully aware just yet, Sabrina stumbled down the hallway of her trailer in her oversized night shirt only to be greeted by Gin and Mo standing in her living room. Fury was clearly pulsing off Mo as he sliced his hard gaze her way. Again, she went with the old standby — "What the fuck?"

Mo's jaw flexed and strained as he gritted out, "Nin has vanished."

"What do you mean 'vanished'?" Sabrina asked with more than a hint of snark in her voice. She didn't like being woken up at the best of times but being woken up to find her best friend was missing was almost too much to take in at that moment.

"I will explain," he stated gruffly, "when Serge arrives. He should be here any moment. Hopefully he will have more information."

Sabrina's mind caught up a little with events and she couldn't help but ask, "How did you even get here in the first place? How'd you know where I live?"

"I tracked your scent from Nin's to here," he shared before turning his head towards the door a bare second before Serge walked through.

There was no sexy smirk or flirty nod this time. He gave a general acknowledgement of everyone in the room with quick eyes before he spoke, "No sign. No trace. Powerful magic was used around the area where we lost her. I could feel that. Otherwise, there was nothing more I could find."

"Okay. Okay. Look. She's gotta be around here somewhere. Maybe she ran from you again? Or, like, went off to check on something?"

Mo was silently seething, so Serge stepped in to answer. "She was taking a moment outside, alone. She shouted something about you and took off too quickly for us to stop her. We found her trail easily enough, but her scent disappeared along the way."

Gin, obviously distressed, turned a bit snarky themselves when they said, "And how, exactly, did she manage to leave without you noticing?"

"She wasn't a prisoner, Gin. She wasn't being restrained or kept in the house. Yes, we would have stopped her from leaving the porch on her own if we considered she would step beyond the basic borders of her home, but we did not. Our talks were going well. We felt she was ready to accept what must happen. We gave her a moment of privacy. When we heard her shout Sabrina's name, we went outside but she was already gone." Serge calmly explained all this, and as he did, Sabrina herself felt soothed, almost entranced by the comfort of his voice. Her body started swaying toward Serge, as if wanting to be closer to the source, when Gin's voice broke over her.

"Now look at what you have done, Serge. Sabrina is nearly swooning. Pull back the magic, cousin. I appreciate your efforts to calm us, but we must all be alert."

"Sorry. Just trying to help," Serge muttered, cutting eyes over to Sabrina in contrition.

She shook off the feeling of his magic and scowled at him, which made him give a small smirk. Having felt what Serge could do when he wished, on two separate occasions, a shiver ran up her spine. She knew to be far more careful around him in the future, a bit more guarded. He was likely a good guy. He was fighting Comus after all. Still, even so-called good guys didn't always think about the damage they caused along the way.

Gin started in on their own round of questioning to an increasingly agitated Mo:

"How much of a head start did she have on you?"

"7-10 minutes. No more."

"She travelled along a normal route?

"Yes."

"The trail ends abruptly?"

"Yes."

"Did you smell her magic?"

"Yes, but others as well, though that was camouflaged so it did not give off a distinct, traceable scent."

"Take me there at once," Gin demanded.

Mo nodded, and all three Fae walked out the front door in a close line. When Sabrina closed the door behind her, ready to come along, Mo stiffened and turned to her. Gin did as well, but there was more regret in their eyes. "Sabrina, love, you cannot come along. It is swifter for us to travel over land in a direct path to the spot."

"Okay, you apparently have Flash speed. Understood. Does that mean I can't meet you there?"

"No," Gin said.

"Fine. I'm in the car. You're on your legs. I'll be at Nin's house when you finish your investigation or whatever. It'll be good to have at least one person there in case she returns."

Mo's silent seemed to mark agreement, or at least acquiescence, but without a word he turned and stalked away. Gin tsked and smiled at her. Serge bowed. All three somehow bled into the night and disappeared right before her eyes.

"Yep. Flash speed. Got it," Sabrina whispered before filing away the odd sight in the part of her brain currently learning to process all these new and fantastical things. With no traffic and a clear night sky, Sabrina flew over the familiar country roads in her own speedy way, and was at Nin's house for a fretful hour when Gin, Mo, and Serge entered, looking too wary for good news.

"So?"

Mo, with his perpetual scowl, gave a violent shake of his head and stalked into the kitchen. Serge plopped down on the sofa and threw an arm over his eyes, looking defeated. Gin was the only one to approach her, and they turned sad eyes her way when they reached her position. "She is not here. And, I fear, not anywhere in this realm."

"She went back to Fae?"

"Was dragged back," Mo ground out, his back facing them, the muscles of his shoulders tense and straining as he leaned over the counter and gripped the front edge of the kitchen sink.

"What?" Sabrina whispered, horror and fear creeping. "Are you sure? How do you know? I mean, she could have just decided to go along without you, right?"

"Yes. She could. Nin is powerful enough to jump back to Fae on her own, especially as she knows this place and the feeling of both realms so well. But, there was something else there, a smell of magic that was not Nin's but was too disguised for any of us to positively identify. It could also not be positively traced back to a source, not without more equipment and time than we currently have. Only a few members of Fae could wield that level of power. Most of them would not do such a thing, as they were aware of our mission here. That leaves only one real option. If she did not leave of her own free will, Comus took her."

"How? She's been here a long time, and he just happens to show up now?" Sabrina snapped.

Gin looked hurt but took the hit well. Mo gave something like a growl from behind Sabrina, but said nothing. Serge continued to lay still and quiet. Gin slowly released a long breath and said, "As I think you imply, it is likely our fault. We may have unintentionally led him to our Nin. Our magic in Fae would leave a trace, as it does here. If he somehow knew who was coming along, the general point where we departed from Fae, what our intentions were, he could have followed us. I masked my magic, but with enough time and motivation, Comus could find traces and follow it like a thread."

"With the wand and chalice, he could have compelled a seer into his service, and we did not even consider those possibilities before we led him right to our sister's door" Serge whispered.

"Maybe, but we cannot know."

Mo appeared to gather himself up and joined Gin and Sabrina. "We leave now," he said. "If she has been taken by Comus and is in Fae, we have little time to stop more horrible events from occurring. We must speak with The Council. It is time for a full attack. Our warriors have been training and planning for this for years. We are ready. I am happy to bring this fight to the Palace gates."

"You are correct that we must leave, Mo. However, a full military attack may need more consideration, given Nin may well be a prisoner inside the Palace."

"I am tired of consideration," Mo stated, then his eyes turned into fathomless pools of dark anger that Sabrina vowed she never wanted turned her way. "He has her again, Gin. He has our Nin. And he is hurting her, no doubt, in many different ways." He quickly deflated, brought his hand up to Gin's shoulder, and on a plea, quietly said, "I did not save her before. Cousin, we must do so now."

Sabrina looked away from that brotherly pain and saw Serge had lifted from the couch and was looking down at his boots with his arms wrapped around his waist, a picture of dejection and sadness.

"Yes, Mosi. Yes. We will help Nin with all our power. We will get her back this time. There is no doubt," Gin assured their hurting cousin. "But we must be smart. We also must trust that Nin has her own plays and powers. She will do much to help herself. She is the strong Little One you taught to throw a spear and block a sword, Serge taught to spy, I taught to recite spells. She is more than you give her credit for in your fear."

Sabrina openly cried at this. She knew, if Nin heard that, she would be overjoyed. She was also worried sick about her friend and afraid there was nothing she could do. Afraid also, win or lose, there was no way she would see Nin again, as she may remain behind in Fae regardless of the outcome of these particular events.

"We will leave shortly for The Falls, as soon as Sabrina has packed a bag for Nin," and here Gin hesitated, turning to Sabrina to be face-to-face, "and hopefully, herself."

"What is this?" Mo retorted.

Gin sighed, looked up at the ceiling for a moment, and then brought a hand up to pinch the bridge of their nose. Finally getting some composure, Gin leveled out and stated the case plainly. "Sabrina is needed. I feel Sabrina should to be in Fae with us, but more than that, I know she has information and specialized knowledge that will be integral in the fight against Comus."

"What knowledge?" Serge asked, his face harder than it had been. Seemed to Sabrina he, like Mo, did not like the idea of her in Fae.

"It is too intricate to explain fully now. She has knowledge I need. She must come."

"No. Absolutely not. This will not stand." Mo held firm.

"Yeah, I agree with Mo on this one, Gin. It is too dangerous right now for any human," Serge added.

"She is not any human. She is Nin's. And Nin is hers. That is important. I know it. Also, you have no say in who comes or goes. She is bound to a Fae and therefore free to enter or leave Fae as she wishes. The real question is — does she wish to come with us?" Turning to her, with their head cocked to the side, Gin continued, "I did not force this issue earlier, as you reacted strongly, but there is no more time for you to become accustomed to the idea. I do not know what will happen or how, exactly, your knowledge will play a role in what shall pass. I just know you will play a role. I feel it. I do not discount such feelings; they do not lead me astray. Yet, I will not force you to come. You must enter Fae of your own free will. Will you join us? Will you come to Fae, stay with us in The Falls, and help us get Nin back?"

"Of course," she stated confidently, though she did not feel very confident at that moment. While she had been shocked before when Gin brought up this possibility, the events leading to this moment had made her choice much easier. She had no hesitation, even if she did have a great deal of fear. She would go, she would do whatever she could, and she would help them not only free Nin, but give Nin whatever she needed to heal afterward. "I'll be right back." She zipped toward the door and her waiting car, off to pack a backpack with a few essentials and a duffel bag filled with Milton books.

She would pack Nin the same — minus the Milton, of course — when she returned. She'd travel to another realm, fight evil with whatever minimal human skill she had, to make sure Nin was safe and reunited with the people who loved her.

CHAPTER 8

To pack as quickly as possible, Sabrina dumped a semester's worth of junk from her backpack onto her kitchen table to clear it for the few personal items she planned to take to the Fae realm. This was a good thing, as she hadn't stopped to think about her students or her job until that moment. She took time to send an email to her department chair. Luckily, she had uploaded final grades as soon as she finished reviewing the last essays her students submitted. That was yesterday morning, less than twenty-four hours ago. It now felt like a lifetime.

She did take the time to send a quick email to her students as well because she knew she'd get the normal grade questions rolling in as soon as final grades posted. She loved teaching, enjoyed her students, but the job itself was hard and grueling at times, and definitely not worth the little pay she received. She set up an away message for her email, crossed her fingers in hopes that her inbox wasn't completely unmanageable when she returned to it, and jumped up to scurry out the door. The digital display on her radio told her she'd been home for an hour dealing with these issues already, so she motored down her driveway with her usual speed, leaving her work, and her world, behind.

When she pulled up to Nin's place, Mo stood cross-armed on the porch with his feet firmly planted shoulder-length apart. She was getting used to his serious expressions and this was no different. He was rigid and his face managed to appear both blank and slightly annoyed, an oxymoron she would believe impossible if it wasn't staring at her from the Fae in front of her.

Sabrina sighed, heaved herself from her car with her backpack and duffel dragging behind her, and walked over to him with her head high. "Before this all really starts, we need to do something about this," she stated, tossing a hand back and forth between the two of them, "whatever it is. I'm not your sister, so I don't have to put up with your shit. Though it didn't seem like Nin did much of that, either. All this to say, we have more important things to do than scowl at each other. I know you're not happy I'm here or Nin did that mind-meld bonding thing with me, or that I'm going to Fae. Tough. You have no say in it. So, can we please just move forward and work together? For Nin?"

Mo looked her in the eyes intently through this tirade and stayed motionless for a few beats afterward, which made Sabrina feel a little antsy under his intense gaze. Finally, he sighed, a sound that mingled both resignation and regret. "Know it is not you. You care for Nin, and she for you. That tells me enough about your character. There are too many unknowns. I did not know what Nin's life was like here in the human world, so I worried for her. And now, my sister is out there somewhere, lost or hurting. I do not want to also worry about you being hurt or mistreated in Fae."

"No one said you had to worry about me. I'm a grown woman. I can look after myself."

"Admirable, but moot. First, I worry for all who hold a place in my family. That is my burden to bear, one I happily place on myself. As you are bound to Nin, so you are bound to me by extension. I will worry for you no matter what comes, so take that as you will. Second, you are confident and strong and competent. I have seen this. Still, you are going to a different world, where you know nothing of the place or the people. Anything could be a risk there. You should be cautious moving forward. Fae is lovely. It is my home and I care for it deeply. It is also harsh, especially to beautiful humans. Your kind in particular tends to attract trouble there. Remember, we are not taking some fantastical, magical trip for our own amusement, but preparing for a battle. I am right to worry. You should be worried as well."

Sabrina flushed hot and red at the beauty comment, but decided it was in everyone's best interest to just plow ahead like she didn't hear it. "I'm not stupid or incapable of learning. I am adaptable. I will be cautious. I'll also be in this fight for Nin. That is the sole reason I'm coming to your world."

"We now know where we stand. You will do and feel as you must. I will worry and act as I should. I acknowledge I can be…negative in my initial reactions to people and situations. I will try to give you space and stop being so harsh and unpleasant toward you. That is not your fault, but my own. I try to do what I feel is right without telling others why it is so. I should have spoken more directly to you regarding my thoughts. For that, I do apologize. I will endeavor to be more forthright with you in the future as you have done with me just now."

He ended with a small bow to Sabrina. This was odd for her. No one bowed her way. When he rose, she, in turn, offered her hand, showing she appreciated what he had said and was willing to work with him from this point forward. His hand was warm, silky, and firm in hers. His eyes were intent and more inviting when he pumped her hand in kind.

She withdrew and muttered, "Okay then," as she rubbed both her hands together. She made it look like she was warming herself by blowing on her palms afterward, but that was not the real reason she started rubbing her right hand. As soon as she touched Mo, a pleasant warmth scored across her palm, heating it in an odd but comforting way. She didn't know if he had felt the same, and she was definitely not going to ask him, so she quickly stepped around him and let the screen door slam behind her as she entered Nin's cottage.

Both Serge and Gin were sitting on opposite ends of Nin's couch but had obviously been listening to her conversation with Mo. At least Gin had the sense to try to hide the fact, busying themself with what appeared to be a fascinating smudge on Nin's side table.

Serge stared at her outright, a wide smile on his face. "Nicely done, Sabrina. Not many have the guts to take on that scowl. You will do well in Fae." With that, he knifed off the couch and stepped towards her, grabbing onto her upper arms and studying her face with a few tilts of the head. "Yes. You will do very well in Fae indeed. If you have any problems, with the grouch out there or anyone else, let me know." He threw a smile at her that was the first Sabrina would call brotherly and not flirty or mischievous. "Mo is right about one thing. Fae is a dangerous place, and it is even more so now. You do not know its ways. I will help you in any way I can." He dropped his arms and turned towards the kitchen, yelling back at them, "I'm taking those cookies with me. They're too good to leave behind. Does Nin hide any more here somewhere?"

"Look in the freezer," Sabrina called, before turning to Gin, who was now gesturing for her to sit with them. "Come," they said. "We have little time and much to discuss." With her backpack still hanging from her shoulders, she dropped down softly onto the couch, leaning ever so slightly against the arm so she could face Gin. They smiled, but it seemed a little strained. "I did not foresee this happening so quickly, although I knew it would likely happen for you one day. I thought we would have more time to prepare you. Alas, that is not the case. We do what we must, and although I am no seer, I feel you are of vital importance for the mission ahead."

Sabrina nodded but remained quiet. There was little she could add, and she was getting more and more nervous by the minute. It was best to let Gin reveal whatever they wished and go from there.

"First issue. We are returning to the greenhouse, and the site of our arrival, in order to rework the spell and get us all to Fae. As I said, being bound to Nin has advantages and this is one: there will be no real trouble for you in being bespelled in general or in traveling between realms. However, you are not familiar with the workings of magic, and a strong spell such as this can have effects. You may feel sick or dizzy. I suggest you keep your eyes closed to help with that. You may also feel other things for a few seconds as we travel between the realms, some of it might be uncomfortable, even painful. This is to be expected. Know it will pass and you will be safe in Fae in mere moments after the spell takes hold."

"So, expect some discomfort, but there is nothing I should be afraid of? No way this can go wrong?"

Gin hedged before they answered. "There are always ways magic can go wrong. It is not like your science; it has a certain element of the unknowable always at play. Some even believe it has a mind of its own — a living, knowing thing in and of itself. However, I am performing the same spell as before, in the exact same location, in an effort to right our position in the universe. All of that helps. Your trust will also help. Think of Nin. Think of your desire to find her. Intention guides the way in any spell. Given all this, you have little chance of a magical mishap." Sitting a little straighter, Gin also added, "I, myself, am powerful and very adept. I will guide you true."

Sabrina reached for Gin's hand and patted it, leaving hers to sit softly on theirs for a moment, saying, "I have no doubts then. You got this."

Gin grinned for a moment, then turned serious again.

"Second issue. You know little of Fae outside of the political turmoil and history I gave you earlier. You know nothing about our culture or our natural world, both of which will hold many surprises for you in the days ahead. I cannot give you these lessons here. We do not have the time. I will guide you while we are there. Mo, though surly, does have your best interests at heart, even if you two would disagree about what that is. You can go to him. Serge has also offered you his aid, which is nothing to ignore as he is very adept at the ways of Fae, both the place and the people, because of his powers and his time in the Palace Court. If at any time you are scared, uncertain, or feel unsure in any way, reach for one of us. We will help you navigate Fae. Other than that, sadly, you must be prepared to learn as you go."

"Good thing I'm a quick study," Sabrina quipped.

"Quite," Gin said in reply. "You are taking all of this remarkably well. How are you feeling, Sabrina?"

"I'm nervous, scared, excited, cautious, anxious, but above all that, I'm ready to go find my friend."

"Excellent. That is the important thing, is it not? We go to slay dragons for our Nin, and that gives us strength."

"Will there be dragons?" Sabrina rushed out on a breath that was part amazement and part fear.

"Sorry," Gin laughed with a chuckle. "No. Just a metaphor I picked up in your realm long, long ago."

With an exaggerated slump for effect, Sabrina groused, "That's kinda disappointing."

Mo interjected with a laugh and a hand on her shoulder, which brought that same odd buzz to the skin beneath her shirt. Sabrina hadn't even heard him come into the house, much less get this close, but he gave her a small, warm smile and that was a welcomed change. It appeared he took their talk to heart. "Do not wish more monsters on us, human. We have enough on our hands. Can you take a moment to put some of Nin's things in a bag? She will have access to some of her older things that we have preserved in The Falls, but she will appreciate you bringing along what she values here. Just remember to pack light."

Sabrina nodded and rushed through the process, filling a weekend bag she found with some underwear, comfortable clothes, and the beauty products Nin favored most. It would be a balm to her, like Mo figured, so Sabrina picked only what she thought would give her the most comfort when she came back to them. "All done," she sang loudly as she exited the tiny cottage bathroom and zipped up Nin's bag.

Serge reached for it, gently touching Sabrina's hand as he did and giving her a reassuring squeeze. She gave a weak smile to Serge, though she did appreciate his gesture, and moved ahead to be closer to Gin. She felt they were the closest thing she had to a friend here, no offense to the others, so she wanted to be with them when her world literally changed. Mo pulled up straight as an arrow, an old soldier at attention, and firmly stated, "We leave."

At the greenhouse, Gin placed everyone in the position they had been in when they had arrived from Fae. Sabrina was added in last, told to stand facing Serge and Mo and hold on to their forearms. Sabrina had her backpack strapped tightly to her frame and Mo shouldered the heavy book duffel after the two bickered briefly over who would hold it. She gripped tight, ignoring the steely muscled forearms under her grip and the tingle she got from Mo as best she could. She heaved out a breath and closed her eyes as Gin began to chant.

In seconds she felt a sharp tug on her navel, then a violent push that threatened to knock her off her feet. Her stomach lurched and bile rolled up her throat as she instantly became dizzy and disoriented. She smelled sage and Gin, felt an electrified wind whip around her face and tangle through her hair, and then her legs took a hard impact. She nearly fell, or would have if she hadn't maintained a death grip on Mo and Serge.

"Sabrina," Mo whispered, putting his warm, firm hand over hers at his arm. "You can let go. Open your eyes. We have arrived."

At that, Sabrina loosened her grip, opened her eyes, and took a step away from the two Fae in front of her. She blinked, from the aftereffects of her transition and because of what she saw. She wasn't in Kentucky anymore. That was very clear.

CHAPTER 9

Sabrina took in the scene around her. The four of them were in a lush, vibrant meadow. The tall grass was ombre, starting a deep bluish green close to the ground and ending in a rich kelly green around her hips. She reached out a hand, skimming it over the foliage and watching it ripple from her touch. It shimmered faintly like a clam shell reflecting light, but instead of hues of pink and white and blues, it was all a riot of greens. It was mesmerizing and unlike anything she had seen before.

When she finally stopped staring in awe at what was apparently just grass in Fae, she saw they stood in a crossroads at the center of the clearing, each of the four paths leading to a different type of tree line. Straight ahead of her was what looked like woods much like the ones in Kentucky, filled with a familiar mix of old, and therefore massive, oaks and elms, maple and walnut. The odd thing, though, was it appeared to be autumn in that section of woodlands. Where she stood felt like a warm spring day, sun shining and grasses swaying in a gentle breeze. That forest ahead was a bright burst of Fall — red and orange and yellow leaves topped each tree and drifted down to litter the soft brown forest floor.

To her left was a stark field of birch trees, although they weren't like the birch trees she knew. They were not slim, but hearty and thick. If she walked over and tried, she knew she wouldn't be able to get her arms around some of those trunks. They did have the regular signs of a birch: white bark curling and peeling away from the trunks of each tree, shaving-like pieces strewn across the ground around them. Only a few yellowed leaves remained, stubbornly holding on to their branches. This was likely because it was clearly winter in that section of forest. Snow, pristine and glistening, blanketed the ground and piled around the trees. She saw a few pops of color here and there and realized they were birds, flitting in and around the trees, their bright pink and purple feathers shaking off snow when they stopped on a bare branch. They were diving, headfirst, into snowbanks, only to shoot out moments later with snow-covered grasses in their mouths. The section looked cold and stark in many ways, but that activity, those birds, made it a little less harsh.

She looked behind her and found a full-on jungle. She'd never seen an actual jungle in person. Had never been much of anywhere in her life, really, so that was no surprise. That grouping of vines and tall, dark trees looked like what she had seen in pictures and on film, so it was familiar enough. It was damp and dark, a place where animals, reptiles, and insects would nest and hide and burrow. She could almost feel the humidity wafting from that spot, a heated wetness that would make her skin slick with a sweaty sheen. She hoped they were not going in that direction. She was well used to the humid summers of Kentucky, the sticky heat that lasted months, but never enjoyed it. A trek through even worse humidity would not be welcome.

She turned to study the last section of woods. This was an alpine forest in the midst of spring. Evergreens pushed from the ground. There were even a few massive redwoods dotted here and there, some she could see far in the distance. Fresh, new grass sprouted in small bursts. Woodland creatures scampered. Like, really and truly scampered, their little furry faces cute enough to squeeze. The vibe of this section of forest matched the meadow in most ways, but also reminded her of fairy tales. It may be cliche, but she had almost thought all of Fae would be like that section. She wasn't disappointed it was not. The beauty of the differences was astounding. She tried to take in the different vistas at once, but the incongruity was a bit too much. She laughed, though. A deep laugh, filled with wonder and awe, because that was what she felt suffuse her in that moment.

As she spent her first few minutes marveling at the new world around her, Serge and Mo stood tall together while Gin tilted their head toward the sky, eyes closed, breathing deep. They snapped their head in place quickly and clapped their hands together. Sabrina noticed it, but was still stuck in awe, until Gin finally spoke, "Yes. All is good. I sense no other unknown Fae around to follow us. We can head to The Falls."

Mo and Serge both moved at once, about to set off on their journey, and Sabrina felt crestfallen when they headed in the direction of the jungle.

"Really? Not the mellow meadowland or the crisp autumn forest? Oh no, it's gotta be the hot, sticky place, of course," she muttered, hanging her head, and steeling herself for what might be a long journey. She shuffled slowly behind the trio of Fae in front of her.

Gin looked back, then held back, and linked their arm with Sabrina's like they were about to take a lovely stroll down the promenade in some British costume drama. "Sad, lovely? Do not fret. We are not at all far from our destination. The Falls is a special place, which requires special natural protections on top of the spells we cast to conceal it — hence, why we chose this section of our realm. The journey for those who know the way is tricky at times, but much easier than for those who attempt to navigate these jungles without our knowledge of the paths."

Sabrina, now more curious than apprehensive, asked, "What exactly is The Falls? You've mentioned it a number of times but haven't really explained what it is."

"It is the place for what you might call the resistance — the group of Fae who are actively fighting against Comus. This includes most of the original Council, Mo and his band of warriors, a number of courtiers like Serge, myself and other teacher-scholars, and any other Fae who wishes to be hidden or to fight against Comus and his tyranny. We have built our own little community over the past few decades, working together to make a contained home we can live in and work from until Comus is defeated."

"Not every Fae is there?"

"Oh, no. Some do support Comus, and those that are most loyal to him stay at The Palace, which is the traditional seat of Fae government. Others move about their lives as best they can, trying to do what they always did and hoping Comus does nothing to hinder this."

Sabrina scowled a bit at this, but Gin shook their head her way. "Do not be angry at those who do not actively oppose. They have many reasons. I still believe most support our cause and would see Comus fall. Yet, people are comfortable with what they know. Others do not feel free or able to fight openly and privately express support. We all have our burdens, Sabrina. Some cannot fight. Some will not fight. Those who can are the ones we need to have. Fate has seen this is so."

Sabrina just nodded and got into step, following closely behind Gin as the group made their way deeper and deeper into the dense, hot jungle. She slowed a bit, lagging behind after a few minutes. She was tired, but also awed by all around her. It was a jungle. Everything was hot and steamy, true, but also vibrant and enticing. Gin's robed back was clearly visible about ten feet ahead, so she saw no need to worry. A chittering sound distracted her and she whipped her head to the right. There, hanging from a branch a few feet away, was a small round ball of fluff, hopping happily along. It was some sort of bird, though its face was far more mammalian. She cocked her head to study it, stopping in her tracks. The animal did the same, mimicking her actions, which brought a goofy grin to her face.

Sabrina heard Gin shout something and turned to him. Then she froze. As soon as her eyes had left the bird-animal creature, it had changed, looming far larger and more menacing out of the corner of her eye. She turned fully to face it, realizing in horror that it had turned from a small, fluffy thing into a four-foot pile of razor teeth and talons that was about to swoop down on her. Before she could scream, the air was knocked from her. Serge landed on top of her hard, and her breath left in a whoosh. Mo, spear in hand, easily repelled the creature, parrying it back, back, back into the depths of the jungle.

"Sorry, love. Should have told you not to look too deep into things here. Sometimes, all they need is your attention to strike," Serge grumbled. It was an honest apology.

"Thanks for the save and all. Appreciate it. Really. But could you please get off me now?" Sabrina replied with gritted teeth. He was heavy and she was pinned between his hard body and the dirt in a way that was not sexy but rather uncomfortable.

"Sergius," Mo barked, now apparently done with both running off that creature and the antics of his younger brother.

"You're welcome. And no harm meant." Serge jumped from her and offered a hand, helping her from the ground. "Though, in other circumstances…" He let that response hang, and Sabrina felt heat rise her cheeks.

"Really, Sergius. Your endless flirting does get tiresome. It is neither the time nor the place," Gin fussed. Coming to her and looking her over, they added, "I am truly sorry. I should not have allowed you to linger."

"Everyone must be more mindful. More vigilant. Fae and human," Mo added, sweat now prickling his brow. A brow that looked furrowed in worry as his eyes assessed Sabrina's form for damage.

"Yes. Everyone. Okay. You did not warn me, and silly human that I am, I was careless. Lesson learned by all, but no harm, no foul. Let's carry on."

"Sabrina, you will now follow directly behind me," Mo commanded, turning to continue the trek through the jungle.

Serge smiled and waved a hand forward, urging her without words to do what his brother said. She did. She had no qualms being protected by these Fae men. The beauty and the danger of Fae was quite clear to her now.

CHAPTER 10

About 30 minutes after that frightening encounter, the trail came to a steep incline. Sabrina was already sweaty, so much so, she had tied her flannel around her waist long ago and her shirt was clinging to her drenched skin. Layers were a usual for her — she had learned this while she was teaching in multiple classrooms where any given day each could be freezing or sweltering on a whim — and no one had told her what to wear on this adventure. She went with a standby: unbuttoned flannel to help with any potential chill, white v-neck tee that wasn't too constricting, old jeans with a bit of wear that was more about age than fashion, comfy-cushioned socks, and her trusty hiking shoes. Her hair was in a sleek ponytail, allowing for ease and movement without sticking out too much, at least in the human world. Here, she had no idea what it would do. Right then, she was thankful for the light tee, even though the flannel and jeans were dragging her down a bit. The hiking shoes were now coming in handy, too, giving her solid grip as she trudged behind the others up the steep hill. She wasn't the most athletic, or the most graceful, so she remained slow and steady, not wanting to fall and roll all the way down, but also wanting to keep her breathing as even as possible while pushing herself forward. At least she'd quit smoking years ago.

They climbed higher and higher for a few minutes and Sabrina was definitely winded when she spotted a plateau ahead. Mo reached it first, turning back and stretching back to take her hand, helping her scramble up those last few feet. By the time she caught her breath and rose to her full height to face beyond the hill, Serge slung an arm across her shoulders, not seeming to mind the sweat dripping off her — sweat that annoyingly was dripping from him

— and said, "No worries, love. We're almost there, and this last stretch is a ride, not a hike."

She had nothing to say to that, as she was too busy staring around in disbelief. What was there appeared like an illusion as it was nothing that could exist within the physical realities of her own world.

The hill they had crested formed a high ring that appeared to have no corresponding decline. The soil, trees, mass of jungle and foliage ended along the six-foot strip of land that made up the plateau. This extended on all sides, curving inward, but disappearing far into the horizon, giving the appearance that it formed a circle or oval of sorts around the space, but one so big it could not be fully seen from this simple vantage point. Out beyond this ring of land was a dense fog her sight could not penetrate at all. She did, however, spy a contraption to her left. Many years ago, on a weekend trip to Pittsburgh, she had ridden a trolley rail up the side of a mountain to see a view of the city and the three rivers below. What stood there was similar in size and shape, a rectangular box with open windows and what looked like bench seating along the four interior walls. It rested on a metal track that disappeared into that deep fog. It was there for a few feet, dipping in a downward motion for just a bit off of the strip of land on which the trolley car sat, but then she could see no more of where the tracks lead.

Mo moved toward the car, with Gin following close behind. Sabrina had no choice but to follow after them both as Serge kept her tucked tight to his side. She didn't know what to expect, so she allowed Serge to guide her along the plateau, into the car, and onto one of the benches. Mo sat on the far bench, managing to look relaxed and at ease even with his perfectly poised posture. He watched Sabrina closely as she began to fidget in her seat, which was on the bench along the far wall. She was close enough for him to reach but not exactly in his space, which gave her some mild reassurance. Not enough, though. She sat ramrod straight, definitely not looking comfortable, as her hands fluttered and twisted in her lap. She knew she looked scared because she was scared. She didn't savor the idea of taking some magical trolley into an unknown space.

"Ease yourself," Mo said calmly. "We are almost finished with our journey. Sit back, close your eyes, and we will be done soon."

"Close my eyes? Why?" Sabrina whispered. It sounded like good advice, and she really wanted to trust and take it, but she had to know whether it was necessary or just to calm her.

"It's just to ease your own mind, Sabrina," Gin called to her, seemingly fully aware of why she asked and what she needed to know at that moment. They were at the front of the car, close to a number or levers she guessed would control this contraption. "I'll guide us through the fog true, but it clearly has affected you. Nothing will happen to you if you keep your eyes open, but it may be better for you to ease yourself by closing your eyes."

With that, Sabrina snapped her eyes closed and started breathing like she did when she practiced yoga — five breaths in, five beats hold, five breaths out. It was a calming mindfulness practice she picked up years ago, and if there was ever a time she needed that, it was in this incongruous trolley car that was about to plunge into a complete unknown. She felt the lurch of the car beginning a descent, heard the clack of metal wheels along tracks, and knew they were propelling forward. They picked up speed quickly, but it was not too much, and she knew Gin was controlling that, though she wondered if they went a little slower for her sake.

Keeping her eyes closed, she asked blindly to the room at large, "What is this…?" though the question trailed off. It wasn't a place, exactly, but she didn't know what to actually call it.

"The fog?" Serge asked, and she felt him scoot closer to her as he did. She nodded, swallowing the lump of fear that kept creeping up her throat. "It is a space filled with protective magic. Only those connected to the magic of the person who created such a fog can enter or exit it, hence, the trolley car. It's more efficient for supplies and larger groups and whatnot. It's basically a magical barrier, a security measure to hide and protect The Falls," he answered. "It was created by a few people, including Gin and my mother, which makes it very powerful. We, as Fae of The Falls, could travel there directly through a portal, but you can't. You've never been, and neither has Nin, and it is her magic that binds you in Fae. Once you get in and meet with The Council, you'll be given that power, so no more fog trips for you after this."

Sabrina felt her body crumple in relief a bit at that news. She did not like this fog, for some reason it disturbed her more than the trek through the strange jungle. She figured it was about both being unable to see and unaware of what would come at the end that ratcheted up her nerves. It was like being in a speeding car on a foggy night on unfamiliar country roads. It felt dangerous. She was glad to know she'd never have to encounter it again. She felt the slowing of the trolley, felt the jerk of a stop, and knew they had to be at their destination. The odd little journey was done.

"It is now over," she heard Mo echo her own thoughts, and he sounded closer than he had been. "You can open your eyes."

She blinked them open, but all she saw was Mo directly in front of her. She reared back a little at how close he was.

He pushed his hands close to her face. "May I?" he asked. She didn't know what he wanted, but she nodded anyway. He smiled at her — an actual smile that wasn't wide or blinding but did show a bit of teeth and joy and made her stomach do a small flip — then placed one hand at her mouth. He muttered a few words in what she figured was Fae, then he took both hands and placed them over her eyes, clearly uttering more words even though she couldn't hear anything. He pulled back and stood tall, offering a hand to her to help her rise from her bench.

"What was that?"

"Something I should have done earlier. I was going to do it, Mo. You did not have to," Gin said this on a bit of a huff, as if they were put out that they had not gotten to do it.

"As Sabrina said earlier, no worries. I was there, it needed to be done, I did it."

"Again, what was that?" Sabrina pressed.

"The basic language spell," Gin replied with a vague flip of the hand. "The one that allows you to understand anything you hear and have your words understood by anyone around you. We are not the only Fae with this spell on us, but there are Fae who do not have it. It's better to put it on you now than run into a situation where you need it and can't get it from one of us for some reason."

Sabrina nodded, but stopped, cocked her head in thought, and asked, "What about spells? I've heard a few at this point. They always sound like they are in a foreign language. I assume that's Fae. Why do I hear them in Fae and everything else I hear from y'all is in English?"

Serge butt in at this point. "Spellcraft is always spoken and heard in Fae, no matter what. There are a lot of theories why this is, but overall, no one really knows. That's just how it is," he answered with the shrug of a shoulder. "Come on. Let's get out of this car and show you The Falls." With what she imagined was his trademark — that sexy smirk — Serge strolled out of the trolley. They had landed on a wooden platform several flights of stairs tall.

As soon as all four exited, the car moved off, climbing up in the sky and then disappearing in the blink of an eye. Sabrina only saw an expanse of blue sky, tufts of clouds dotted here and there, and sunshine glowing down at her as she searched for the car for a moment. It was no longer in her sight and neither was the fog. She shrugged and decided to let it go. She shook off any lingering questions and heaved a sigh of relief the trip was done, at least for the moment.

CHAPTER II

Sabrina shielded her eyes with a hand placed at her
brow and surveyed the scene around her. It was loud
and vibrant, both audibly and visually. She saw
bright green tracks of grass with intersecting pink
sand lanes. Strong oaks and elms, willows and
magnolias dotted the landscape. They were on a
small hilltop, looking down on what was a settlement
of sorts. There were houses with stone walls and
thatched roofs, but they weren't small. They looked
like rambling ranch-style homes that would easily
accommodate a number of people. These were no
simple single-room structures, but thoughtful homes

crafted to be both lasting shelter and family space. Flowers, in pots and in clusters in the ground, hugged wooden porches constructed with wide and steep overhangs to help block the elements from those entering or exiting the home.

Along with these flowers, the arched doors added pops of swirling color. They were not simply red or blue or yellow. Some had churning mixtures of colors, flowing like Van Gogh paintings in matching but varying hues of blues, greens, reds, yellows, pinks, and purples. Others had geometric designs, chess boards with brightly colored squares, circles intersecting and breaking in contrasting colors, waves and stripes and plaids. While each house was similar in structure, the doors obviously told a story about who was inside, what they were like. It was pure personality expressed through paint or wood dye.

These houses were an outer perimeter. Beyond them, in a blank open block of space marked by a much larger expanse of the pink sand, was a bazaar. Tents of all colors and designs, held up with sturdy poles, sheltered tables where Sabrina saw figures chatting and shopping. She couldn't see what was sold from her vantage point, but Fae moved in and out, some loitering and some quickly going about business, like any merchant center of any town she had ever been to in her world. She wanted to peruse those stalls and see what she could find, touch, taste in this new and exciting place.

Right in the center of it all, past the houses and the marketplace, a huge stone tower loomed. It wasn't exactly foreboding. Colorful banners that flew from the windows dotted the exterior of the structure and it looked like the Fae of The Falls hung news and announcements in bright paper along the outside. But it was definitely a place of defense. A heavy wooden door was propped open now, but if shut it would be hard to breach. The widows allowed banners that added bursts of color to the gray stone, but the first sets started a few stories up the sides. Overall, it looked like a smaller version of siege castles she had seen in old sketches or Hollywood recreations, but without the additional turrets or square footage. It stood alone as a single citadel of defense, and as such, Sabrina guessed it was the place where community events and meetings were held and decisions were made, just like secure courthouses and town halls in her time, or similarly structured castles long ago abandoned in the human realm.

Behind her, however, was the source of the thundering rush she heard. It was a giant waterfall, cascading blue-green crystalline waters down into a pool that drained directly into a glistening stream that surrounded the settlement. The roar of rapidly falling water crashing over jutting rocks and a cropping of huge boulders at the bottom of the drop was oppressive from where she stood, a testament to the might and power of that water as it flowed over the ledge. She couldn't see where the water originated, she could only see the place where it fell over an edge, but it was loud and seemingly endless. However, that churn and force became a calm pool at the bottom, then a gently babbling brook as it eased around the town itself. The noise likely lessened the further you went down, away from the wild edge of the falling waters. She hadn't heard the waterfall in the trolley car either, which was something else she didn't question about that space.

Mo said, on a shout, "Let us go," and she followed without a word, not even trying to be heard over the crash of the water around them.

They moved closer to the outskirts of the town, and as the roar faded and the Fae figures could be more clearly seen, she saw that many looked just like her companions. They were racially and physically diverse, had various genders and ages, but for all intents and purposes, they looked human. She began to see others, though. She tried not to stare or gawk — that was just plain rude in any world — when she first noticed the tiny flying figures that zipped around the town. She saw rocks with faces that moved and ambled upright. She noticed miniature green men and women scurrying around like everyone else, and a couple of figures laughing while smoking long pipes who looked suspiciously like garden gnomes with their small stature, long gray beards, and pointed hats. Gin had used the phrases "noble" and "lesser" Fae when they first discussed this realm, and she had a sinking suspicion she knew what that meant, both in the description and possible treatment these beings faced in their world.

When a small flying figure careened a little close to her head, she jerked but successfully fought the instinct to swat. She caught a tinkle of laughter as the miniature woman, no more than three-inches tall from pointed toes to gently-swaying ponytail, zipped around her head and came to hover a foot in front of her face. The tiny person wore a toga of sorts, but also sported shiny armor across her chest and

shoulders and a metal headpiece with just enough
room for that jaunty ponytail to escape out of the top.
A small sword hung from a leather belt at her waist.
It was miniscule, but Sabrina saw a glint that hinted it
was also wickedly sharp.

"A human," the small flying soldier laughed,
clapping her hands together. "Haven't seen one of
you in so very long."

Gin stopped, gave a small bow to the tiny
woman who looked like every fairy she ever
imagined as a child, except more heavily armed, and
gave introductions. "Chieftain Allera, I am happy to
introduce you to Sabrina of Nin."

Sabrina smiled and gave what she felt was a
respectful wave, but that was ignored. The miniature
figure gasped at hearing her name, flew right up into
Sabrina's face, and stared straight into one eye.
Again, she fought the urge to duck or swat. A
lifetime of only being concerned with winged insects
flying around her face wasn't exactly helpful. She
knew it was a conscious, thoughtful being. Her words
and actions conveyed as much. As did her
scrutinizing stare. It was disconcerting; the types of
stares she was used to were eye-to-eye after all.
Allera's stare was eye-to-whole-flying-body.

"My word," the woman muttered. "Does this mean…"

Gin shook their head sadly. "More news will come, but spreading this through your ranks will help hasten it. Sabrina is Nin's. We have seen Nin. But our mission was not fully successful. There is much we have to do, quickly, in order to save Fae."

The small woman hugged herself for a moment, then straightened her spine, floating tall and proud. "As you wish, Gin the Scholar. I will ensure the message is received among my people and those who abide within our grounds. We will be available for assistance should you need it."

"I fear we will, long before this fight for Fae is complete."

She nodded at that, turned back to Sabrina, and offered a small bow. "Sabrina of Nin, it was a great honor. Know the Wisps will be at your service in your time of need."

Sabrina looked to Gin wide-eyed as Allera flew away. "What was all that?" she gasped. There was a lot to process from that very brief introduction.

"We have fallen behind Mo and Serge. We must continue forward," Gin asserted, walking away while keeping their face turned toward her. "In brief

— you met Chieftain Allera, leader of the Wisps and The Falls liaison for the Lesser Fae. She will spread word quickly, to Lesser and Noble Fae. They knew our mission, now know you are here and Nin is not, and will be prepared for more information as it comes forward. The Council should have been notified first, but the opportunity arose, and I did not wish to squander it."

"A Wisp Chieftain?"

"Yes. You humans called them that at one point in time as well. They've also been known as fairies and the little folk by your kind. They don't linger in the human world much any longer. It is too dangerous for them. They are a small, but mighty and fierce people, with enough magical strength and courage to be a great help in any fight ahead. As Chieftain, Allera is their leader in life and war."

Sabrina had many, many more questions about those "Lesser" Fae — a term she figured was not the greatest and did not bode well for inter-Fae relations overall — but the group had moved purposefully toward the town center and were about to cross a small footbridge currently guarded by a Fae leaning on a tall wooden staff. Gin halted for a moment to take a position by Sabrina, and she didn't look down as they grasped her hand tightly. The Fae guard nodded at Mo, Serge, and Gin, noticed Gin's grip on Sabrina, and cocked their helmeted head in a bit of a question.

Mo barked an order of attention and the guard snapped to, straightening from their lean and looking away from the group to stare ahead at the empty lane in front of the bridge. Mo muttered something about vigilance, Serge smirked, and Gin released her hand. Sabrina looked at them with a question in their eyes.

Gin answered without the words needing to be spoken. "Two reasons, Sabrina. First, there is magic in the stream that requires a physical connection with someone of The Falls or a specific binding spell in order to allow you to enter successfully. It's another security measure. Second, the guard would know you were human but not who you were. Me taking your hand showed trust and respect, which would help ease the guard and forestall any questions upon entry, at least for now."

Sabrina nodded, but then let her attention wander more across the people and structures of The Falls. She was so immersed in taking in as much as she could that she nearly stepped right into Serge's back when he abruptly stopped in front of her. It was only when she righted herself from her stutter-step that she felt the tension in the group. Standing a few feet in front of a frozen Mo was a gorgeous Fae woman. Like, the most gorgeous woman Sabrina had ever seen in real life. If she was of her world, Sabrina would say she was Persian. She'd always loved Persian art — illuminated manuscripts, tapestries, sculptures, etc. — and this woman looked like she had walked straight from an illuminated page of Rumi's love poems.

She was clothed in sweeping and flowing red and gold fabric that both moved around her with the breeze and highlighted her curvy figure. She was short in stature, but poised, standing straight and tall in a pose that was the embodiment of dignity. Her hand fluttered with grace up from her waist to her cheek, touching her face lightly and highlighting her golden complexion, her rounded and pursed lips, her dark and intelligent eyes, her brows that were deep slashes topping the loveliness that was her face. Her hair, a fall of waves in a brown so dark it was one hue away from black, framed all of this. Then she spoke, and Sabrina's knees locked and her stomach started a churn.

"My sons?" she asked, a hint of sadness and hope in her voice as she looked at all of them in the party and most assuredly noted the one person missing from the group. She didn't obviously take notice of Sabrina at this point, who now felt very much like an interloper in a tense family scene.

Mo, now unstuck, moved slowly forward and, with a crack in his voice, whispered, "I am so sorry, Mother. She was taken."

This beauty in front of her, the woman who was her best friend's mother, seemed to crumble while she stood, deflated into herself, hugging her own stomach and shuttering out deep breaths this harsh news. Mo continued as Sabrina watched tears slide down her cheeks, "Please forgive me, Mother. It is my fault."

Her head snapped straight again, and it was like a steel rod rammed right down her spine. "Mosi — say no such thing. Did you abandon her? Did you push her away from you? Did you allow someone to take her right in front of your eyes? I think not. That is not you, my son. Whatever happened to our Nin is also not you." With a sharpening of her eyes and a hardness to her voice she added, "I think we all know who is to blame, and he will be dealt with very soon."

With that, she shook herself and said, "Come, boys. Greet your mother properly."

Mo, then Serge, moved into their mother's open arms, squeezing her tight and with obvious affection. "You, too, Gin."

They muttered a "Yes, Auntie," and offered some softly whispered words to this woman before pulling away and turning to Sabrina with a smile.

"Aunt Inanna, please meet Sabrina of Nin. Sabrina, this is Inanna of the Night Sky. She is my aunt, mother to Mo, Serge, and Nin, and a member of The Council of Fae."

Sabrina bowed because she really had no clue what she was supposed to do in this situation. Gin had not covered Fae etiquette in their brief discussions. Inanna moved closer, studying Sabrina with a small smile. When they were just a step from each other, she stopped her appraisal and started the questions.

"Hello, Sabrina of Nin. You smell of my daughter's magic. Your name also tells me you are bound to her. True?"

"Yes."

"How long have you been bound to her?"

"About a day," Sabrina stated nervously, thinking it might look bad that this was so new.

Gin interjected here and gave some explanation, but the whole time they talked, Inanna remained fixated on Sabrina. So much so, Sabrina could not look away from her intense stare. "We surprised Nin, and Sabrina came to her defense not knowing what was happening. She was injured, Nin decided she could not have her cleared, and thus she was bound not too long after we came to the human realm."

"Hmm," she answered. "And what are you to my daughter? Lover? Friend?"

At this, Sabrina bristled a bit. This was Nin's mother, yes, but Nin was important to her too. And she was important to Nin. Important enough to do the binding on even. Staring right back in the woman's eyes and crossing her arms defiantly at her chest, she said "She is my sister. Not blood sisters, obviously, but still a sister."

At that, Inanna let out a husky laugh that sounded so much like Nin's that it made Sabrina's heart ache just a fraction. "I can see the family resemblance. We're all too stubborn for our own good at times. Come, then, Sabrina of Nin, and hug your new mother for the first time."

Sabrina was stock still as Inanna moved in and took her in her warm arms. That maternal hug, something Sabrina had not felt since her Gran passed, brought tears to her eyes. She hesitated only a second before wrapping her arms around this woman she just met and allowing her warmth to seep into her body in an oddly healing way.

Inanna pulled away, but kept Sabrina at arm's length, showing understanding and sadness in her dark eyes when she saw the tears shimmering in Sabrina's vision. She said no more, just squeezed her shoulders, gave a quick nod that looked eerily like Mo's curt movements, then stood to Sabrina's left side, hooking them together elbow-to-elbow. "The rest of The Council waits in the tower. Sten felt your arrival on the trolley, so we gathered quickly. I wanted to meet you before. I did not feel Nin with you, but sensed traces of her magic. I needed to know what had happened to prepare myself for the Council Meeting. Now I know and we must proceed with haste. There are many things to discuss and many decisions that must be made swiftly if we are to offer Nin the help she needs."

Inanna allowed the three in front of her to turn and proceed, pulling Sabrina back a few steps so they could linger just slightly behind the others for a few private words.

"How long have you known Nin?"

"About two years."

"How long have you known of Fae?"

"About a day."

"You are holding up admirably, then. You carry yourself well for someone unused to our place, people, or ways. Shows my girl chooses her people wisely. However, please do not take offense in this question, why are you here now? Why did they bring you? It is not the best of times for you to visit the Fae. Do you have magics?"

"No," Sabrina sighed. Inanna was not trying to be rude, and Sabrina understood why she asked the question. It must seem odd to her to learn an unknowing and non-magical human was brought along. Yet, the question beat right to the heart of something Sabrina had been stressing over in the back of her mind since she agreed to come along. She was not magic. She had no fighting skills. She had little skill, in fact, beyond a weirdly specific knowledge of John Milton that appeared somehow applicable to this situation and an ability to write, do research, and come to the defense of someone she loves without hesitation.

Sabrina knew none of that was small or insignificant, but when your enemy used powerful magic and thwarted others with magic time and time again, it made her doubt she had anything to really contribute. "Gin asked me to come and I agreed. I have some human knowledge they believe will be crucial in the current situation. I told them about some strange connections between Nin's story and some human writing I studied. Because of all that, they told Mo and Serge they felt I was important, whatever that means, and both seemed fine with bringing me along after that, though there were some grumbles about it. To be honest, I fear I won't be very helpful here."

Inanna gave her a dazzling smile and a pat on her cheek. "If Gin says it is important, it is important. Fear not. They are rarely wrong about such things. You will be of use. We will all help our Nin together, yes?"

Sabrina sighed but nodded. She wasn't totally reassured, but it was nice to hear.

"Now, I must tell you something quickly, before we reach the Tower, as I doubt the boys or Gin mentioned it. There are those in Fae who look down upon humans because they lack magic or long lives. One of the most egregious of these sits at the head of The Council. Steel yourself. He may shoot venom your way, but Gin, the boys, and I will stand with you. He would also never dare hurt someone bound to Nin, as he respects and fears power above all else. You are safe, but you may be annoyed very soon."

Sabrina swallowed hard. She was already worried about many things. She didn't need to add prejudicial men to that list. She was an academic, so really, it would be an all too familiar annoyance. That was at least a comfort, having a bit of experience about the next obstacle in her way. It seemed condescending men were just hard for women to escape in whatever realm they found themselves.

CHAPTER 12

Sabrina has steeled herself a bit after her chat with Inanna, but the lovely breeze and pleasant company of Nin's mother eased her mind as they walked toward the looming Tower. Once they neared the structure, Sabrina saw that, like the small footbridge, there was a guard outside the massive and heavy-looking wooden doors. This guard, however, seemed more attentive than the other. She guessed that was likely due to proximity to power — like Foucault said, people are more likely to behave in certain ways if they know they could be watched by some form of authority at any moment. Given the direction of her thoughts and the fact that they were strolling toward a tall, foreboding tower, Sabrina muttered "The Fae panopticon" to herself before snorting at her own, admittedly very nerdy and very niche, philosophical joke.

"What was that?" Inanna asked, still holding on to Sabrina's arm as they moved to pass through the threshold.

Sabrina was about to wave her weird academic joke away as unimportant when she felt a physical jolt. It was like a small shock wave traveled up her backbone, making her stretch up on the balls of her feet, an almost-jump caused by a tiny prick of pain and a whole lot of surprise. She looked around, eyes wide, as they passed through the open doorway, and it was Inanna's turn to give a small laugh. "Oh, that looked funny on you. Sorry, dear. I forgot to warn you. This is our most secure communal location in The Falls. It has extra magical security, which is what you likely felt because you are not officially a part of The Falls. If you had not been connected to me, or someone else connected to leadership in this place, jolt would have been much more aggressive."

Sabrina nodded. That level of security, and Inanna's position in this place, made her consider for the first time the fact that she was walking into what was ostensibly the headquarters of a rebellion and a place of peace and respite from tyranny. It was like journeying to Hoth or joining the followers of Earthseed in Acorn. It was a heady thing, knowing she was about to be part of the political workings in a new world full of powerful and dangerous magic. It made her stand a bit taller and look around more sharply so as to take in everything that she may need in the future. If she was there to help Nin, in any way, she needed to remain alert and at the ready.

Directly across the doorway was a small foyer with three doors: one each to the right and left and one massive door, just slightly smaller than the one guarded on the outside, directly in front of the entrance. Beyond that, there was nothing else. No bold and colorful banners, no tables or chairs, just doorways, walls, floors, and ceilings. It was a no-frills entrance that was purely functional, and that function was to simply direct individuals left, right, or center. Their party of five moved toward the center wooden doors. These were closed, latched with metal bars that made a massive, seemingly impenetrable grid across the entire expanse of thick wood. Inanna patted her hand once then disengaged from her elbow, moving around Gin and Serge to meet Mo at the front of their little group. At the same time, she and Mo held their hands palm out, shoulder width and height in front of them, and chanted in Fae. Magic was being called.

Sabrina watched, struck by the shimmer and shake of the metal as it seemed to fold into itself. It did not melt away but contracted to reveal hinges at the sides and a large center split marked with two intricately woven metal handles. Mo grasped one, Inanna the other, and they pushed inward at the same time. Sabrina imagined she heard a bit of a hiss of air, as if a seal had been broken, but that could have been her imagination.

She was so engrossed by the magic she hadn't noticed Gin move back to her side until she felt their hand at her shoulder. "Impressive bit of magic, if I do say so myself," they said on a beam.

"You did that?"

"Yes. It's a true seal, and only the spell uttered by two designated authorities of The Falls can make the metal casing recede. Otherwise, the metal is cursed and will cause serious physical damage to any who touch it directly. That's one of the reasons for the guard back there," they added, "to make sure no random Fae accidentally touches that door. The second layer requires the two authorities who spoke the spell to each push a handle simultaneously, of their own free volition, to allow the seal to break and the doors to open. Once we have passed, the door will seal itself back up. It will also only unseal on this side through the touch of one of the authorities who last opened the seal. One of my more intricate theoretical creations, and I did not actually cast it on my own. It took a number of spellcasters, metal mages, and Lesser Fae to get it in place and working correctly."

"What authorities?"

"There are certain Fae here who are appointed leaders. You have The Council, but also Mo, because he is considered the head of our fighters. He is like a general in an army. As the leader of the scholars and teachers here, I also have that honor. There are others, too: leaders of the healers, merchants, growers. All together, there are about twenty Fae who are designated authorities who can open that door, and do any number of other things for the people who live here."

"How many Fae live here?" Sabrina asked.

"I do not know for certain. The numbers change as more and more people ask for refuge. Numbers for the Lesser Fae are always hard to pin down precisely because they have a warranted fear of the Noble Fae and are not always that forthcoming with information their leaders may view as tactical. If given a general estimate, I would say between five and six thousand out of the approximately twenty-five thousand total Fae."

"Why is the overall Fae population so small? Your realm is large, right?"

"In terrain, yes. Our land could sustain many more Fae, but we have always had factions and those factions have always valued their own spaces. It's also often hard for Fae to reproduce. No one really knows why, but both Noble and Lesser Fae usually only have one child every few hundred years, even if they were to try to have more."

"Huh. Okay…" Sabrina wandered off at the end, letting her sentence hang. She had finally switched her gaze from Gin to the room where they stood. It was a massive semi-circle that took up at least half of the total diameter of the tower. They had stopped at what was basically a landing. To the right and left, wooden spiral staircases curved up and down the length of the entire tower. You could also see the tower not only extended up for several flights, but also down. The floor they were on had to be the central floor, because it held a constructed dais that looked as if it could be viewed from staring over the railing that surrounded the floors of each level. One on top of the other, the floors themselves were held together and connected by the spiral staircases at the end and massive wooden pillars that stretched up and down the length of the structure. Each floor was the same size and shape — a large rectangle with railings set out a few feet from the stone walls. The only difference was this level, the platform extended and slightly slanted outward at the far wall, giving this particular floor the shape of a semicircle and making that extra section visible to the levels above and below.

This was obviously where The Council met. Sabrina knew this not only because of the logic of the space, but because she watched Inanna walk to an empty seat in a row of five exquisitely carved and lushly cushioned chairs that were presently filled with other Fae. Inanna was in a chair on the left hand side, marking only one Fae to the left of her and the three remaining forming the rest of the semi-circle of poised and intently gazing Fae to the right of her.

The sole Fae on her left was massive, even seated in his chair. A hulking pile of muscles that held equal amounts of deep scarring and tattooing in thick black loops and swirls, he was intimidating even though he smiled more than any of the other Fae seated before them. To his right, leaning against his chair, was a huge broadsword that looked heavy enough to hurt someone if it simply knocked into them, nevermind the gleaming, menacing edge that was razor-sharp. He would be a giant when he stood, because Sabrina saw his knees were elevated, hovering inches above where the seat of the large chair was located, making him look like a kid who hit a growth spurt attempting to sit still and at ease in a middle school desk chair. His chest was mostly bare, which was why Sabrina could see all those scars and tattoos. They were clearly on display over the hides and furs that skirted his middle and slung haphazardly across his left shoulder. He had a tangled mass of blond curls and frizzes that engulfed his head because of his thick hair and beard. The only nods at grooming were three braids: two were intricate and oddly delicate 2-inch wide strands that started at his

temples and were pulled back, presumably to meet up
again somewhere at the back of his head; one started
about 3 inches from where she guessed his chin
would be (and that was just a guess as she had no
idea what was under all that beard), was woven with
blue and black clay beads, and was a good six inches
long. In all, this Fae was a lot to take in. Most of it
was intimidating at first glance, until you noticed the
expression on his face — a beaming smile and a
laugh in the eye that was a bit more soothing than
Sabrina would assume from the bulky frame and
aggressive weaponry.

Sabrina had been trying her best not to
rudely gawk at the giant Fae. She knew she failed
when he gave her a wink and a smirk.

Flustered, she looked around and noticed
she had been left behind. Mo, Serge, and Gin had all
moved forward about six feet and all three were
bowing toward the members of the Council. She
rushed forward, did a quick bow as well, and heard
an exasperated sigh in response. This came from the
man in the middle of the arc of chairs, to the left of
Inanna. He was dressed much like Gin, in a robe
reminiscent of a monk. Unlike Gin, his robes were
white with a large hood at the back. A thick gold

chain sat at his waist and only his face, hands, and sandaled feet were visible. That face, scowling at Sabrina, could be described as cherubic. Round and rosy cheeks, bright blue eyes, and sandy brown hair with small wisps of curls added to this effect. He had a young face that seemed frozen in adolescence. Only his height, which Sabrina judged by his long arms and legs and his rigid frame, belied that. He may look young and innocent at a distance, but there was more there in his eyes. All that arrested youth was marred by the disdain that clearly showed on his face when he looked towards Sabrina. This must be the one Inanna warned her about.

Next to him, things seemed a bit friendlier. A woman sat to his left dressed like every image of Queen Elizabeth Sabrina had ever seen. It was almost costume-like and included the starkly powdered face, brightly rouged circles on her cheeks, bright bowed of a mouth painted in the same vivid pink as her cheeks, stiff ruffled collar, and jewels pinned here and there. She was, however, not a redhead, but a brunette, with chestnut waves pulled back artfully from her face and cascading around her shoulders. She also had a beatific smile directed right at Sabrina. A giggle — very unexpected — fell from her mouth, which she quickly covered with a lace handkerchief in her hand. She then waved at Sabrina, issuing an obvious welcome, even if it felt too informal and out-of-place from her position on the platform.

Last in the row, at the far left end, sat a man in leather breeches with a half-opened and billowing linen shirt that perfectly framed a scattering of black chest hair on full display. His face was devilish — literally. He was smoldering, olive-toned, and sported a sharp black Van Dyke that matched his black arched brows and black slicked-back hair. It was a weird mix, the vaguely timeless (at least historically) garb on a Hispanic man that had artfully groomed himself in a deliberate way. He had a smirk like Serge and roved half-hooded eyes over Sabrina languidly. He was also the only Council Member not seated upright. Instead, he sat with legs across one arm of the chair, one arm thrown over the back of the chair, and his back resting against the other arm. He was lovely and sensual and the interest in his eyes may have been something Sabrina would awkwardly respond in her own time if there weren't far more pressing matters to deal with in the here-and-now.

Gin finally piped up, clearly their throat quickly and saying, "Council, may I introduce you to

Sabrina of Nin." At this introduction, there was a
flutter from the Elizabethan and the Norseman leaned
forward. The monk-man in the middle tsked in
obvious judgment, but the only one who said
anything was the man on the far left.

"How lovely for Nin. Found a human to call
her own. Will she share?"

"That is a ridiculous and inappropriate
question, Andrés," Monk Man snapped.

The Elizabethan lady tittered a bit. She then
swatted towards his chair with her lace handkerchief
and whispered, "Always so bad, Dre."

Gin hid a smile with a bow of his head but
then went straight back to business. "Sabrina, allow
me to introduce the Council. On your far right is Sten
of the Salt Seas." The giant stood and proved his
stature, nodding toward Sabrina with kindness in his
eyes and a soft grunt.

"Of course you have met Inanna of the
Shores. In the center, at the Council Head, sits
Michel the Learned." The robe man stood, haughty
and proud, but offered nothing to Sabrina. She looked
to Gin, who gave her wide eyes and a swift bob of the
head. She rightly took that to mean she should do
something to acknowledge this guy in an official

way. As they bowed before, she did so again, thinking it best to just go with what she knew. He stiffened, sniffed her way dismissively, and eased back down in the chair.

"Next, you have the lovely Jane of the Dale." When the Elizabethan woman rose at her name, Sabrina decided to give a low curtsy. It likely looked a bit absurd, curtsying in her jeans and t-shirt, but it seemed a fitting response to this gowned woman in front of her. Another giggle, a sparkle to the eye, and a wave of her lace handkerchief was her dismissal, but Sabrina had a feeling she'd done well with that greeting when she saw Jane's smiles and Michel's obvious annoyance.

"And finally, may I present Andrés of the Mountains." The man with the smooth eyes had an equally smooth gait, which Sabrina noted because he was already walking toward her before Gin had finished their introductions. He reached for her hand, which she gave on a bit of a blush. He bowed over it low, kissing it and letting his lips linger a touch too long. It was just shy of lecherous, so Sabrina pulled her hand away as he murmured, "Please, call me Dre. A pleasure, lovely Sabrina," before turning to swagger back to his lounging position in his chair.

"Enough introductions. We must have reports. Why have you not returned with Nin? She was summoned by this Council to appear," Michel boomed out, sucking the energy from the room and immediately focusing everyone, in a negative way, on the business at hand. Yes, they needed to move forward quickly. No, he did not need to be a complete ass about it.

"She was taken, sir," Mo clipped out as he stared straight ahead at attention.

"You allowed her to be taken?" Michel hissed.

That caused a stir. Sten and Inanna both jumped from their seats, staring daggers at Michel. Jane muttered, "Well, I say," and Dre perked up a little, swinging his legs forward so he actually sat upright in his chair and leaning down like he was readying to watch a boxing match.

"Do not say such to my son, who has served this Council and all of Fae with honor and courage for many, many centuries." Inanna seethed.

Michel looked sullen at the overt attack directed his way and crossed his arms in a pout. She had seen him in action for only a handful of moments, but Sabrina knew his type too well. He did not like contradiction at all. He would also place blame, always, but never take any himself.

Mo, meanwhile, stayed stoic and at attention. That only broke when Sten reached him, clapping a hand on his shoulder and leaning down deep to whisper in his ear. Mo's shoulders sagged a bit at this. He looked to the man that had to be a friend, and nodded before coming back to attention, ever the good soldier. Serge and Gin, however, were clearly on the alert and had closed ranks around Mo. Sabrina even caught herself moving closer to him, that dig from someone she did not know but already disliked making her feel protective towards a man she barely knew but still, somehow, felt connected to on a variety of levels.

"Do not listen to Michel, Mosi. You are a soldier of honor; you obviously would not let your sister go. What do you believe happened?" Sten asked gently once he was back in his seat.

"Obviously, Comus took her," Serge answered quickly before Mo could say anything. "Who else would or could have traced Gin's magic?" He cut his eyes toward the center of the arc. "Save Michel, of course," he added at the end, his words dripping with disdain.

"Is that an accusation, Sergius?" Michel demanded.

"No, sir. Just a statement of fact. You could trace Gin's magic, correct?"

Michel was stymied and Sabrina held in her laugh. For a man like that, it would be hard not to admit to any level of perceived power. In this situation, however, admitting that would be a bad thing. It was a crafty take down on Serge's part, and it made Sabrina like him even more.

"Well, of course, but maybe not, who could really tell with such turmoil these days?" Michel blustered.

"Enough. This is tiresome. No questions are necessary. Mo, just give your report and let us be done," Dre stated, now obviously tired of the meeting itself and ready to be done with it.

"Yes, sir. We found Nin with Gin's magic. Our initial encounter caused an accident that then led to Nin binding herself to Sabrina. Sabrina was then told of Fae. I discussed current issues and concerns with Nin. However, before she could return with us, she was somehow led into a smattering of woods outside of the wards surrounding her human home and taken by someone powerful enough to track us to the human realm and disguise the normal scent of their magic. It appeared there was also a struggle. All of this points to Nin now being a prisoner to Comus."

"Poor Nin," Jane whispered, putting her lace up to her eyes to catch a small tear that threatened to fall.

"Fine. I expect a scroll reporting all details of the conversations you had with Nin and her disappearance," Michel barked toward Mo. Mo did not verbally answer, just gave a swift nod in acceptance. "However," Michel continued, now turning snide eyes right at Sabrina, "that does not at all answer why you would bring a human woman here to Fae, much less let her enter the highly secured realm of The Falls."

"Human" dripped like acid from Michel's tongue, and Sabrina's back shot ramrod straight, ready to defend herself if need be.

"I am here for Nin," Sabrina proudly stated.

"Who is not actually here. And whose whereabouts, it seems, are currently unknown. Therefore, human, you have no reason to be her in Fae in general or here in front of this esteemed Council, specifically. You should not have been allowed into this Keep," Michel said, openly lashing out with every staccato word. He was very angry to have her in his presence.

"I was asked. Invited, even. But I don't need to explain my actions to you. If I've gotten right, I have certain protections because I am bonded to the Princess of the Green." Michel huffed at this, about to retort, but Sabrina cut him off. "I am Nin's. She is mine. Our relationship is not for you to understand or interrogate. I am here to help my friend and I'll do whatever I have to do to accomplish that. You don't need to know anything else about me."

"Not true, human." Michel sneered. "As head of The Council, I can ask any question I see fit, especially as it pertains to Fae safety."

"And I'm a threat? To you and Fae?" Sabrina laughed. She'd seen enough of the people and place at this point to know that was a joke.

"Humans are always a threat. Nin scurrying away to the human realm, much less bonding with an actual human, is beyond my imagination."

"Don't you dare start on Nin," Sabrina seethed, fist clenched.

Before she and Michel could escalate their back-and-forth, Gin touched her arm to calm her. Then, they spoke to the Council at large. "It was I who invited Sabrina to join us in Fae. I informed Mo and Serge she must accompany us. I said it was a feeling she would be useful, but truthfully it is more." They let out a deep breath and softly continued. "Sabrina has knowledge of a human text that I believe to be a Fae prophecy."

And with that quiet announcement, chaos ensued.

CHAPTER 13

Michel sputtered and rose from his chair, now staring daggers at both Sabrina and Gin. Sten sat back hard against his chair with a thud, shock written across his face. Inanna shook her head with a look of wonder towards Sabrina. Jane fluttered her lace even more, fanning herself as quickly as she could as if she were trying to ward off some escalating physical reaction. Dre was fully leaning forward, hands gripping the arms of the chair, and giving Sabrina a more assessing look.

She heard rumblings off to her side and looked to Mo and Serge, seeing that they were also deeply concerned by this announcement in ways she would not have guessed. Mo looked at her in amazement. Serge looked angry, furious even, before schooling his face and turning away from Gin and Sabrina. This was the most shocking reaction, as the easygoing Serge seemed unlikely to care about things like texts or prophecies or whatever, much less a human being knowing some old play, but it helped ground Sabrina in an odd way. If Serge was upset, this was serious. She turned to Gin, clearly needing more explanation, but so did everyone else in the room.

"I demand an explanation this instant, Borjigin!" Michel bellowed as he landed back into his seat hard.

"You can demand nothing of Borjigin as it pertains to a found prophecy, Michel, as you well know," Sten snapped back. That received a hurried nod and harrumph from Jane, accompanied with a narrow-eyed glare at Michel from Inanna. Dre slowly sat back in his own chair, adding nothing to the conversation, but looking at Sabrina a bit too intensely for her liking.

She, in turn, looked to Gin, hoping for some answers to what just happened and why it was so damn important. They opened their mouth to speak, but before anything happened, a seething Serge rounded on his cousin and hissed loudly, "Why were we not told?"

Gin softly said, "Sergius. I am sorry, cousin. I just…" and reached for Serge, who quickly stepped back to avoid Gin's touch.

"Son," Inanna called in a soothing voice. "You know Gin cannot reveal such things unless given direct permission by the person who has found the prophecy or first realized its significance. As that was likely Sabrina, and she has no knowledge whatsoever of these rules and rituals, that did not come. You were all also distraught from Nin's disappearance and tired from your quick return to Fae. This is not about you, my heart. It is a series of events that resulted in little time for anyone to fully understand what was happening."

Serge demurred to his mother but turned away from Gin and Sabrina to stomp across the room in a bit of a huff. It was odd, and so against the Serge she thought him to be, but then again, she had only known him for a little over 24 hours at this point.

Still wondering about Serge, and a little hurt by his odd reaction, she wasn't paying attention and was once again surprised at Mo suddenly being at her side. He still stood at attention, ever the soldier in front of his superiors, but he now posted so close to her side it would be hard for anyone not to take a hint: he was positioning himself to protect her. This, coupled with Serge's level of anger, made Sabrina truly frightened. The Fae looked human, but she had to remember they were not. Mo's superhuman speed made that very clear. She could easily be hurt or even killed in this new place with all this strange, wonderful, and exceedingly powerful magic. At these thoughts, she herself scooted a little closer to Mo, trusting him to keep her safe in this new and uncertain situation.

Gin shook his head on a long-suffering sigh before addressing The Council again. "You, above all others, realize that I have a scholarly responsibility to not reveal an unverified prophecy until research is completed, and only then when the original point of contact agrees to the revelation of specifics or reveals details themselves explicitly. As Inanna so accurately deduced, the past day has been hectic and uncertain. The position of the prophecy is sound, but not yet tested. Sabrina, knowing nothing of the place of prophecy in our world or how prophecies are treated here, could not do that. I needed time, but sadly had none. She showed me the human text I believe is a prophecy while I was away from the siblings, at her home. I did not tell anyone I thought this was a prophecy — Mo, Serge, or Sabrina herself — only that I thought the text would reveal much to us about the situation we currently find ourselves navigating. I am sorry this upsets you, but I am more sorry that all of this has been thrust onto Sabrina without her fully understanding what was happening.

"In fact," and at this point, they looked toward me with a hint of regret in their eyes, "I did too little to prepare overall. She has no knowledge of what Fae prophecy is, why this text seems to move beyond basic coincidence into prophecy, or the power of true prophecy in general in Fae. That is not a part of the human world outside of the stories they tell for entertainment. She came solely to help her friend, because she was asked and because she was told she could be of some service. That is who and what Sabrina is — a loyal and fierce protector at heart. That is all that can be spoken of here and now, and you know you must trust me in this."

This seemed to calm many in the room, but Sabrina still bristled. She was more than a little annoyed by this apparent bombshell. She didn't like being left in the dark on important things. Knowledge is power, and she was powerless enough in Fae. She also understood Gin had little time to get into nitty gritty details with her before their whirlwind travels. Sabrina had to shake off her annoyance and hope Gin would answer all her questions about this big reveal sooner rather than later.

Michel looked angry but chastised enough to give a sharp nod as a nonverbal form of acquiescence.

Surprisingly, at least for Sabrina, Jane then spoke up for her. "She must be inducted and allowed free passage to and through The Falls."

Sten called "Here, here," accenting his agreement with loud stomps of his feet. Inanna smiled toward Sabrina, nodding in agreement.

Neither Michel nor Dre responded, but no one paid them any mind. It seems three overt agreements were all that were needed.

"Allow me?" Inanna asked The Council, even though she had already risen and was walking towards Sabrina. Standing in front of Sabrina, only a step away, she smiled warmly and said, "Please, Sabrina. Close your eyes. Trust me for a moment."

Sabrina had known her practically no time at all, and she was not a trusting person in general, but she had felt the love and warmth from Inanna earlier. Had seen her acceptance and her defense. She closed her eyes, took a deep breath, and decided she had to trust both her own instincts and the Fae she felt were good and true, and that included both Inanna and Gin. She heard Inanna speaking in Fae, casting her spellwork. She felt a tingling warmth, the same feeling she had when she sipped a good bourbon, when Inanna put her hand over Sabrina's chest, directly above her heart. Her hand was warm and firm in and of itself, but also emitted a flash of power that sent heated pulses through Sabrina's system. After a moment, Inanna's hand moved to her mouth and the same feelings were repeated there. She moved her hand to Sabrina's forehead and the process started again. When she finished there, she moved her hand away and her chanting changed in cadence and tempo, to end on a semi-shout that seemed to blow a wind across Sabrina's entire front, a force so strong she almost had to go back on a foot to keep her balance.

Then, it was all over. "You may open your eyes, love," Inanna softly said, taking Sabrina's hands in her own. "You are now a part of The Falls. You can exit and enter as need be. You can lead certain others here and help them enter at your side, but no more than two individuals at the same time. You will always know how to return to The Falls no matter where you are in Fae, but you cannot reveal that knowledge to an outsider. This is what our spell does, so use it wisely and guard our refuge well. I trust that you will, my brave new daughter." With that, she leaned up to plant a soft kiss on Sabrina's cheek.

"This ridiculous human business should be concluded for now. The woman is spelled, let us move on," Michel said dismissively. "We must think more on Comus and what to do next."

"Yes," Sten interjected. "The time of caution is over. Our plans have been in place for a while. We have the means to wage a full attack. It is time we ousted Comus from The Palace."

"I'm unsure a full-scale battle is truly necessary," Jane interjected.

"Even with all the evidence before you? Bah. Like most women, you are too squeamish, Jane. You just do not wish to see a fight" Michel growled her way. At this sexist dismissal, palpable anger rose from everyone in the room.

"And what fight have you ever actually seen, Michel?" Dre interjected while looking entirely too fascinated by his fingernails.

"Stop. Sniping and arguing will not help this matter. Planning will," Inanna stated, and Sabrina felt that was the wise path even though anger at Michel's words was still hot in her.

"Yes, planning is important, but Inanna, you must see that we now have to bring a fight to Comus? Force is what he knows and what he will respond to in the end."

"Agreed," Mo answered.

"Even if we need to plan an assault on The Palace, which I do not know for certain is the case, we need to decide exactly how that would work," Inanna answered.

"Oh, please, come now. This grows even more tiresome. Mosi is our established military leader. He already had plans in place. He should just adapt those plans to the current moment and we should move forward decisively so we can be done with all this," Dre stated.

"Mosi is capable, yes, but we are The Council. It is our responsibility to sanction all plans in order to ensure the safety and preservation of all Fae." Michel added.

"Yes yes yes. Okay. Mo creates a specific battle plan to confront Comus, oust him from his position of power, and get Nin back," Inanna suggests. "He presents that plan to The Council, we vote on it, and move forward or regroup as needed. How does that sound?"

There were ayes all around, and Michel then demanded to hear back from Mo within the next two days.

"I have much to still discuss with you, Council," Michel added on a wave towards Mo, Serge, Gin and Sabrina, "however, you four are no longer required. Dismissed."

Sten snorted toward Michel, Jane smiled brightly and gave a grand wave goodbye, and Inanna rose to lead them to the chamber doors. She had to help them exit, just as she helped them enter. She gave her boys and Gin quick hugs, then reached for Sabrina as she tried to exit. Holding her tight, she whispered, "We will talk soon, you and I. Leave now knowing this: you have a purpose here. Continue to be brave and thoughtful, that will guide you through."

Sabrina nodded and exited, feeling the weight of those wooden doors shut and seal behind her. She met up with the group outside The Tower.

Serge looked a little less pissed off, but not by much. "We will have words, cousin," he clipped to Gin. "What you did not reveal could have had dire consequences for us, and for Sabrina. You should have told us. Sabrina, I will see you soon, I am sure. Until then…" He let that sentence trail off as he turned away and left without a wave or a solid goodbye.

"Do not mind him, Sabrina. He is angry with me, not you, and he has some reason. Rest assured, his anger burns bright, but also burns out quickly. He will be back to apologize for his behavior and be of further use soon," Gin revealed with a pat on her shoulder.

"What of Sabrina now?" Mo asked.

"In The Falls she is safe. I will take her. She is needed in my library. That is where we will study this human Fae prophecy more closely."

Mo nodded in agreement and took his own leave after a quick smile and bow to a blushing Sabrina.

"He has much to plan, and little time to do it," Gin explained, "but he will come see us soon as well. Now, however, we head to my home, and my library. I am so happy to show you my library." Gin added the last with a grin and led Sabrina away by her hand.

Sabrina, still reeling in many ways, had a lot of unanswered questions, many things Gin would need to reconcile for her. Despite all that, she wore a bright grin that was part excitement and part nervous energy. They were headed to a Fae library to study Milton, which was apparently some Fae prophecy she now needed to use to help her friend. Sabrina felt the weight of that on her shoulders, but they remained squared. She even felt a little more self-assured in this new place now. If she knew anything, she knew her way around a library. How different could a Fae library really be?

CHAPTER 14

Gin chatted cheerfully the entire time the two made the trek to their home. Other Fae they encountered were hesitant and curious, but no one seemed hostile. Actually, they mostly minded their own business and went about their day even if they noticed a human in their midst.

"The Fae are like all beings," Gin said when Sabrina asked about this, "they are concerned with the business of daily life most often and have little time to contemplate a small change or addition. If it does not directly affect them, it is of little concern."

They led Sabrina beyond a ring of Fae houses, to a small stone structure on the outskirts of The Falls. It was bordered by the stream on the outside, making it the very last house within the barrier. Past that stream was a small thicket of woods that teemed with life, inviting exploration and promising enchantment, until you realized one step into that woods, outside the protective ring of the stream, was a step into a more vulnerable place.

The house they moved toward was a squat, rounded single-story that rose from the ground like a small, perfectly aligned hill. It was made from stones gathered in various shades of brown ranging in color from Mississippi mud to beach sand, a kaleidoscope of neutrals that put the mind at ease. The pathway to the front door was pink sand. This narrow lane was outlined by a long, yellowish-green grass dotted with the occasional orange flower. The front door was an arched explosion of yellows and oranges and stark whites that at first looked chaotic, but upon closer inspection formed a pattern, like the fractal that emerges when you look at an ice crystal under a microscope. It was web-like but also starry, a complex pattern but a natural pattern nonetheless, organic and comforting. It fit what she knew of Gin perfectly.

They reached for their door, muttered a few words, then swung it open. Seemed magic worked just as well as locks in Fae. Gin grinned shyly, dipped their head, and extended an arm into the shadow of the doorway and said, "Welcome to my home."

Sabrina stepped inside and could think of no other word but cozy. What greeted her matched the outside in many ways. It was a giant circular room with curving walls. Wooden floors were topped with full, richly patterned rugs in a multitude of colors. Tables were stacked with books and scrolls. Overstuffed chairs and one very fluffy looking floor pad made up the seating in what would be called the living area.

A large fireplace, about twice the size of the average American fireplace and tall enough to stoop into, roared to life at her right after Gin said a few words, and she could see a cooking set-up there with a weathered Dutch oven, a teapot, and even an old toast turner for the fire. The vast interior of the fireplace was blackened by prolonged and consistent use, but was pristine on the outside, constructed with the same variety of stone as the exterior of the house.

Further in was an intricately overlaid table about thigh-high, surrounded by cushioned seating. Cabinets lined the far wall, interrupted only by a small modern sink that looked a little anachronistic in the otherwise pre-industrial home. There were three other doors in the space, one next to the giant fireplace on the right and two closely situated on the curved wall to the left. Given the kitchen set-up, Sabrina really hoped one was an anachronistic bathroom that matched that out-of-place modern sink.

"Tea?" Gin asked, bustling towards their fireplace to grab the iron teapot.

"Yes, please." While Gin moved to fill the teapot from the sink and make other preparations, Sabrina wandered over to the nearest overstuffed chair. The side table next to it held a mountain of books, scrolls, and loose papers. Some were clearly in English, some were in other human languages she recognized, and others were in scripts she did not know. They could be archaic human languages or Fae languages. She did not know for sure. This made her give off a bit of a huff. She hadn't really considered the logistics of books in Fae, which was a very

American thing for her to do, she knew — not think about the barriers and uses of other languages beyond English.

She was fluent in French, passable in Spanish, but beyond that she would be completely lost and of little use. After picking up one of the texts in an unknown language and leafing through the pages, she let her shoulders sag a bit and placed it back down on the stack where it came.

"Oh, Sabrina, love. Do not worry," Gin asserted when they looked up from tea prep to see what she had been doing and apparently feeling. It must have been written all over her face. "May I?" they asked, nodding toward her and their hands. "A spell." They offered for clarification before Sabrina could ask.

"Yeah. Sure. Okay, go ahead," she said, straightening herself and closing her eyes.

Gin chuckled before beginning, saying, "See? You are already so very good at preparing for a spell." They reached a hand forward, laying it gently across her eyes, and muttered in Fae. Sabrina felt a tingle, then a more persistent burn, then a burst of white light even though her eyes were closed. She heard Gin give an okay and she blinked her eyes open, trying to push away the starbursts flashing across her vision. When they were cleared, she looked back at the pile on the table beside her and, sure enough, all of it appeared in English.

"A handy trick for a researcher," she whispered in amazement, thinking about all the wonderful things she could easily read with this new power.

"Yes. One of my favorites for that very reason. Before we start talking about reading and research, please, have a seat and tell me how you take your tea."

She plopped herself down in the chair at her side. The kettle was ready, the tea seeped, and Gin poured it into very delicate Asian tea cups, a lovely shade of jade green painted with a thick, glossy black band at the bottom and a more fine black lip at the top. "It's a blend of something very similar to your green tea, with a few other herbs mixed in to help calm you. I think you may need it after all that has occurred today."

"For sure. Good looking out, Gin. If you have a little sugar or some form of sweetener, I wouldn't mind that."

Gin nodded and finished the tea up, handing the cup to Sabrina. She felt instantly better, the comforting and familiar warmth of the tea seeping into the palms of her hands as she smelled a lovely blend of sweet and floral scents wafting from the cup. She took a tentative sip and let out a sigh of relief when the hot, tasty liquid began to warm her from the inside out. "Perfection," she said with a smile, turning fully to Gin, who was observing her with a smile of relief in their own comfy chair opposite her.

"Rough day?" they asked with a bit of a laugh in their voice. Sabrina let out a harsh psst sound while running a hand through her hair. "First, let me apologize. There is much I did not warn you about before coming here: what we would go through on our journey here, the protection wards, some prejudiced Fae, the importance and meaning of Fae prophesy and your connection to that…"

"Yeah, all that was left out," Sabrina deadpanned, but she softened when she saw the regret plainly written on Gin's face. "Look, it's not really your fault. You told me a whole lot the other night in our chat. We had no idea that Nin would be taken and I would need to know so much about Fae and magic and … whatever else so quickly. That's not on you."

"Thank you for saying so, but…"

"Nope. No 'buts,'" Sabrina added, firmly but without malice. "The things with magic and my experiences seem like they would be easy for you to forget, overlook, because they are such a part of you and every Fae's daily life and I get the feeling you haven't hung out with a human in a while."

"Centuries," Gin added, then sipping their tea slowly, letting Sabrina continue.

"Okay. Centuries. Jeez, y'all are very, very old. Wait. We'll circle back around to that later. Not important now." Sabrina rambled but then reigned it in with the wave of the hand and an intense refocus at Gin. "What is important is this prophecy business, which seemed to freak everyone right the hell out. You were prepared for that response. That tells me you knew, likely from the moment I told you about the Milton play, how important it actually was. You did say that to me, but not in any truly forceful way. Definitely not with the gravity that everyone else's reaction to your little reveal would warrant." Sabrina paused, reeling in her annoyance a bit because there were a lot of different factors to consider and while she was annoyed, she couldn't totally blame Gin for

not being chatty Kathy when so much was happening

at once. She took a beat, had a breath, and carried on.

"I don't know much at all about Fae, the

people or the place, but everyone in that room earlier

seemed very upset with you about this prophecy

business. It must be serious. And if it involves me,

and could have had consequences on our journey,

which Serge implied, I really should've been told

more about it from the jump. I feel like there is this

big thing I don't know guiding me, circling me, and

not only do I not know that thing, I don't even know

why it would be so important or significant in

general. Like I'm a bird, unknowingly trapped in a

glass dome. They don't know what cages them, or

even that something does cage them because they can

see the sky, but it limits them in a way that can hurt

them if they try to go beyond it. See what I'm saying

here, Gin? This was apparently a big deal, it involved

me, and you didn't tell me about it or how much of a

big deal it was before I agreed to come. I'd still fight

for Nin regardless, but I had the right to know all that

I was getting into here first. We call it informed

consent in human research or medicine — the idea

that you should always be aware of the pros and cons of a thing before you agree to do it."

"You are correct, Sabrina. Again, I do very much apologize for all I did not reveal, but the prophecy issue was the biggest omission. I should have explained I thought the play was a Fae prophecy, what Fae prophecies are, and what that means for you and all of us. It is a lot, but all of it is important to you and Nin and our overall fight against Comus. Even if I didn't have time to tell you every detail, I should have told you more."

"Okay. Now, we move forward. I understand that a lot of different things converged all at once to cause this issue, but please don't withhold something so important in the future. Really, just don't withhold anything that may involve me. I'm a person that likes to learn in general, but right now I'm also a human woman who needs to know what's happening around her because I'm mostly flying blind here."

"Yes, Sabrina. Like any good scholar, I, too, learn, and I will not make this same mistake in the future."

With that, Sabrina raised her teacup toward Gin in a quasi-salute, acknowledging without words that she forgave, that she still trusted even if that trust was now a little brittle. Like all things, trust can ebb and flow, depending on circumstances and events over time. Sabrina had a feeling her trust in Gin was not misguided, that it would be fortified and grow even stronger after this.

"Right," she clipped, setting the teacup down on top of a book, which was sadly the only place to rest it, and leaning back in her chair. Crossing her arms and cocking her head, she added "Now about that prophecy business…"

"Of course," Gin interjected, nearly jumping in their seat at the ability to answer some questions, to impart some knowledge. "You were correct in your observation during Council — they were all shocked by my additional information about a possible prophecy. This is because prophecies derive from a very old and still unknown source of natural magic in Fae. They are written down by seers, sealed away so as to be found only by the right person at the right time. Seers themselves know nothing of it. The magic takes them, they know they lose time, sometimes hours and sometimes days, and that is the only clue they have that they wrote a prophecy. Everything else is gone from their memory. This happens so rarely that whole generations of seers can go by without one having a prophecy."

"What does a seer normally do then? What makes a prophecy different?"

"Seers normally only get glimpses into the immediate future, and that is only connected to people they know or are in direct contact with in order to help or hinder. Also, visions are more malleable, they can shift and change based on decisions that individuals make for themselves or others. Prophecy is more like fate — it will come to pass no matter what decisions are made. Unlike visions, however, prophecies are obtuse, sometimes overly vague, written in riddle form, or even so specific in their allusions that it is hard to tell what fits until after the fact. If a possible prophecy is found, scholars try to decipher it as best they can because it is a direct knowledge of the future that usually involves very big events, good or bad."

"And you think Milton's masque is a prophecy?"

"Yes. Not only does it have too many matching details to be pure coincidence, but the manner of Fae discovery is an important indication. I only discovered this play because you, a human who happened to form a deep and loving friendship with a Fae Princess, is an expert on this very particular text. A text that directly relates to that Fae Princess you befriended, although you did not realize that until a series of events unfolded that made it clear. That series of events that seems serendipitous is a mark that this is a prophecy. Without fate, without something guiding so many over such a long period of time, none of this could have happened as it did."

"Therefore, it has to be a prophecy, because fate or some form of cosmic whatever caused all of us to meet, interact, and discover this esoteric play that lays out issues connected to Nin and Comus — the central struggle that seems to be rocking all of Fae at this moment."

"Exactly. Fate, destiny, whatever you will, it was meant to be presented by you to me in our very hour of need, created and somehow transmitted by some seer long ago who didn't even realize what they were doing."

"Is it that combination of fate and unknown magic that makes people pay so much attention to these prophecies?"

"That and the fact that in recorded Fae history, which goes back a very, very long time, there has never been a prophecy discovered that did not come to pass."

"Oh, wow. Okay. Does this mean Milton was Fae? Or even a seer?"

"It is a possibility, but it's a very, very small possibility. As you have said, he was a famous human only a few hundred years ago. No Fae has risked human notoriety since long before then. The more likely scenario is that a Fae seer gave him the prophecy, or he found the prophecy hidden somewhere and used it as the basis for his drama. That would make this even more complicated. The play would then be a secondhand prophecy, taken from its already cryptic original form and made even more obscure through translation and a writer's creative liberties with the original material. It is something unheard of in Fae until now."

"That's, well…shit. Gin, that's heavy and weird. That means we'll have to treat this differently than other prophecies while also getting as much information from it as possible."

"Yes. Exactly. On top of this, prophecy is only ever fully confirmed after the fact, so other Fae will not believe in what we have discovered until much of the events of the play come to pass in one way or another. All of this means you and I are on our own. We must use both our formidable skills as scholars to better understand this text in light of what has already happened and what we know may happen while also taking into account that this Milton fellow may have changed some things around. We must also do this as soon as possible, giving everything we uncover to Mo and The Council and convincing them of its accuracy as best we can in the hopes it will help save our Nin."

Sabrina moved from her chair, seeing the sadness in Gin's eyes and needing to do something about it, and came to kneel by them, placing her hands on theirs, now folded still in their lap. "We got this, you and I. I feel that. We'll do whatever we have to do, use whatever tool is at our disposal, to make sure Nin is safe again."

With a look of worry, Gin said, "I have the same drive and hope, but we must also be realistic. What is to come will not be easy, emotionally, intellectually, or even physically if we find we are called to the fight. Our victory is not at all guaranteed. It may all be even harder on you because you are a human in Fae. You need to also acknowledge this."

"Thanks for the pep talk," Sabrina sarcastically stated, trying to lighten the mood a bit, but she saw that Gin needed some reassurance. "Yes, Gin. I know this. I knew this when I agreed to come, even without all the more dire specifics. I also know we will stand together, we'll do what we must to get Nin back and beat Comus' ass!"

Gin finally cracked a wry smile at that last bit, which made Sabrina beam back at them. She was fine with kicking some ass, she thought, if that ass needed kicking. If she herself was kicked around while doing it, that was a small price to pay to help Nin and her family, who were becoming more and more important to Sabrina by the minute.

CHAPTER 15

They both finished their tea in comfortable silence, taking the opportunity to decompress. It was nice. Sabrina appreciated that she and Gin could sit quietly and not chatter. It helped her find some mellow and feel more tightly connected to this Fae she was coming to respect and care about in a very brief amount of time. Sabrina knew, however, they had little time for these small luxuries. She stood from her and gave herself a big stretch. Turning to eye Gin, she said, "Let's do this. And by this, I mean start researching. I think that may be where the two of us do the most good for any coming fight."

"Okay. Let us begin. As you were kind enough to allow me in your library…"

"Office," Sabrina corrected with a laugh. "Not exactly a library. Just a collection of a few bookshelves packed full."

"Still a library of sorts. All libraries, offices, and bookshops are special, no? Any place that stores writing, the knowledge kept on paper to be preserved and passed down, is an important place."

"This is true."

"Quite. Now, let me do a brief tour of the house and we will end in my library." Gin proceeded to basically point out areas to Sabrina in the big open room where you could find everyday items or where they would take their meals. The door next to the fireplace was Gin's bedroom, and when they opened the door to show her, Sabrina saw a swirl of more bright yellows and oranges that matched the door painted along the walls. This brightness made the space feel huge and special even though it was small and sparsely furnished. The painting was the focus, and the wide bed, bedside tables, and single chest in the corner all seemed to blend into the effect on the walls. Again, it felt very Gin, or what Sabrina knew of them so far — a bright spot of calm and focus that made you smile a bit just being in that presence. Soothing, just as Gin seemed to be.

The door on the opposite wall, closest to the entryway, was in fact a bathroom. It was basic — toilet, small pedestal sink, single shower stall — but functional. Like the kitchen sink, it seemed off in this place, but Sabrina was very happy to see it. It did make her ask, "Why do you have a contemporary human bathroom when you haven't seen a human in centuries?"

"Fae and humans both have the same bodily functions and needs. We also value hygiene. Bathroom facilities have been standard here for a very long time, longer than with humans in fact. This bathroom looks contemporary to you, but if you look more closely you will see that there are different technologies that keep it all together and functioning. It's not magic, just a slightly different approach based on the way our realm operates similar to, but different from, your realm. A lot of things are like that, Sabrina. It is why our food and drink are safe for you, as is our air, but they might smell or taste or feel a little different. There are many things we share as our realms are alike."

This made logical sense to Sabrina. If the two different realms functioned like some theoretical physicists and science fiction writers conceived of parallel universes, then the Fae world seemed like a smaller version of her world, more contained and with fewer people, with the one major functional difference being the existence of magic. Fae looked human, knew a lot of humans because they had the ability to go between worlds, but were just a little different in their progress and functioning because of the inclusion of magic.

Moving on, Gin came to the final door in his small cottage. Sabrina figured this was the library, which was probably like her own office, a small room with some seating but mostly packed bookcases, seeing as Gin called her small office in her tiny trailer a library. It couldn't hold much in the space, and the overflow of books around the open-space common area in Gin's house also pointed to this. Regardless, Sabrina was excited to see Gin's collection of research materials, to dig into the old texts and see what she discovered.

"I do not let many in here. It is a sanctuary of sorts. It also houses some very old and very rare materials, which is why I have it spelled closed. I will

lift that spell for you so you can enter as you wish.
You can even stay in here if you like, there is a space
to sleep. I will ask that you be very mindful of what
you do and say in here. Fae books can both hold and
unleash magic. Some can cause havoc just from
being read. Mind all warnings on or at the beginnings
of books, papers, or scrolls and you should be fine.
You told me of your years working in a library at
your university, so I feel like you will treat the books
well. A part of me is excited to share this space with
someone who loves books and knowledge as I do."

That last was said with a sly, private grin
before Gin turned to fully face the closed door. They
cast a spell much like the one she had seen Mo and
Inanna perform at the Tower, but less complex in
language and action. Gin waved a hand over the
wooden door while chanting, gripped the brass
handle, then stopped speaking when an audible hiss
of a seal opening could be heard, and the click of a
door latch sounded. Gin pushed open the door and
stepped aside, giving Sabrina a silent signal to enter
the room before they did.

She walked through the door and was
stunned. Before her was an actual library, one like
you might see in the old, large English manor house

of a rich nobleman who enjoyed books. It held
gleaming wood stacks of bookcases that rose four
stories in the air. A small, staggered staircase and a
square gangway at each floor level allowed you
access to all the books. On the ground floor there
were massive oak tables strewn with open books,
loose papers, scraps of notes, quills and pens both,
and squat chairs. A large fireplace, flanked by a
massive set of windows stretched on the wall
opposite the door lit and warmed the space. She stood
there, mouth literally agape, unable to comprehend
the beauty of owning such a place.

"What do you think?" Gin asked quietly,
seeming to really want a positive answer.

"I think it's the absolute, hands-down,
greatest personal library I have ever seen, in real life
or in TV or movies. It's…magnificent." She beamed
over at Gin, who grinned back with pride, and took
her hand.

"Come," they said in reply, "Let me show
you more."

These are, of course, study tables. I will
clear this one on our left for you to use exclusively.
There, in that back left corner, is a catalog of the
books."

"A card catalog!" Sabrina gasped and ran over to it, having completely missed this treasure when she first took in the space. It was tucked into the far corner, flush with the bookcases built into the wall. Each small shelf that she pulled out showed cards and cards and cards directing her towards books by subject based on floor, bookcase, and shelf numbers she now could see marked with small brass plates all around the room. "I haven't seen one of these since I was a little girl, looking up books in Wilde's old library, which had them for so long only because it took a while to raise the money for a digital conversion. All libraries I know of are digitized now, which is great for ease and accessibility. But there was always something about the physical action of flipping through the cards that I missed."

"Some do not think about the tactile pleasure of research, of holding paper in your hand and learning. There is a special feeling that gives you."

"So very true," Sabrina replied on a happy sigh, giving the catalog a loving pat as if it were a good pet that needed rubbing. "Okay. What other surprises are here?"

"It is just a basic library. A lot of material, most is from Fae, but there are some human texts here. You can use the catalog to find any additional materials or references you may need, although you yourself brought the most pertinent materials. There is a pulley system in the far corner there to help you cart books up and down the floors. Sorry to say there is no pulley system for us, we must walk the steps. Oh, and there is the sleeping space. Let me show you."

Gin moved to the right and opened another door Sabrina had completely missed in her initial excitement. Inside was a small room, about 8'x8', with a heavy wooden double bed, a small bedside table with a lamp, and a squat three drawer dresser. The bed, table, and dresser were all a gleaming and bright pine, and the curtains over the tiny window high above the bed, the bedding, and the small cloth draped over both the table and dresser were all a soft, butter color, a yellow so smooth and light it was just shy of cream. Sabrina said nothing as she took in the space, and Gin began to talk.

"It's not much, I know. And I do wish I had a better room to offer, but I get so few guests staying here it has never been an issue. If you wish, I will

217

take this room and you may use mine. It is brighter and…"

"No no no. This is great. It's light and airy and secluded. Like a little Scandinavian offshoot of your very dense and heavy and beautiful library. It's perfection."

"I am pleased you enjoy it. If you do need anything, at any time, you be sure to let me know. However, I have a feeling you may need some alone time. I myself need to rest for a bit before we begin our work. Would you like a shower, a nap, some food?"

"All of the above would be great."

"Excellent. You take the first shower, and I will prepare a small snack. Then, we'll have a little time to rest on our own and meet back up here later."

"Sounds like a plan," Sabrina replied, moving out of the bedroom and making her way to the library door. "I'll just grab my backpack and head to the bathroom if that's okay."

"Yes. Go right ahead."

Sabrina stopped at the door, took another look around the massive library, and turned back on Gin. "Okay, one last question from me before I go to clean up. How is this hidden? Why is it hidden? I mean, I know it's magic, but I'm just curious about the literal process."

"My library is massive and well-known, even if there are not many Fae who have been inside of it in the past. It needed to be hidden to be untraceable to a certain degree. Some of the books can be tracked, and a cloaking spell on the entire structure of the library was required. The house was constructed on the outskirts, the library was magically moved from my old home to this cottage and connected after it was built, sealed and cloaked so no one could see or sense it. Fae in The Falls know it is here, somewhere around my home, but they don't even know the full details of it beyond a few close to me. It is a special place with a purpose and is therefore protected."

"Makes sense, I guess. Fae magic doesn't have to conform to human ideas about physics, right?" She made her mind calm the other questions she had. They could wait. What needed to get done so they could start good, solid research could not. "Okay. I need to clean myself, eat some food, and take a power nap. In that order. Let's get to it." Sabrina went to retrieve her bag and take the hottest shower possible while Gin prepped a snack and fussed around the house being a good host.

* * *

She didn't waste time in the shower — she had no idea about the hot water situation in Fae — and exited the small bathroom with a puff of steam wafting behind her only fifteen minutes after she entered. Sabrina was toweling off her clean hair, scrunching it to mop up excess water, and talking to Gin without looking around her.

"Okay. That was ah-mazing. Really needed to wash the travel off my skin. I was so damn sweaty." When she looked up from drying her head, she froze. She was a deer on the backroads of Wilde, trapped in headlights, because Gin was nowhere to be found, but Mo stood staring at her.

He hovered between the armchairs in the living room. Sabrina felt heat in the stare, which made her stiff and unsure. She also felt a wave of embarrassment. She looked like a wet, dripping fool of a human, having just pulled on a bright pink tank with a shelf bra and lightning print capri leggings after her quick shower. She went for comfort over fashion when she could, but it didn't make her feel better when this beautiful and dark Fae man stood staring at her while her hair dripped and her chubbiness was on full display in this tight get-up.

"Oh, hey," she muttered, slouching a bit and throwing the damp towel across her shoulders. "Where's Gin?"

"They…" Mo started, but his voice was rough and scratchy. He cleared it and started over. "They had to briefly step out to gather additional supplies."

"For me or in general?"

Mo, looking away finally and studying a pile of books on a table, said, "I believe both."

Sabrina didn't want to put anyone out. "Unnecessary, for me at least. I'd manage fine. But what are you doing here? Shouldn't you be planning?"

"Gin did not wish for you to be alone, even if only for a few minutes."

"Kind, but again, not necessary. Also, why you? You're super busy. You don't need to babysit me. I'm good." Sabrina plopped down on a chair to help prove her point.

Mo looked up then, heat in his eyes, a gaze that pinned her to that chair. "It takes time to gather forces. I can wait here as I can wait there. There is little difference for now. And I did not wish for you to be alone."

"Well...okay," Sabrina muttered, looking away when she was finally able to do so. She was flustered, unsure of how to proceed. Mo did things to her, emotionally and physically, when he was around. It was unlike any feeling she'd had for a man before. He was still Nin's brother, though. They were also in the middle of some very serious business. It was not the time to explore those feelings. She could even admit she may never want to explore those feelings. They were big and bold and more than a little overwhelming.

"Sabrina, I..." Mo began, moving closer to her, smiling with a little hesitancy, when Gin burst back into the house. They smiled broadly but they stopped, bouncing a look between Sabrina and Mo.

"I do apologize," they said, but Sabrina was done with the beginnings of conversations she really did not want to have.

"No problem. No problem at all, Gin. I just got out of the shower. Mo told me where you were.

Hope you didn't go to too much trouble for me. Like, I'm fine. Totally good. No need to bother yourself." She knew she rambled when she was unsure or nervous, and she was both in the moment. She moved toward Gin, who now looked closely at Mo. He turned away from everyone in the room when I started speaking with Gin.

"Yes. All is well, cousin," Mo said, turning back to Sabrina and Gin, now both standing just inside the door. He moved forward swiftly, stopping short. "I am afraid I must leave immediately. There is much to do."

"Yes. Quite," Gin chirped, plastering a bright smile on their face. "Do let us know if we can be of assistance. And we shall inform you when we learn more from the potential prophecy."

Mod gave a curt nod, then turned to Sabrina. His face softened a bit, although worry or confusion or something else she could not name made his forehead wrinkle and knitted his brows. "Sabrina," he said with a gruff voice. He snatched her hand, bent low, and brushed hot lips there. She started, warmth tingling up her arm at the feel of his lush lips on her skin. "A pleasure, as always, dear lady." He exited, leaving both Gin and Sabrina gaping in his wake.

Gin opened their mouth, a smirk forming there before words, when Sabrina brought up a hand. "Nope. Not now, Gin. Maybe not ever, but definitely not now. Now I need food and a power nap. In that order." She turned to walk further into the house and hopefully Gin left the conversation they wanted to have at the door. There were more important things to concentrate on at the moment.

Research would start soon but having food and rest after such a long day was important. Brain-scattered research, based in exhaustion or hunger or desperation, would help no one, and they all needed to be at their best to save Nin. Though too much time spent on these things was out of the question. They had a Lady to save.

CHAPTER 16

It was after her disco nap. Both Sabrina and Gin had been going for over 24 hours at this point and Sabrina knew that she needed some sleep to be of any use in the library. Luckily she had put her phone in her bag out of reflex. It didn't get a signal in a parallel world, obviously, but it still had a functioning timer. She woke with a start when a blaring sound similar to the alarm on a nuclear reactor filled the small space. Swiping her phone off, she stumbled from bed and did a few yoga stretches to stretch her body and get her blood flowing. She was about to head out of the room when a soft tap sounded at her door.

"Yes?" she called hesitantly, stopping just shy of opening the door. She figured it was Gin, but surprises had been popping up everywhere, so precaution was a good idea in Fae.

"Just me, dear. Wanted to see if you needed anything. Tea? Water? Another snack?"

Sabrina opened the door with a wan smile. She liked Gin and she wanted to be their friend, but she was living on little sleep in a brave new world and a bright, big smile was just too much to muster at this point. "No, Gin, but thank you. I figure we should get started on some research." She noticed the high dark outside the library windows when she entered the chamber. "Is time here the same?"

"Depends on where you are and what your comparison is," Gin stated while ushering Nin to a seat at a cleared research table, "but if you mean the same as when we left the human realm, then just about, give or take a handful of hours. And time passes at the same rate."

"So that means Nin has now been gone for about 24 hours."

"More or less, yes. A day with Comus must feel longer than 24 hours for her, however."

Sabrina gave a sad nod. "True, true. Now, where do we start?"

"That is the question, is it not? Where does all good research start? With what we already know."

"Exactly! And what we know, on my end at least, revolves around an old play I studied as a grad student. Let me think about reality versus fiction for a minute before diving in. Bear with me. Our purpose is to save Nin, who is being held by Comus, who is, as you confirmed, the son of Bacchus and Circe, who I cannot believe were actually real, Fae or not. He is in the Fae Palace, acting as a Prince, having taken it over in some form of coup after the Mae Queen disappeared." She trailed off there, thinking quietly to herself now.

"Yes. We know Comus holds great magical power himself, especially from the chalice and wand he wields, leftovers from his mother."

"Which brings us all back to Milton. That's directly in the play. Comus is the main bad guy in this play. He kidnaps a young woman and that woman's two brothers and guiding spirit go off to find and rescue her. Comus has a cup and a wand that help him wield magical powers. The cup comes from his mother — Circe. In the end, the young lady is freed by some river goddess named Sabrina. It's all there." Shaking her head in disbelief, she mutters, "It all fits. Don't know why, but it all fits."

Pulling the purple Norton edition of Milton's works out of her duffel, she handed it Gin's way. "I remember a lot of this. It's kinda trapped in my head from repeated reading, so you take this. I'll start reading through some of this Milton research to see if anything outside of the text points us in a particular direction."

"A sensible strategy. However, you'll need your own version of the play to reference. I'll copy this quickly." Instead of heading to a copy machine, they muttered Fae over the open book. To the right of the text, an exact replica of the Milton collection materialized.

"Huh. Well I guess that's a little handier than a Xerox machine." Sabrina said to a confused Gin. "Nevermind. A very human thing that's unimportant right now. It reminds me, though. Before we begin, you're sure Milton wasn't a Fae seer or human prophet? That could affect our understanding of things."

"Highly unlikely. He was probably human. Some humans can see some shadings of the future, but no human has true prophetic ability that we've ever seen. No. It was discovered by or revealed to the writer somehow, written by him, then published."

"Not only published, Gin. Performed. For centuries. Not many people know it now, *Paradise Lost* is usually the only thing people know of Milton, but John Milton is considered one of the biggies in British literature. People study his work extensively. It gets put into production at national theaters to this day. Hell, my entire thesis was on how Milton portrayed women in his texts — including The Lady and Sabrina from this particular play. I have books and books and papers upon papers here with me and it's just a drop in the bucket compared to all that people have said about Milton and this play in the past few hundred years of human history. I wish we had access to more here."

"If this is Fae prophecy unearthed, as I believe it to be, we have all we need between the two of us," Gin replied in an effort to reassure her the two of them, working together, were enough.

"Okay. I'll skim through these other texts but come back to the play and do a quick re-read. I'll just take the Norton copy. We can come back and discuss what we think after, yes?"

Gin nodded and, reaching into the folds of their robe, held out two large fountain pens. "For notes," they added.

Sabrina grinned as she took a pen. "I knew I liked you, Gin. Notes in margins are absolutely necessary."

"Yes. Marginalia can be most effective."

"No pristine books here. Books are to be used, read, learned from and written in when necessary. Annotate away!" She shouted this as she moved to sit on her own at a cleared table, underlining text, taking notes, muttering to herself, and chewing on the end of the pen Gin gave her as she thought hard about what Milton wrote, what others had said about it, and what it all might actually mean.

Luckily the play was fairly short, Sabrina was already familiar with all the books she had brought along, and both of them read at dizzying speeds. They both finished reading quickly, even with writing notes and underlining and staring in dumbfounded awe at some of the similarities that popped up in this Milton drama from nearly 400 years ago. Sabrina looked up to see Gin was done and patiently waited for her to finish her review of the extra materials. They motioned for her to join them.

She sat down with a thump into an overly large leather chair and started, "First of all, just have to get this out there: all that virginity business is ridiculous."

Gin gave a quick laugh. "I never understood humanity's general obsession with virginity over the past few thousand years."

"Me neither, friend. Milton was a man of his time, though, and a political man to boot, which is obvious here in some of this. Being a political man meant being a religious man then, and these English protestants separating from the monarchy and the Church of England in the 17th century were no joke. They literally took off a king's head right in the middle of London. Milton himself wrote an essay about how necessary it was to execute that king. Wild stuff. But, general ideas of bad people in charge and tyranny aside, not really important for our situation. If we take out the religious references and the more specific political dynamics associated with England in the early 1700s, there's a lot here that directly corresponds to what is happening here and now."

"Yes. There is all you listed earlier from the top of your head. There is the guilt the brothers feel."

"Although them being barely in puberty definitely does not describe Mo or Serge."

"Not quite. There is the spirit guide, who seems to be like an angel of sorts. I think that might be me?" Gin looked sheepish here, wanting Sabrina's thoughts on the matter.

"I figured the same thing. The best guide and source of knowledge around, my friend."

Gin blushed and moved on, "What was fascinating to me was the description of the cup. The wand is a bit of an afterthought, though it is important it isn't taken in the end. The cup, however, seems to be the source of Comus' power to transform and entice in the play."

"For sure, but what could that mean? I don't know enough about actual magic and these objects of power to add anything here. Sorry."

"Do not apologize unless you have wronged someone, Sabrina. Your lack of understanding in this area is perfectly understandable, but your willingness to learn means you will pick up much of this quickly. As for objects of power, they all differ. They can be imbibed with power through spellcraft or created at magical locations or forged at a time when magic is high and seeps into the object. It varies from piece to piece. What we know of the cup is that it belonged to Circe, she did use it in a way as described in that old human poem…"

"*The Odyssey*?" Sabrina scoffed at it being called an old human poem. When they nodded, she asked, "Circe actually turned people into pigs?"

"Not exactly. They were more similar to what is described here, humans that took on some animal characteristics in physical appearance and in behavior, but who were not fully transformed. It was a potion that did this, not the cup itself, but using the same object over and over again for such strong elixirs would definitely leave a magical trace. Comus could very well use it to create feelings of loyalty in his followers. He could also use it as a proven vessel for some other concoction of more strength or more devastating effect for our Nin."

"Like in the play, we need to warn Mo and Serge to watch for and destroy the cup and the wand."

"The two should know to secure such powerful objects already, but it will not harm us to add it to their thoughts before they leave. The most

233

important thing, I think, is making sure Mo and Serge neutralize both objects of power and capture Comus himself. We do not want this ending to come to pass."

"No, definitely not. We can't have Comus sneaking away, ready to pounce whenever he finishes licking his wounds. How do we do that, though? Can we even do it, if this ending is written?"

"We must work on the assumption the play shows us what could happen, not what will happen, and therefore work for a better outcome. We bring what we learn from the play to The Council and advise a more measured and highly planned attack on the Palace. It seems haste is what was the enemy of the brothers here."

"Okay. That sounds good, but what if? What are our contingencies?"

Gin thought for a moment and a sad look entered their eyes. "One part resonates in an unexpected way. I had a lover for many centuries who was a healer. He taught me what I know of healing magic and medicinals, as my original gifts were in spellcraft and construction of new spells — magical theory of a sort. He taught me much, as the drama says, but sadly he did not teach me the name of this plant that would help."

"Are you talking about the reference to the plant that supposedly helps against Comus enchantments? The 'Hæmony'? I think it's goldenrod."

"Goldenrod?"

"Yeah, do y'all not have that here? It's all over the place in North America. It's even the state flower of Kentucky, where you found me and Nin. It grows like a weed, and some call it a weed, but it has its beauty." Flipping through her pages, she came to the lines and pointed to her notes. "Look here, Gin.

> "   *Amongst the rest a small unsightly root,*
> *But of divine effect, he cull'd it me out;*
> *The leaf was darkest, and had prickles on it,*
> *But in another Country, as he said,*
> *Bore a bright golden flowre, but not in this soyl:*
> *Unknown, and like esteem'd, and the dull swayn*

Treads on it daily with his clouted
shoon,
And yet more med'cinal is it then
that Moly
That Hermes once to wise Ulysses
gave;
He call'd it Hæmony, and gave it
me,
And bade me keep it as of sovran
use
'Gainst all inchnatments, mildewe
blast, or damp...'"

"Goldenrod grows in many places in the human realm, but at this point in history I don't think it had been introduced to England yet, so it would definitely be foreign and unknown to Milton. It's also been used as a medicinal plant, for teas and such, for many, many centuries. It has a bright golden flower, and spiny little leaves that can be bright green or dark green. The name Milton uses here is like hominy, a type of food native to North America. That word, hominy, would even be unknown and maybe a bit magical to someone like Milton; it comes from the Powhatan word 'chickahominy,' and most men like Milton knew very little, and cared to know very little, about Native Americans. All this says goldenrod to me."

Gin sat, thinking deep thoughts, with a hand at their chin and a distant look in their eyes. Then they rose without a word and headed for the door, coming back minutes later with a rolled leather carrying case in their hands. They unfurled it and inside were glass vials, all meticulously labeled in handwriting that, from their notes on the Milton text, Sabrina could clearly see was not Gin's.

They scanned the contents and then brightened, reverently pulling a vial from a row and handing it to Sabrina. To her it clearly read goldenrod, and she beamed. Gin appeared happy, but also a bit bereft, stroking the vials softly as they looked down at them. Clearing their throat, they added, with head still down, "Philo was very dear to me, and it seems he is of help once again, so long after his passing."

Sabrina knew the pain of loss too well and reached for Gin's hand to hold it tight, to squeeze, to acknowledge without words an understanding.

Gin shook off their thoughts, sucked in a breath, and turned to Sabrina with a shaky smile. "It seems we have something that will help Mo and

Serge deflect Comus' magic, if the text is to be believed. That is a good thing." They rose again, a little heavier with thoughts even though their mission had already been heavy and packed away the leather case. "I will return these to their rightful place. Goldenrod tea, you say?'

Sabrina cleared her throat, feeling the weight of Gin's sadness on herself as well. "Yes. I'd say mixing it with green teas should do the trick. Or if you want to give them something nasty to suck down, just brew it solo. I suspect it should be ingested right before they go off to fight to ensure potency."

Gin shuffled out of room to return in moments, having deposited their treasure back in its place and sliding the vial of dried goldenrod in some pocket in the folds of their robes.

"Okay. So. We have some tea that may or may not help. We have the outline of what could happen, which gives us a guide for what not to do in many ways. What else do we need from this?" Sabrina asked.

"What can you give? What could be the key to unstick Nin if she is bound in some way by

Comus? If we go by the structure of the play, it is something that must come from you, Sabrina."

Sabrina blew out a loud breath and rammed a hand through her hair, haphazardly pulling her topknot loose as she did so. "I have no idea. I'm no goddess. I have no magic. I do not know what magical potion I'm supposed to have to help. The lines aren't adding up for me:

> "   *Thus I sprinkle on thy brest*
> *Drops that from my fountain pure,*
> *I have kept of pretious cure,*
> *Thrice upon thy finger tips,*
> *Thrice upon thy rubied lips,*
> *Next this marble venom'd seat*
> *Smear'd with gumms of glutenous heat*
> *I touch with chaste palms moist and cold,*
> *Now the spell hath lost his hold;'"*

"Let us break this down," Gin asserted. "This much we know — if Nin is stuck in some way, shape, or form, you are the one we must call on for aid in her release. You will sprinkle some liquid of some sort, lay hands, and she will be freed. That, at least, is a reassurance all is not lost if Nin is found in the midst of some magical binding or hold."

"Yes, but, we have to figure out the liquid. As before, that virginity issue is out of the realm of reality," Gin snorted a bit at this and Sabrina managed to crack a bit of a smile, "and I'm sure my hands will be clammy enough from nerves that they will be both 'moist' and 'cold.' The process of laying, some on her chest, some at her fingers, some at her lips, is clear. What to use is the sticking point."

"Sabrina, you will come up with the answer. It has to be something you have or know of. It is something directly related to you in some way. It will come to mind in time. I trust in this."

Sabrina had little faith herself. She racked her brain and came up with nothing, and the more nothing she came up with, the worse she felt about the situation. Gin and Sabrina talked more, hashed out minor details from the text, and made a plan.

"We must meet with The Council immediately. They should be hearing Mo's plan for attack, soon as it is. We can attempt to slow that process in some small way with this information. More time and care is clearly needed to plan an effective offensive. The haste to attack is the downfall at the end of this play. We do not want to repeat that mistake."

"But…" Sabrina hesitated. She tried to push away thoughts about the actuality of Nin with Comus. It was clear from their reading of the play that whatever might be happening at the Palace, it would not be good for her friend. Gin saw this in her eyes, likely felt the same, and they deflated a bit.

"We must trust in Nin's strength," Gin finally said, "and trust in our own ability to help her through whatever happens in these times, emotionally and physically. For now, it is better to plan and execute effectively than to rush forward. Nin is strong. It may be unfair, and it may seem callous, but we must work for what is best for her and Fae, even if it goes against our initial instincts."

Sabrina nodded with tears in her eyes. She understood the point. It was valid. It didn't make her feel better, though. She excused herself, saying she wanted to freshen up for the Council meeting. She shut the door to her room off the library, slid down into a crouch with her back to the door, and let herself cry for a time. She shed tears of frustration, pain, sadness. Then she rose up and did what needed to be done.

CHAPTER 17

Gin tried to contact Mo to see when they were meeting with The Council but found he had already left. That meeting was already happening, so Sabrina and Gin raced towards the Tower. Gin contacted the leader of the Merchant Guild for help. Gin said the Fae, Manny, owed them a favor — and a very serious favor was needed to convince another leader of The Falls to interrupt a Council meeting already in progress. Mo was likely debriefing the Council at that moment, and Gin and Sabrina needed to get into that room so they could discuss what they knew. The way was shut for them without another leader to help open the door. Apparently, Allera could help.

"Borjigin the Scholar, Sabrina of Nin. It is a privilege to help great thinkers such as yourselves in your time of need. As long as I lead the Wisps, you will have our arms," Allera gravely stated, hovering in front of Gin and Sabrina, who stood before the enchanted doors to The Council Chamber.

"You honor us with your words and your aid, Chieftain Allera," Gin added. "As a Falls liaison, you can help me complete the spell which will allow us entry into this space."

"As is right and true. Let no Fae say the Wisps did not help in an hour of need."

"Hear, Hear," Sabrina added, hoping to offer encouragement of her own.

Allera gave a quick dip of a bow her way, then turned fully to Gin. "I can and will aid you in this, Gin. I, however, cannot enter with you. I must gather my forces and wait with my people for word from Mosi. If the battle is imminent, we must prepare. You will need others to exit this place."

Gin gave his assent and the two turned to open the door. They completed the ritual Sabrina had seen Mo and Inanna perform earlier, and the door unbarred and open, just as before. However, their reception was a little chillier this time around. Gin marched into the room as if they had every right to be there, and Sabrina figured that was true. Gin was a Fae leader and scholar and belonged, if not on the Council, at the very least in front of it. Sabrina did not have that position, so she did not share in their confidence at that moment. In fact, with Michel staring daggers right at her, as if she and only she was the reason for this interruption, she had to swallow down a bit of nervous fear and anxiety to put on a strong front for Gin and their findings.

Really, this was nothing new to her; she had performed in very similar circumstances many times in her academic life. It was part of the front she had learned to put on — a poor Kentucky girl who was a first-generation college student, she had felt decidedly out of place and out-gunned many times, but she never let it show. Just like in graduate school and academia in general, Sabrina faked it 'til she made it, projecting strength and knowledge and confidence she very much did not feel.

Mo, Inanna, and Sten looked at them with curiosity. Michel looked enraged. Jane looked slightly anxious, but Sabrina thought that may be how she always looked. Andres just looked bored, and Sabrina knew that was an effect he likely projected for a variety of reasons. Of course, Michel was the first to speak. His voice was a whip-crack of pure privileged indignation, repeating the same thing that many old white dudes in power had said in many places throughout history, in Fae and in the human realm.

"What is the meaning of this?"

Sabrina would have laughed at the cliched absurdity of that phrase coming from him if the outcome of this conversation wasn't so crucial.

Gin hurried to stand beside Mo, who was at attention close to the center of the arch of Council seats. They gave a quick bow and began, "We do apologize for the sudden intrusion, Council, but"

They weren't allowed to finish just yet. Michel began to huff more. "Well, I never. We are in the middle of very important and strategic discussions that are to be only between The Council and our military leader. You two have no right to be in this meeting. You were explicitly not invited. You know this because you obviously knew when the meeting was taking place but were not rightfully admitted." Michel's eyes narrowed then, scanning the room behind Mo, Gin, and Sabrina, who hovered a step behind the two Fae at the center of the room. "And who, pray tell, allowed you to enter? What leader agreed to such an egregious step? I see no one else with you."

Sten entered the fray then, and Sabrina suspected that Fae had not missed Manny's coattails as he hurried away from the scene of the magic. "Michel, please. Gin would never enter the Council chamber in session without just cause. You know this. Stop blustering and allow them to state their case."

"Thank you, Sten." Gin began again. "As I was about to say, Sabrina and I have spent the time since our last meeting attempting to decipher any messages that could possibly be gleaned from that human play that appeared so oddly prophetic."

"Yes yes yes. We know that much, Gin," Andres replied a bit sharply. "Get on with it. We've already had to sit here and listen to Mosi's military strategy and Michel's endless barrage of questions to him about that strategy for what feels like eons. To the point, then, so we can hopefully be finished with this meeting."

"As you will it. We discovered a number of things. We still maintain that Mo should wait a little longer to engage Comus in battle, at least until we have had time to debrief him fully and learn more from the text. We do not ask for long — a day or two at most."

Mo piped up at this. "Nin needs us now. Nearly two days have passed since Nin was taken. I will not leave her unprotected any longer. All of Fae needs us to keep Nin from Comus in case he can somehow acquire her powers. He'd be too powerful to contend with then. We must act swiftly."

"Of course Nin must be rescued as soon as possible," Sabrina gritted out, angered at the implication that she wasn't thinking of Nin. That was the only damn reason she was in this strange place to begin with. "We just feel you need to remain mindful of the possibility presented in the play. We can tell you what we have figured out, but you need to read it too, just in case. You need to think about it and use it as you plan. We're not military strategists, Mo, we're scholars. You may be able to find more value if you take the time. Without sufficient planning and joint action, Comus can escape and retain some power.

That leaves both Nin and Fae vulnerable even if you win this one battle."

Mo looked annoyed but he nodded, a sign he wasn't exactly ignoring these issues, but was not taking it as seriously as Sabrina felt he should. He hadn't taken the time to read the damn text himself, so he had no idea what information it held. The least he could do was the basic homework, right? Sabrina shrugged at this. There was little she could do to make him listen; she just hoped her and Gin's reminders would penetrate and Mo and Serge would not make the same mistakes as the brothers in the play.

"Stop this in-fighting. Please," Inanna said, her voice a little chillier than Sabrina had heard from her at this point. "My daughter is at that Palace. Who knows what is being done to her? We must act now. We must know what you and Sabrina have discovered, Gin."

Gin nodded and went for a more direct approach this time. "Sabrina and I have discovered that goldenrod, likely in tea form, a common plant where Sabrina and Nin were in the human realm, is mentioned as an antidote of sorts in the play. We believe this will help inoculate those fighting Comus from the magic produced by his objects of power. It may even reverse effects for anyone under their spell. It will surely protect anyone facing Comus one-on-one."

"Excellent," Mo stated. "Give me what you have and I will disperse it through my men before dawn."

"Dawn?" Sabrina said. "But you haven't even heard the rest."

"It is of no consequence. Regardless, we ride to The Palace at full dark tonight and strike before the sun fully rises."

"That is too soon. The brothers in the play confront Comus too soon and he escapes. Nin may well be saved, but she wouldn't be safe."

"She'll be safe if we oust him from The Palace and she takes her place as leader," Mo retorted.

"Damnit! Listen to us. She may be safe in the moment, but the long term is important too, Mo. She was snatched from the human realm. Do you think Comus wouldn't do all he could to take her again if he's allowed to escape? She'd be in danger still. All of Fae would still be in danger."

"You seem to underestimate my abilities. I'm a trained warrior of Fae, leader of The Falls guard and military. I know how to plan an attack. I have been planning this specific attack for a long while. We have finally acquired the information and magics needed to ensure success, which makes the timing perfect. I have worked through cases and contingencies in my head countless times. I thank you for bringing additional information to me, but this attack can go forward smoothly without delay. I know this."

"I get it, Mo. I don't deny you your expertise. You know much more about battles and strategy and magic than I ever will. I know you have been planning this attack, and that planning had to get amped up once your sister was taken the second time. But there is more to consider than strategic weaknesses and battle formations. Give Gin and I our dues as well. We've studied this text, which Gin believes is Fae prophecy. We've thought it through together and I've known a great deal about it for years. It connects to what is happening right now in Fae and it clearly shows there are missteps ahead if you rush the offensive."

"I cannot plan based on a strange human book, even if it may or may not be a prophecy. I must go with what I know. This offensive is not rushed. Sabrina, please believe this is no disrespect to you or Gin. It is what I must do as a leader and a brother."

Gin, seeing that the argument would not be won any time soon and that another approach was necessary, jumped in with Mo. "If you refuse to cede time and study the text with us, Sabrina and I must be there during the charge."

Mo shook his head firmly. "Gin, you have seen battle. Of course you may join. However, Sabrina is a liability we cannot have."

"Excuse me?" Sabrina huffed, offended by the off-handed way he behaved.

"I completely agree," Michel sniffed.

"Mosi," his mother said with a chastising tone. Turning to Sabrina, she gave a small smile. "Dear, he says it far too harshly than he should, but his point is not without merit. You have never seen a battle. You do not know that pain and horror and chaos. Your heart is willing, definitely, but even beyond the physical reality of battle in both realms, Fae battles include magic. You have no defenses against that. It would make you, and anyone tasked with protecting you, vulnerable."

"I must disagree with you all," Gin interrupted. "I understand your concerns, but if things do not go as planned, Sabrina is our only hope for saving Nin."

"How?" Jane asked hesitantly.

"The play clearly states that Sabrina is the only one who can free Nin if she is somehow magically trapped."

"But how can that be?" Jane asked with a tilt of the head. "She herself has no magic. What is it she has that will help Nin if she is confined by Comus' powerful magics?"

"Well…" Gin said at the same time Sabrina muttered, "Thatwedon'tknow," in a quick breath.

"What did you say?" Sten asked, perplexed.

"We don't know, okay? We knew we were out of time, but I have not quite figured out a crucial component to my contribution. There is an allusion in the play I have yet to suss out."

Michel laughed. "Of course you haven't," and Sabrina wanted to walk right up to his high wooden chair and punch him in the throat.

"If you do not even know what this component is, how can you be sure you need to physically be there to make it work?" Inanna asked.

It was a logical question that Sabrina could only refute with, "I know I need to be there."

Gin echoed that same sentiment, but given Mo's objections and their lack of information and time, it was not looking good for their case.

"This drones on," Andres interjected. "A vote then. I propose Mosi be allowed to go forth as planned, with the addition of taking this goldenrod with him for added protection and allowing Gin to be a part of the campaign, as they have the concrete knowledge from this human play that seems oh so important. Sabrina will stay behind for her own safety and the safety of others. All in favor, say 'Aye.'"

She watched as one-by-one the entire Council said "Aye." Sabrina was hurt by Inanna and Sten's agreement, although she logically understood why they would give it. Michel smirked at her failure, and that chafed. Jane looked ready to bolt, as did Dre, though for very different reasons. Mo whispered with Gin in a huddle, likely planning what to do next, and Sabrina felt unmoored, unaware of

what to do now that events were rapidly escalating
but she was benched.

She was ushered out of the Council chamber
by Inanna, who invited Sabrina to wait for word on
the Palace attack with her at her home.

Gin popped up and grabbed Sabrina. "That
is a lovely idea, Aunt Inanna," they stated, "but I'm
afraid I need Sabrina to do a little more research for
me."

Pulling her out of the Tower and along the
road towards their home, Gin began to give rapid-fire
instructions. "I am sorry they do not believe you
should be present, but in some ways this is good. It
will give you time alone to think, and you need to do
so. That is the only way to discover what concoction
could help Nin. Once you have it, you can wait for
my call if you are needed."

"Call? You have phones here?"

"No. Better." Gin pulled Sabrina into the
house and closed the door. "I knew this was a strong
possibility. I also truly believe you will be needed in
that battle. A link is required. Comus is not the only
Fae who has personal objects of power. Philo and I
had a pair we used many times." From their robes,
Gin pulled out what looked like a flint rock, white

and shaped in a flat oblong that felt jagged when they placed it in her hand. "This is like chalk. I have mine here," they added, patting their robe. "This piece is for you. Just in case, but I doubt you will need it. It works powerfully and simply enough that even a human can use it. It requires no incantation or spellcraft, only intention. Imagine who you need in a moment and draw a crude door on any surface. It will open and take you directly to them, but only if they are in Fae and in an area not barred to you through magical wards. I will use mine to directly come for you if Nin needs you. This I swear to you, Sabrina of Nin. I will not hesitate."

Sabrina nodded, slipping her half of this powerful magical object into the back pocket of her jeans. "I know you'll come for me if I can help."

"As for now, do what you will in my home. You are welcome to it. I must fly in order to meet with Mo and his band of men."

Sabrina nodded and offered Gin a quick, tight hug before they left. Turning then to Gin's empty home, Sabrina went to her room in the library. She had only her thoughts now, and those thoughts were dark with worry. She needed to push that aside, take up the riddle of the goddess' potion, and see what came up with a bit more thought. She doubted it would help much. She'd mulled over it for hours at this point. Sabrina was out of ideas and out of the battle for now. She needed inspiration, but all she had rattling around in her head was worry and doubt and sadness.

CHAPTER 18

Sabrina lay alone on the guest bed, flipping the flint stone Gin had given her over and over in her hand. She was trying to do anything to clear her mind in the hopes an answer would come. What was this potion she would need? What were those drops from my fountain pure? "Milton and his damn obsession with purity," she muttered to herself.

Her frustration grew, and she began to handle the stone more and more aggressively until it slipped right from her fingers. It looked like a fragile thing, even if it was some sort of object of power, and Sabrina's breath held tight as she watched it quickly bounce from the edge of the bed and hit the hardwood floor of the room with a thud. She closed her eyes and told herself it had to still be intact, that it was a good thud rather than a harsh shatter she heard. Peering over the edge of the bed she saw it there, whole, and let out a long breath of relief.

"No need to go breaking magical objects that are likely irreplaceable," she muttered to herself, scooping it up from the floor and moving it gently to the front pocket of her backpack.

When she placed the flint there, she heard the ring of jostled metal and fished into the bottom of the pocket, pulling out her car keys. Like her phone, throwing her keys in her bag was a habit. No need for car or house or office keys in Fae. She should have left them at Nin's cottage, but she was so used to throwing them into the front pocket of the backpack when she got out of her car that it had been muscle memory that placed them in that bag. As she closed her hands around the mass to put it in a different pocket so they wouldn't do damage to the stone, she felt it — the small glass vial she'd so reverently placed there a few months before. Memories and ideas and connections flashed before her in quick succession, leading to one blinding revelation.

She helped her Gran make dandelion wine many times. "It's my own religious experience," Gran would joke to Sabrina in the spring whenever she began the process, "my own small form of the divine. Turning water into wine is a godly trait after all."

Gran would gather the usual ingredients for the wine, but she had her own rituals as well. She added other flowers to soak in the water — dandelions were always the main component but also anything that was in or around her house at the time was thrown in, like pansies and roses and such.

"Of pansies, pinks, and gaudy Daffodils," Sabrina whispered now to herself in the quiet of the room as the memories continued.

Gran also always used water from the Kentucky River. Not much, especially after Sabrina nagged her numerous times about pollution and contamination and how the river was not what it once was. Too much pollution along the Ohio had seeped down through it. Too many coal mines had misused it.

"It's a bit of the land and water where we grew," she claimed, and even if she had to boil it for a while and only add a few drops, that river water, that connection to what could be seen as an old River Goddess' domain, was there in that potent mixture.

Her homemade dandelion wine was something Gran gave Sabrina even when she was child, though in much smaller doses. A piece of her own familial love wrapped up in tradition and care from one woman to another. It symbolized a lot for Sabrina even before this point, and she had watched reverently as her sick Gran had gone about making what would be her last batch. After her death, after Sabrina's grief had waned a bit and she had grown close to Nin, Sabrina had shared. She shared the stories of the dandelion wine, and in the end, she shared the last jar of wine she had.
Gran had spent many a night with friends, laughing and drinking that brew. She knew the value of friendship and showed it regularly when she was alive. Had instilled it in Sabrina so she knew a good friend like Nin when she saw her and would hold on tight to that special connection.

She thought it fitting to share. Gran wanted others to enjoy her creation, to live a little when they tasted that wine. Who better to share it with than her new friend, so quickly like a sister to her, someone who had not known Gran in life but appreciated her after death? They'd sat in Nin's cottage on the Winter Solstice and drank the last of the drought made by the last of her blood family. They didn't get drunk, just pleasantly fuzzy. Sabrina spent time both crying and laughing, telling stories of Gran to her friend.

The following afternoon, Nin came knocking on Sabrina's door. She'd managed to save a tiny bit of the dandelion wine and presented a gift to her friend. It was a thick glass bottle, sturdy but tiny, with a deep cork sealed over in a greenish wax. The wine was perfectly golden with an odd shimmer and there was only a tablespoon at most in the bottle. In the middle was a miniature, floating dandelion. It never sank down or rose up, but stayed suspended always, a tiny little version of the flower that many called a weed.

Looking back with her present knowledge, she knew Nin's magic had to be in this bottle somehow. The preserved flower had been a wonder to her when she stopped to think of it before. Now it was a note of the magic Nin secretly used to give her friend something special, a token to remember her Gran and to show her appreciation for being a part of that last ritual sharing of the wine. It was a tangible act of remembrance, a solid object that demonstrated

binding love from past to present to future for
Sabrina and Nin.

"It all fits. It all fits! Gran and the river, both
my fountains. The charm that must be on this bottle,
the intention and care it took to make and my
memory of all of it. It's my potion, my drops of
magic!" She plopped down on the bed, awed by what
was in her hand, a thing so special to her for so many
reasons, but also now that she knew, a thing of even
more magic. "Thanks again Gran — helping me out
even here, even now." She kissed the bottle after
taking it off the key ring, then put it in her pocket.
Now she was ready to meet whatever came. She was
ready, with Nin's own love and care from the past, to
help her friend if it actually came down to it. She
hoped it didn't, but Sabrina knew that preparation
was half the battle already won.

For now, all she could really do is wait,
though that waiting was anxious and worrying.
Sabrina's past few days had been rough, but Nin's
were likely tragic, and she hoped it was not too
much, that she and Gin and Mo and Serge were not
too late to save Nin — physically or emotionally.

PART 11: THE LADY

RISES

Come, lady, while Heaven lends us grace,
Let us fly this cursed place,
Lest the sorcerer us entice
With some other new device

John Milton, *Comus*, 1634

CHAPTER 1

Nin started that Saturday like all the other Saturdays she'd spent in Wilde over the past ten years. She greeted the sun with a smile, letting the wooded air wash over her as she drank a cup of strong tea and rocked gently in her porch swing. She loved the solitude of her little slice of Kentucky. Her life had not been lonely up to a certain point, far from it. She had family and friends and duties to her land. She was raised to believe she had an important calling that made some people want to be around her and some others look up to her. She found both more than a little exhausting. Even before her life took a drastic and traumatic turn, she had sometimes thought her calling, and the expectations of others that came with it, may be too much for her.

That word — calling — was something she had learned here, in this human realm. It meant a divine influence pushing you in a particular direction. It was fate, but with a driving hand that Nin felt was forced. Being forced into things, cowed and controlled, had also been a large part of her life before.

On her porch though, in front of this tiny home and in view of her lovely greenhouse, she was not forced to be anything other than Nina, the woman she had fashioned herself into on this plot of Earth. She was not forced to bend to the sick pseudo-love of a tyrant. She was not pressured to take on the cause of all her people. She had stepped outside of duty and chosen a way that left her alone, ignoring her calling. Some may view that as selfish, but it was more complicated than that, as most things in this realm of the other so often were. Hiding in the human realm helped her, yes, but it also helped others. It was part self-preservation, part survival, and part rebellion. Like so many women before her, Nin had been told again and again that her sacrifice - of time,

commitment, love, skill, family, friends, etc. -
benefited the community. Like so many women
before her, in this land and her own, she had been
asked to give up anything that was her own in order
to help the whole — family, community, relationship.
It was an old story, equally shared in human and Fae
circles. Women were to give until they could give no
more, all in order to help others, while doing nothing
to help themselves become whole or to live in their
own truth.

She felt guilt. Of course she did. Guilt was
drilled into most women early on in any number of
societies. She also felt safe and free in the here and
now. The allure of those things, at least for the past
decade, had been enough to make her stay in this
realm and let go of her connections in her home
realm. It was good to be Nina here, not Nin there.

Padding barefoot across her porch, she
returned inside to throw on her work clothes. No one
was likely to come out on a Saturday morning, at
least no one she couldn't hear coming from far off, so
she pulled her hair back in a ponytail. It always
helped to get the hair out of her face while working
with earth, but the points at the tips of her ears were a
little too pronounced for a ponytail most days. She

quickly learned that there were a lot of things humans did not notice, or willfully ignored, but physical imperfections were not one of them. Odd ears stuck out to people, who then felt the need to ask questions or start whispers. It was easier to avoid all together and work through the annoyance of hair in her face than to try to deflect curiosity once it was sparked in a human.

In fact, she took great pains to hide both her physical and magical differences. It was one reason she had few clients, and of those few clients, fewer still actually came by her nursery. She did not need the money. She'd fled dripping in gold and jewels that she paid for in blood. She'd used a bit of her Fae glamour and charm to part some Wall Street men from just a small fraction of their wealth. She had no qualms with this after spending a few months in America and seeing how they used and abused their financial power. All this meant she paid for her land outright, built her cottage and nursery out of pocket over time, and sat comfortably on a solid savings while she did work she enjoyed. She did not live in luxury as she had before, but safety and freedom were well worth the trade. Besides, she had always found more happiness in getting dirty than in lounging in gowns, though the latter was something she enjoyed every now and again.

The only person who very well could show up unannounced would be Sabrina, and that would just be a happy surprise for Nin. She'd been in this realm for around ten years, avoiding working with the same people for long and trying to not make long-term connections so she could stay on this plot of land without too many questions being asked when she failed to age.

Sabrina was an oddity, a human she wanted in her life in a more permanent way. That first phone call had been the beginning of something, though Nin did not realize it until she was actually in Sabrina's presence the next day. The call showed Sabrina to be thoughtful and connected with her piece of land, something Nin appreciated. When she had jumped down from her truck and turned to Sabrina, blurry-eyed but giving a slightly crooked smile and small wave her way, she felt something in her stir. It was not lust or romance, but something else warm and comforting. It was endearment, as if she knew this human would be important to her in some way.

Very old and powerful magic moved through Nin, so she learned to listen to her feelings as

they were her strongest instinctual connection to that
magic. Because of this she stepped up to Sabrina
happy and a bit hopeful that she had found a woman
she could befriend, and was glad for it in the two
years since. Her magic had not been wrong. They
were now precious to each other, a balm each had not
realized they needed until they connected. Sabrina
was still grieving the loss of her family, current and
past. Nin was nursing old wounds through distance
and solitude. Each learned comfort and a new form of
grace through with no expectations or reservations. It
was the easiest friendship, likely the easiest
relationship of any kind, Nin had ever known.

However, a cloud hung there for Nin. A
proverbial shoe ready to drop at any moment. Sabrina
did not know who Nin was, or more aptly, what she
was. There was no reason why she would guess, and
Nin struggled with telling her friend. Because of this
secret, there were also pains Nin had not revealed to
Sabrina, such as the reason she left her realm behind
and the trauma she had fled. While it was likely
Sabrina had no idea about her magic or the fact she
was not human, the other she guessed at but had
never pressed the issue. She knew "Nina" did not
date, did not allow anyone other than Sabrina in her

home, did not stand too close to any person, did not allow touch or contact unless she initiated it.

One painful night, Sabrina had suggested they watch some old 90s movie Nin had never seen because it was added to Netflix. *Sleeping With the Enemy* felt very, very real to Nin in a way that caused a physical reaction. After the woman was left crying in pain on the ground in the first ten minutes of the film, and her husband whispered to her with quiet menace, "I'm so sorry. Will you smile? Hhmm?" Nin hit pause and got up to pace the room, counting steps and breaths to calm herself even as a few tears slid down her face.

Sabrina had offered a hug, which Nin accepted even though she felt almost too vulnerable for touch at that moment, then held her close, rubbing her back and her hair gently. Nin hadn't cried in a long time, and it felt good to release those tears even though the real fear that swelled up when she saw that on the screen was unwanted. Sabrina sat holding Nin and whispering, "I'm so, so sorry" over and over again until she calmed. That sorry had not been just about playing such a movie without warning, but an acknowledgment that Sabrina now knew, without words being spoken, the flavor of Nin's pain.

Sabrina had slept on Nin's couch that night, staying close to her friend in case she needed her again but not demanding the story of her past. All this showed Sabrina's loyalty, care, and concern. All of it made Nin love her even more.

Nin wavered often. She had almost told Sabrina who she was, what her past entailed, many times over the past two years. She knew it would eventually happen, but a part of her was afraid of rejection. Sabrina had never shown herself to be a person that would push a friend away because of who or what they were, but the sliver of a chance and her own lack of self-esteem held Nin back. One day the truth would out, but Nin held on to Sabrina tightly, appreciating all that they were in that time and place, before truth would change that. While Sabrina may not reject Nin outright, she knew that somehow, Sabrina finding out the truth would cause a shift in their relationship, one way or another.

She also knew that, technically, it was dangerous for Sabrina to know of Fae. It was against Fae rules to tell humans who and what they were. Humans outnumbered them, and they were violent creatures. Magic could not always save them, and humans had killed plenty of Fae in the past —

particularly Fae women who were burned at the stake as human witches. Rules were in place to help prevent this from happening. In order to tell a human about Fae without painful consequences, you had to lay claim to that human, in front of Fae witnesses, swearing you would be responsible for their actions and use of that knowledge. Otherwise, magic was used to turn memories into hazy dreams if a human saw or learned too much. Nin had no problem swearing on Sabrina. She trusted her friend in all ways. She had a very big problem bringing Sabrina into a realm she had run away from herself. It was too dangerous in Fae for her, it could be lethal for a human like Sabrina.

These concerns were often running idle in the back of Nin's mind. It was at the forefront today for some reason, as she went about greenhouse maintenance and worked her hands into soil to re-pot a number of ferns. She figured it was because she had spent a lovely, practically carefree evening with Sabrina. The more time that passed, the more guilty she felt about her lies of omission, and Nin usually contemplated her options for a while after seeing Sabrina. She also felt something stir in her, a warning of some kind that somehow hit on the connection between her and Sabrina. She could not pinpoint what the cause was, it was just a vague sense of dread that somehow involved both her and her friend. She wasn't a seer, though supposedly dream communication between earth magic wielders from different eras was said to have occurred in the past. That was not the case now. She had no premonitions or magical conversations, just a magical hint of intuition. Whatever it was, the feeling needed to be examined, and Nin was becoming more and more certain she would have to confess all to her friend very soon.

In that moment, though, she was content to let her mind drift away from such topics as she worked with her hands and her magic. She whispered softly to the ferns in Faeish as she repotted, chanting for them to grow firm and strong, to solidly take root in their new home. It was both a wish and a promise — a wish they would do what they could to survive and a promise that Nin would do all in her power to help them thrive.

The ferns returned her chanting in their own language, one that Nin didn't exactly know but could interpret nonetheless. They agreed to the bargain, trusted Nin to help them, and thanked her for her care. It was a special moment only earth magic wielders knew, the unspoken communication that occurred between something of the earth and yourself, and it was something that nourished Nin's soul as it nourished the roots of the plants she helped along.

Suddenly, she sensed growing magic in the air that was not her own. It made the hair on her arms stand up, and she quickly scanned her surroundings. Wiping soil from her hands onto old work jeans, she became frantic as the soft static stirrings of magic pricked her ears. She smelt a bit of ozone, the charred electrical smell that clung to air after a lightning strike, which marked a fissure being created. Someone or something was coming and it was almost here.

She internally screamed, unprepared for what was to come because it was unknown, when she caught the faintest scent of myrrh hanging in the air. That jolted her spine straight as she saw the first invisible waves shimmer in the air at a crossroads in the greenhouse walkway. She narrowed her eyes and planted herself firmly, hands on hips. She knew who was coming, and she was ready for whatever they might bring her way.

CHAPTER 2

There was no flash of magical light, no loud boom to announce they had ripped through realms to reach this plane. One second the cross path was empty and the next it was not, filled instead by three figures: Mosi, Sergius, and Borjigin.

Mosi stood tall and proud in the middle, staring right at Nin without hesitation. Not even a blink or a look around the nursery. He was pure focus, intent on the task at hand, whatever that may be. She was not surprised by this. Her oldest brother may be affectionately called Mo by his family and few close friends, but he consistently carried the air of a vigilant soldier about him, always dedicated to any mission he committed himself to complete, whether it was confronting a Fae traitor or scolding a younger sister. Nin was uncertain which mission he was currently on, but either way, she would not be cowed by a man she had known as focused and strategic, but fair, her entire life.

To his right stood Sergius, who had no qualms showing his interest in his new surroundings rather than in his little sister. He may have been older than Nin, but Serge was no strict disciplinarian with a single-minded focus. He was the chatty one, the peacekeeper, the consummate politician in the family. He was also a bit of a hedonist, preferring whatever was new and shiny and momentarily entertaining over any form of confrontation. All of this made him the perfect courtier in Fae — ready to ease any ruffled feather with a smooth word and equally ready to laugh and be merry at the drop of a hat. Because Serge was here, Nin suspected this was more of a diplomatic mission.

Mo could rely on him to fight if the need arose in most situations, but though he was older by several hundred years, everyone (including Serge himself) knew he was no match for Nin in any type of battle. Her words and her blows were heavier than he preferred.

The third figure, though, eased Nin's worries the most. She may not know how Mo viewed her, and Serge could just be along for a ride into the human realm, but Gin would not be part of any mission that involved hurting Nin. She knew that to her bones. Her cousin, older and wiser and kinder by far, would never force Nin to do something she was unwilling or unable to do. They had been her teacher for many years, training Nin from the age of seven to thirteen, before she was given the highest honor — working directly with the Mae Queen, who was, at the time, the only other living earth-magic wielder in Fae. Gin's magic was strong, their knowledge of magic and Fae even stronger, and they were clearly here to ease Nin's mind. She knew this when they gave her a quick wink with their left eye so Mo wouldn't catch the cue. Gin was here to test waters, to help all parties, and to make sure Nin was fine. That much she knew before anyone even spoke.

"Nin," Mo clipped tersely. "You were not easy to reach."

"Why should I be? I am in hiding," she barked back. She'd use sarcasm, a trait she adored in human communication, but she felt it wouldn't work here. It was something foreign to many Fae who were not that familiar with the human realm, and Mo was too rigid and literal, though it would give Serge and Gin a good chuckle.

"Nin, lovely Nin. How glad I am to see your face," Gin called to her. Gin's words — both the message and the basic sound of their voice — felt like a touch, a caress of care Nin had not realized she missed so very much until that moment.

Tears pricked the back of her eyes, but she shook them away. Gin did not deserve tears, even if they were about love and longing. She just smiled a weak smile their way and gave a nod of her head. Gin was smart enough to see the rest plainly play across her face, so there was nothing she needed to say. Gin bowed their head in return, then breathed deep and let out a slow breath, showing Nin that they too felt loss during their separation.

Serge was being Serge, looking around the greenhouse with a languid gaze to discover what the space had to offer. He did eventually turn to Nin with a smirk and a cock of the head, drawling, "What a lovely space you have here, Little One. So lush and warm. Your skills still serve you well, I see."

"I have not lost skill, brother. It is important you remember that." This was a direct answer to Serge's comment, but she stared straight at Mo as she said it, making it very clear she directed it at her oldest brother. In this room, he was the one she would have to fight, verbally or physically. She wanted to get this done as quickly as possible and warning him in no uncertain terms was the opening salvo in what may well be a hearty battle of wills.

"Of course not, little sister. But have you forgotten where those skills came from? Or where you are supposed to use them?" Mo questioned back.

"These skills come from me," Nin asserted, going forward with her position and staking her own claims. "I was born with them. You, Mother, Gin, the Mae Queen — all of you helped nurture and hone those skills. For that I am forever grateful. However, they are still mine. I would have them regardless of what you did or did not do in my younger years. I do not owe myself or my magic to anyone, family, friend, or foe."

At that, a muscle twitched in Mo's jaw and he clenched his teeth as if physically forced to hold back one of his lectures. It would be one of obligation and responsibility, Nin knew that. The same old song was sung to her from a young age, when her specific magics became apparent. It was never malicious in intent, but still always painful, and made resentment rise in Nin quickly. Gin knew what may be coming soon, too, and stepped forward a bit to head that tirade off at the pass.

"Mo. Nin. Come come. It has been too long since we have seen one another. Let us have at least a moment to share together before we bring up old divisions and strife."

"Hear, hear," Serge cheered. "Can't we chase joy for a bit before we get down to business?"

Mo cut eyes at his two companions and firmly said, "No," with a quick shake of the head. "Time is limited. We must speak of what has passed and what may be done. Nin must…"

"I must what? What must I do, oh wise and powerful brother?" She couldn't help the sarcasm this time. "Please, do tell me exactly what I must do as I cannot possibly make any decision on my own."

Serge shook his head and hid a smirk at her bite. Gin looked sad. They knew this fight would come, and in all likelihood both sides had valid points. Nin understood she was dug in, and some of that was willfulness. Some of it was fear. However, it mostly came from her own plans, knowledge, and first-hand observations, which Mo would not acknowledge as valuable for some reason. She just didn't know if Mo would ever be able to recognize his own entrenched ideas or move to any type of common ground.

"Go ahead and tell me what I owe to Fae," Nin said defiantly, but she deflated a bit, burned by memories that started to crash in around her. She began to whisper then, "I know my debts, but how high is their price? How much should I have to bleed, broken by a man who said he loved me as he loved Fae? All was proven false, and I lived under a literal chain for year, without succor or safety."

At this, Mo faltered for the first time, reaching a hand up as if to pull in Nin and bring her close. He shuddered a bit, but fell short, and pulled himself back. Nin did not know if she would welcome his touch, or if she could even stand it at that moment, but she still desperately wanted him to try. It pained her to see his hand drop as he pulled himself back away from her.

"Comus is no longer biding his time. We have word he is ready to strike to ensure he takes complete control of all of Fae, not just The Palace. This cannot stand."

"It would be so much worse if I were by his side," Nin stated plainly.

"You will not be by his side. You will be by ours."

"That is not his plan, nor his will, and I have seen with my own eyes what he can do to and with me. If he gets me in his grasp at the height of his power, all is lost for Fae. It is better I flee, hide in the human realm until others bring him down. Trust when I say it is better this way, brother. Please."

"Fae may not have the time to wait," Gin interjected, but they held sadness in their eyes as they spoke this. "I may have been happy to see you well and away, in hiding for what would pass, years ago. Now, all signs say Fae will fall, with or without your magics, if something is not done to halt Comus."

"Sorry, little one, but it appears to be so," Serge agreed. "It is why we are here. Mo might want you back regardless, but Gin and I now are in agreement, as is The Council. The plan to hide can no longer work. Action must be taken."

"No, there has to be another way," Nin said, shaking her head in disbelief. "There is too much risk in my return."

Mo huffed in annoyance, clearly ready for Nin to just fall in line, as per usual.

"You know…" Mo began in what Nin thought of as his scolding voice.

"Yes, I do know. I know as no one else knows. You are the one who does not know. You come here and ask too much of me, not knowing what awaits all of us if I go and fail."

"You? Fail? Psst. Not happening," Serge scoffed, falling into human mannerisms quickly. Nin wondered why, but had no real time to think about how Serge knew so many human colloquialisms and behaviors before Mo dismissed his younger brother with little fanfare and stepped closer to her. He was locked on her eyes, but addressing Gin.

"Borjigin, I tire of this just as you must. Explain to her what we have seen and heard. Make her see as we do. She must come with us. Now."

"Mo…" Gin cautioned, shaking their head.

"You think you can make me go back? You think you have that power?" Nina scoffed at her brother. It had been a long time since they had traded blows in practice, but Nin knew she was stronger than Mo in her magics, even with his decades of battle experience.

"Oh, Little One," he half chuckled to her, her ever-present nickname grating her in this moment, "you have been so long in this land, amusing yourself with these plants, you have forgotten. Not all things bend to your will so easily, and there are those who were a match for you."

"Were being an important word there, Mosi," she snapped back, annoyed that he casually dismissed her power while simultaneously claiming she was the only answer to Fae's problems. It was either absurdly hypocritical or delusional. She couldn't decide which, but both options were infuriating.

"Now, now, do I have to stand between you two like…" Serge said, moving up a bit to get between his siblings.

"Don't, Sergius. She needs a reminder, and I am fine with offering that here," Mo bit out. She hadn't been in the presence of another's magic in so long that, although she knew it was coming, she was still surprised when she felt Mo's power spring forward, static humming a soft vibration across her skin. It was a sensation so lost to her over the past years that she wanted to cry when she discovered it again, but it meant Mo was ready to spar, so she couldn't let her defenses down. As bold and seemingly threatening Mo's talk of teaching her lessons had been, she had no doubt it would be a sparring match only. Mo would not hurt her — he would not want to because of his sense of honor and responsibility and love. And, whether he wished to admit it or not, he flat out could not because of her own power.

She braced, thinking to let him have the first shot as he drew out his spear and shield, old talismans he used to help channel his magics and deflect the magic of others. Nin needed no props. Her fingers flexed at her sides, her hands a far more formidable weapon than Mo had likely seen in a while.

Just as the tension was cranking to a crescendo, the muted clatter of something hitting the concrete outside her greenhouse door reached her ears, and Nin's blood ran cold with fear. In that instant she also caught the now-familiar rosemary and mint smell that marked Sabrina's shampoo. Nin froze with her back to her friend, wishing she were not here at this moment. It was so unfortunate, for both of them, that she had come. Nin heard the unmistakable twang from Sabrina, the happy accent she often loved, shout "What the fuck is going on here?" with a mock bravado that made her so proud of her friend, and also so sad this was happening.

She could also see that Mo, Serge, and Gin were frozen, but they were more startled that a human happened to surprise them. Serge's freeze melted more quickly and turned into a slow, seductive smirk. Not good. Mo became narrow-eyed, cocking his head and focusing on this new addition to the fray, evaluating a new threat. Gin blinked, genuinely shocked to see a human.

Nin had no idea how long it had been since Gin had visited this realm — they tended to stay away in their personal library or close to their few friends, not venturing out much. It had likely been a few hundred years since Gin had encountered a human, maybe longer. Nin turned then, staring straight at her friend, and Sabrina's step stuttered when she finally saw Nin's face. If Nin had a mirror, she knew what would be there, so the hesitation did not surprise her. The fear and sadness that had

287

suddenly jumped to the forefront inside was likely written all over her.

Behind her, she heard Mo's "Take care of this," and Serge's innuendo-dripping reply, "Oh, I'll take care of this."

Nin moved swiftly, knowing this unnerved Sabrina when she jumped at Nin appearing so quickly by her side. There was nothing to be done for it. If Serge could, he would have fun with Sabrina, if she wished it. Sabrina could even use a little fun, in Nin's opinion at least. But as soon as Serge tired of her, and he tired of women very quickly before moving on to the next, she would be cleared. Her memory would be erased. Not just her memory of Serge, but her memory of any and all things related to Fae, including Nin herself. The idea of Sabrina not knowing her, not being with her in life, was too difficult to bear. It was part instinct and part rational calculation, but really, in either case, it was love and need that drove her in the next few moments. She held her friend's hand, looked her deeply in her eyes while willing her to come along with what was about to upend her life, and whispered, "Please forgive me Sabrina. And understand."

Then, dropping to a crouch, she reached past the small pebbles of the greenhouse pathway and touched the bit of soil she had spread across the framework just in case she ever had need of it, calling on it to connect to what was beneath it.

She chanted softly, asking the Earth to meet her, to bend and fold to her needs in that moment. Of course it did. It always had for Nin, at least when she wasn't bound by another. Serge went flying back, pushed away by a wave of soil that popped the foundation swiftly, like a graham cracker crumbling in the fist of a child. He spun out of free fall easy enough. Like a cat, Serge always landed on his feet, both literally and figuratively. The push had corralled him away from Sabrina and in proximity to the others. She knew not what they would do to her friend, so she caged them in, adding to her call in midstream, extending the roots and leaves and shoots of plants growing around the pathway where the three stood, creating a thick wall of living green that began to cocoon her family in and force them in place.

Mo pushed at the wall, funneling magic into his spear to try to wither the plants or stop their growth. It did him no good. He could divert what was there, but not stop the progress, and Nin pushed growth and claiming into the spell she continued to weave, hedging Mo, Serge, and Gin tighter and tighter in a small cluster. Fae generally bristled at any type of cage, even a living and breathing green thing, and when she saw the flash of annoyance grow in Gin's eyes, she knew she had a choice to make: dominate them fully or stop completely.

"Enough. Mo, put away your weapons. Serge, no games with the human. Nin, stop this nonsense. Call back the earth. Let us all talk in peace. No force. No harm. Your human can even stay, for now at least."

Nin heaved a sigh at the first "human." She knew her friend would pick that up quickly. Sabrina looked at her, wide-eyed and confused. "Human?" she asked, likely bewildered and a little afraid. It made her heart hurt to hear.

"Yes, Sabrina. Human. Unlike me, or the three other people here." Nin caught the wobble of her friend's legs a second too late. She shouted her name, but Sabrina was already falling, and her head hit the corner of a plant rack with a sickening crack as loud as a gunshot in the now-silent greenhouse. Sabrina was clearly knocked out and seriously injured, as blood began to pool out from a gash in the side of her head.

Nin bent beside her. For not the first or only time in her life, she lamented that she had little healing power. "Quick, Gin. Help," she croaked out, but her cousin was already there, holding a slender hand above Sabrina's head and willing the blood to slow. When it was just a trickle, Gin took out their medicine roll, folding it open on the pathway and beginning to mix ingredients into a paste.

"Now, it's been a long time since I worked on a human, but this mix should do the trick rather quickly. It will close the wound and prevent any swelling. She'll still have a nice headache when she wakes, but she should be fine." Gin smiled up at Nin through this information, offering reassurance to their cousin. She gave a quick thanks and brushed hair away from the wound so Gin could work without obstruction.

"No worries now, little sister. She will be fine," Serge said, crouching beside her and patting her shoulder in an awkward form of comfort.

"It is fortuitous. She is already out. Now it will be a simple thing to clear…" Mo started.

"No," Nin asserted.

"Nin..."

"No more lectures, no more attempts at showing force, and no more talk of clearing," Nina countered, looking down at her friend's head now cradled in her lap as Gin slathered a yellowed paste on her wound. She looked up at Mo, right in his disapproving eyes, and picked up a rather sharp piece of gravel. Nin speared Sabrina's blood on her palm and pricked her own skin, swirling her and her friend's blood together when the wound welled in her palm. Then, she said the binding words, though she wished she had been able to talk to Sabrina one-on-one before she did. "I, Nin, Princess of the Greens, daughter of Inanna and Fannon, vow Sabrina, the human, is mine. She is of me, as I am of her, from this day forward."

Serge gave a low whistle, Mo looked annoyed, but when she looked at Gin, they stared at her quizzically while still touching Sabrina's head. They gave a slow, wide smile, wiped their hands on their robes, and began to gather their medicinals.

"You heard Nin. She made the vow. Sabrina is hers, now and forever forward. No clearing will occur. We should take her somewhere more comfortable where her body can rest."

"To my cottage," Nin replied, bending to easily lift her friend off the ground. "Follow me."

"Will there be tea?" Gin asked, getting in step beside Nin. She smiled at them as she heard her brothers grumble from behind.

"I was thinking wine," Serge quipped.

"Harder spirits are needed," Mo muttered.

CHAPTER 3

Sabrina and Gin had left, after much stress and explanation. Nin and the others had made headway with Sabrina. She seemed a little less apprehensive. Seemed to believe them and was not ready to call in the human authorities at least. And she said she was okay with Nin. It still felt slightly stilted when she and Gin left Nin's cottage.

Nin asked for a moment alone with her friend. Gin made their way up to Sabrina's car in the greenhouse parking lot and Nin pulled her friend along the side of the house.

"Sabrina. I...it...you…" she stammered, so unlike herself.

"Well, now, look who's acting all awkward," Sabrina teased, showing a small smile. Teasing was good. They had fun with that over the course of their friendship. However, Nin needed more assurance.

"Yes. I am at a loss, Sabrina," Nin admitted. "Before you go, I must tell you that this secret I have kept has weighed heavily on my heart."

"But not heavily enough to let it out," Sabrina countered.

"True. For that, and the way in which you discovered it, I am sorry. I should have trusted you with this long ago. It is just, there is so much danger in the knowledge. For you and I both."

Sabrina looked at her friend with sadness and concern. "Nin, I understand that. I really do. I can logically see why you didn't tell me. That doesn't make it sting any less, though. What I said before still holds. We're okay. You're still my sister. I just need some time to wrap my head around all of this and fit it into my concept of you and me as BFFs. I'll get there one hundred percent, I know this, but you gotta give me that time to think all this through and get used to a shit ton of life-altering things."

Nin nodded in understanding. She knew that was logical and rational. But as her friend admitted, that did not make the sting of it any less harsh. "I love you, my Sabrina. My sister. Know that my time in the human realm has been most rewarding because it led me to you."

Sabrina grabbed her friend's hand and squeezed it tight. "Same, lady. You have nothing but love from me. All the other stuff may be new and a little scary, and I may need to get used to it, but that hasn't changed. Promise."

Nin let her friend go, watching her trudge up the gravel drive toward her old car, toward Gin and even more information about Fae. Nin was happy to let Gin take on all of Sabrina's questions. They were both teachers and scholars. They would likely relate to one another well. Gin had taught her so much over the years. They would teach Sabrina well for the brief time they were here.

After Nin watched Sabrina crest the hill, she turned to go back into her cottage and begin discussions with her brothers. She was nervous with them in her home, even if she loved them all, so she needed a bit of a break before she began another heated debate over whether to stay or go back to Fae. She also had Sabrina's blood smeared on her in a number of places, so she announced she needed time to take a bath.

Mo waved her on with a hand, obviously annoyed by this delay, but Serge shrugged and leafed through a book while lounging in her living room. In her small bathroom, she allowed the water to heat almost excessively. Stream billowed from the tap as her tub filled slowly. She had a large garden tub, great for soaking and relaxing, a place where she washed away any troubles from the day, feelings of homesickness or loneliness, and the dark memories that clung to the edges of her mind always, breaking in with a disturbing frequency. She eased into the clean, steaming water that carried a soft lavender scent from the bit of oil she had poured into the tub. Nin tried to relax, and she partially did. The hot water and steam were physical things that could not be denied, and it felt damn good after the morning she endured. However, her mind did not quiet. Instead, her brain focused on the arguments already made about her needing to return, and how she could convince Mo and the others it was safer for her to stay behind.

Nin was no coward. She was scared. Terrified, even. That terror for her own safety would make her hesitate. It would not cause her to dig in, to refuse, if her refusal would hurt those she loved in some way. Nin, however, was privy to Comus' plans. She had sat in on strategy meetings, heard his nightly musings while she laid rigid with fear or cowed by pain. She'd bore his collar, had her own magic dampened, which meant that, along with the pain he inflicted on a regular basis, Comus truly believed she was fully cowed, controlled, and no longer a threat. This is why he had let slip the real plan: Nin's magic could be drained and funneled into him. All Comus needed to do was decipher the process as outlined in a pair of old scrolls he had found. It was forgotten magic, and very dark indeed. Comus would need to know exactly how to do it step-by-step in order to pull off such a complicated feat.

It would drain Nin of all magic and the outcome of that was frightening. Not only because her magic was a physical and mental part of her, something innate to who she was as a being, and as such would be like losing a physical piece, but also because she was what she was, a Fae. There were no non-magical Fae. Some had more or less, depending, but no Noble or Lesser Fae was void of magic. Would this process, then, make her human? Or maybe it would just kill her, make her nonexistent. Comus dampened her magic with the collar. It was more akin to suppression, making it stay within her with no release. That was bad enough, not being able to connect her magic with what it longed for, the physical manifestations of the earth. She couldn't fully fathom what removing her magic altogether would leave. It would rip a hole through her, but whether that hole was survivable was a matter of debate.

This was all personally devastating, which was bad enough to contemplate. The real issue, however, is what would happen to Fae if Comus succeeded in acquiring that level of power. Nin was Princess of the Green. No one in Fae had her level of power besides the Mae Queen, and given some events that occurred during her training with the monarch, that may even be questionable. She rarely let her full power have free reign and she had learned to control it long ago, but Comus would have no qualms using all the magic at his disposal to make all of Fae bend the knee to his every whim. He was already formidable, what with his own high level of personal magic, his overall knowledge of dark magics others dared not use, and his acquisition of the wand and chalice, two very potent magical objects that amplified his powers and gave him new ones to boot. If he could actually succeed in absorbing Nin's level of magical power on top of what he already had, he would truly be invincible, even if the Mae Queen returned.

That was the real reason why she stayed away from Fae after her escape. She had not stayed to fight when she fled. She had not sought out her brothers, mother, or father for help in defeating Comus after she recovered and settled into the human realm. She fled and hid in this world because she saw it as the only real way to actually save Fae. As much as she argued with him and chafed at his bullish orders, she trusted in Mo's strategy and fighting prowess. She also trusted that the true Council, which included her mother, would figure out a way to defeat Comus despite his formidable position at that time. What they could never do is defeat a Comus with more magic than any Fae had ever wielded in recorded memory — and Fae memory was long.

When she broke from her collar and found herself in the woods of Kentucky, she made the conscious choice to go into hiding because she truly felt that taking herself completely out of contention would be the best way to ensure a future victory for those fighting Comus. Her personal fear helped her make that decision, most definitely, but she still, a decade later, did not fault the logic of her choice. It was the right thing to do.

Now, though, the right thing to do would be to listen to Mo's arguments, and whatever information Gin had acquired, in order to reevaluate her self-imposed exile. While hiding had been a good thing in the past, she could also recognize it may no longer be a viable option in a Fae present she knew little about. On this thought, she let out a deep sigh and pushed herself up and out of the tepid bath water. She'd had a moment to think on her own, which is what she needed. Now it was time to face what was likely to be a very long, very annoying, and emotionally devastating conversation. She toweled off, donned her fluffy pink robe, and exited the bathroom. She'd give herself a moment to dress, to collect herself further, but only a moment. Then she had to move forward as best she could, for herself, her family, and her realm.

When she finally emerged from her room, freshly dressed and ready to face what came next, she noticed it was rather late in the day, and her father's love of hosting, as well as his many lectures on the responsibility a home had to its guests, made her change course a bit. They could take some time to eat something other than cookies, but they also needed to get down to business.

Nin declared they all had to eat and then made sandwiches for herself and her brothers. Serge relished his, but that was no surprise. Any pleasure was the true domain of her middle brother, and she had discovered long ago that a turkey pastrami, stacked high with pickles and greens and Swiss cheese and mustard between two pieces of strong rye bread, was a thing of pleasure.

Mo, remaining rigid and unyielding, ate in silence without comment or any outward indication of enjoyment. That was the province of her older brother, constant seriousness at the expense of all else in life. It made Nin sad for him in a variety of ways, but it was also a large source of annoyance. This firm adherence to an idea or action, while commendable in and of itself, was not something she liked to take head on, and she would have to do that today.

Serge stretched back in his chair, patting his stomach and praising the sandwich he just demolished. Mo tsked at his brother and said, "Nin is aware her meal was very good, given your zealous need to moan and fawn over it for the past ten minutes."

Serge let out a soft grunt but nodded, moving to stack all three plates together before heading into the kitchen to linger by the sink and dishwasher. Nin saw he was not actually doing anything about those dirty plates — no surprise there — but he was giving Mo and Nin a little space to talk one-on-one while still being present enough to step in if the need arose.

"So…?" Nin let that unspecific question hang, as she looked at her brother. He sat poised and rigid at her kitchen table. A stark difference from the ease and languid nature of Serge or the comfortable lounge of Sabrina, the person who, until then, was the only being to occupy that particular chair. "You and Gin both hinted at some new information. Something that would somehow change my perspective on the matter of my exile. I would like to hear this story before we debate any more or you start barking orders my way." She then propped her elbow on the table while resting her cheek on her fist, obviously waiting for a story to unfold.

"You have been gone for years, and much has remained the same in Fae, for good and bad," Mo began. "We fight in scrimmages with Comus' soldiers and hold our ground. We continually thwart his plans for expansion but have yet to fully oust him. The Falls remains a refuge that is securely protected. Comus still rules from The Palace and controls big events outside of The Falls. The Fae join our resistance, bow to Comus' will, or persevere as best they can. However, a few months ago, the tide turned. Fae from outside The Falls, those who had been directly held by Comus for a time for some small infraction or another, began to spread tales of a new torture Comus devised. Apparently, he learned how to take magic from other Fae for himself."

At this, Nin gasped, bolting up right with a hand to her throat. "No. Say it has not happened. Tell me I did not leave for nothing!" she let out in a horrified rush.

"You knew of this possibility?" Mo asked.

"For me, and me alone. His goal and, I thought, the only possibility, was to drain and acquire my magic. That is why I ran. That is why I hid. It was safer than him getting my magic and destroying Fae as we know it with that power. Please, tell me what is happening so I can fully understand."

"As we've grown closer to penetrating the strong wards of The Palace, the ultimate goal of all our military strategy and one that is soon to be realized, we became aware of a new threat. It is but whispers now. Tales of demonstrations he held before his Court where he takes a Fae and shows how they can no longer perform even the most basic spells. He then shows how he, himself, can now perform magic they are known to do, spells that particular Fae is known to have mastered. We have no proof, and our few servant spies in the Palace can only confirm such events have been discussed openly. They cannot offer details, as no servants or outsiders beyond those being punished for whatever infraction are allowed to see the actual process — the siphoning of power or the demonstrations in the Throne Room. It is only Comus and his wild Court, jeering and cheering as he uses the pain of others to make some sadistic entertainment out of his new power."

Faced with this new information, Nin felt a sharp sensation in her chest, a literal heartache caused by the pain inflicted on those poor, poor Fae. Tears streamed down her cheeks, and she looked away from her brothers and out her front window at the quiet woods that she now loved so much. "I should have never come here," she said flatly. "I should have found you. Found the Council. Told you of his plans." After a heavy pause, she softly added a whispered thought, "I should have…ended it another way."

"If another way means what I think it means, sister, it is heartbreaking to hear you say such things," Serge inserted. She turned to her normally calm brother to see hurt and anger on his face. "I would never consider that an answer to this mess in Fae, no matter what Comus has or will do. To me, you are more important, Little One."

Mo grabbed her hand, and she saw softness in his face for the first time since he arrived. It was the face he had when he taught her spear and shield, when he laughed at her childhood antics. It was pride and affection. "No, Nin. That was not the way. That is never the way for you. Your logic was not flawed. If you believed, from what you learned directly from Comus, that you were the sole Fae this could happen to, then you were right to hide. I do wish you had told us why, said goodbye to us before you fled, but I also see the wisdom in a clean break. You never know where Comus may have ears to listen or eyes to watch. You sent us the message when and how you could, we eventually knew you were safe and free and that gave us peace."

"But if I had told…"

"Any number of things, good or bad, could have happened. You do not know that. Don't let decisions made in the past lead you down the path of 'what ifs' to a possibly different, rosy future. They could have equally led to disaster."

Nin nodded, but still felt no better about the situation. "As of now, there are rumors only, yes? You and Gin have heard from and about these Fae, obviously, but that is all the proof?"

"That is all in terms of proof. That is not all Gin has learned," Mo stated, leaning back into his chair again and letting go of her hand. "They found precedents, evidence in dark tales of old that this draining has been attempted before. It has even worked before, in some ways, although those accounts of its success are vague. All this means it is possible Comus is doing this as there is proof it has happened, although the process was thought to be lost long ago. This is why we had to come to you now."

Serge slid easily into a chair at the table, but his look was not easy. It was serious, something she had rarely ever seen from this brother, but a look that had up to this point dominated his face during this whole exchange. Serge took this seriously and that made Nin feel even more conflicted about all of this. "To be honest, little sister, Fae is a mess. Has been since the Mae Queen up and vanished. The Court, before Comus took over, was an ugly place full of vicious rumors and backstabbing. The Council, as you likely recall, was bickering about what to do, divided because of both loyalty and fear. The Mae Queen left a whole in the fabric of Fae politics and someone was always going to fill it. Many thought then, and still think now, you are the rightful heir to that throne."

"How can I lead when I let all of this happen?" Nin cried. "Comus' rise, all he has done and still does, is on my head. If I had not loved him, he would not have been poised to take control as he did. If he did not have access to me, he would not have been tempted to acquire more and more power. He likely would have not even sought out whatever dark crafts allow him to take the magics of other Fae. This is all on my head and, ultimately, proof I am not fit to lead in any way."

"Again, you speculate on outcomes and events in a way you cannot know, Nin. You have mighty powers, but you are no seer. Mo and I are your big brothers, we will always see you as a little sister, but even we know that you were born to lead us through this moment."

"It is true, Nin," Mo stated. "I do not give praise lightly, and I would not falsely lead you to believe you are capable when you are not. But we are at the end of our resistance. We have a plan, a way forward, and we are ready to fight. All I need to do is rally the troops. What we lack, and what you can give, is a power and grace similar to the Mae Queen. Fae will respond to this, rally behind it. Your earth magics are more than a match for our adversary. You can save Fae. I know this in my bones. I would bet my spear and shield on it. And there are many, many others — in and outside of The Falls — who know the same."

"What of The Council? Gin? Mother? Hell, either of you? All are powerful. All can take on Comus."

"But we are not as powerful as you," Serge interjected, "and that's fact. We also lack your direct connection to the Mae Queen, your given title, the air of mystery and awe that still surrounds stories of your power. Trust me, Nin, as this is my specialty: in politics, a good story always wins out, and you have a story many wish to follow."

Nin hung her head in defeat, realizing she must return and face her abuser head-on in what would very likely be a physical and magical fight to the death. She may not believe in her ability to face him and win, but apparently everyone else did, and as Serge pointed out, that was a large part of the political battle already won. They needed her to physically be there, to do the work, and to have others see her doing it, to get most of Fae to declare a side.

As these scenarios, good and bad, played through her mind, she felt Serge move to her side. He crouched beside her and lifted her head slightly so she met his gaze. "Sister. We are here. We will help.

I promise you, here and now, what happened to you in the past will not befall you in the future."

Mo added, "Nin, you will be protected. Trust that."

Nin smiled weakly at one brother, then the other, loving that they felt that, feeling their love suffuse her and seep into her bones. "Brothers, I do not need your protection. It is not required. It is also likely a hindrance in the fight ahead, so put that thought away. I do, however, require your guidance, your help, your support, and your love."

Serge smiled and moved away. Mo crossed his arms and gave a quick nod which clearly expressed he did not like what she said about his protection. The three siblings continued talking into the night, when darkness fell around the forest and cottage, enveloping them in the quiet goodness of the Kentucky woods. There were some laughs over old stories told again and again.

Mo asked for more than Nin could give in terms of what her past with Comus had fully entailed. He did, however, get enough to silently simmer in rage. Serge told of his more recent escapades in Fae and the human realm, which he seemed to visit far more often than they had ever known. They all bonded again, finding their footing together as brothers and sister, becoming reacquainted with the familiar bonds of siblings who can grow apart, live apart, but still be a part of one another.

CHAPTER 4

It was the dark of night when Nin said she needed a bit of fresh air. She was having a good time reconnecting with her brothers, but they were a lot to take in, and for someone who had avoided interacting with the majority of other beings over the last decade, it was more than a bit overwhelming. Plus, she had always been a little quieter, a little more reserved, a bit more introverted, so taking a step away was something her family members were used to her doing even before she left them for The Palace, long before the real trouble started and she had to flee Fae altogether.

She wandered out to the front porch, pulled the quilt off the back of the swing, and closed it around her shoulders as she used her toes to give herself a gentle push so her body slowly began the back-and-forth sway that often calmed her. There was a lot to love about her land in the human realm: the rolling hills, the thickets of old growth trees, the general expanse filled (most of the time) with only herself, the animals that passed through or burrowed deep, and the plants that flourished. It was peace for Nin, a place of communion that she felt connected to because of her earth magics. She knew every inch of it, the surface and the deep magic within, and that swing on that porch was a tapping point for her. It was a place she could meditate, feel at one with the land and all in it, and find a little solace in that connection, the cyclical feeling of her magic touching the magic of what was beyond her and out in nature.

She slowly swung, eyes closed and content to listen to the woods around her and the soft mummers of her brothers inside her home, when a shrill ring hit her ears. She reached in her pocket quickly, having completely forgotten she had her cell phone on her. It was one of those human requirements that became a part of her in a way, and most people to be honest, but so few people actually had or used the number, she rarely was called.

The bright screen vibrating in her hand said Sabrina was calling and this made Nin's eyebrows knit together in worry. It was not abnormal to receive a quick call from Sabrina about plans that she wished to make or confirm, but neither friend was a chatter. At least, not on the phone. It was quick calls between them or funny exchanges via messages. They had no plans already in motion and, given the events of earlier, that was unlikely to change. Or so Nin assumed. Then again, new issues or questions could have come to light within Sabrina's discussion with Gin only Nin could rightly answer. Her mind did not wish to jump to conclusions, but there was also danger in Sabrina learning certain things, and that brought its own brand of worry with it.

She answered with a formal hello, which was a habit of Fae etiquette she could never drop, no matter how often Sabrina laughed at the way she greeted people, even those few she knew well. There was static, a weird blend of jumbled words and silence and noises. Reception was not always the best at Sabrina's home, but it was never this bad, and that made Nin listen more closely. She jumped down from the porch and stalked up her driveway, searching for higher ground in case it was her phone. Nin made out "Gin," "wreck," and "help" before the call ended. She tried to call her back, but it went straight to voicemail.

She was running up the hill, fear causing her chest to become a sinkhole, a blank void ripped through the middle of her. Then, she got a quick text. It read, "Gin and I in accident at the intersection of SR 104 and Ludlow Lane on our way back to you. Need help. Gin hurt." It didn't read like Sabrina's normal quick bursts, but Nin didn't need more explanation. Her friend and cousin were in trouble. Gin was hurt. Sabrina may even be hurt and downplaying the situation, which was something she would do. Nin thought of little else after this. Getting to them quickly was all that mattered in the moment.

Nin shot off a short "On my way" and took off at a run before thinking on it. She had no need to hide her abilities from Sabrina now, and she knew it would be quicker for her to move in a straight line across fields on foot than go back, get her keys, get in her truck and travel the roads. She was across one field, still on the land she acquired but at least a half a mile from her cottage, before she thought of Mo and

Serge. She was so used to doing things on her own at this point, used to having no other Fae help in the human realm, that they came as a passing thought. She yelled out behind her, hoping they would hear. If it came down to it, she could carry the most injured back with her immediately the send one of her brothers to get the other. They'd likely not even realize she was gone if they did not catch her leaving.

It a few seconds, a mile more in distance, to reach the small ditch marking where her land ended and her neighbor's fields began. As soon as she crossed the border, the place she protected with specific wards when she first settled in that area, she felt a pop and smelled the stink of unknown magic. In that instant, right before everything became chaos, she knew she made a grave mistake.

That thought was barely realized when she was pulled off her feet, doubled over with a jerk as if some rope had been slipped around her midriff and she reached the end of the line. She landed on her back, the force knocking the air from her lungs in an audible whoosh. She heard scampering near, in the bits and pieces left in the spring field not yet plowed and planted, so she had no time to plan an attack or clearly discern her targets. All she had time to do was call with her mind. She lashed out at whatever was within a few feet of her prone body with a torrent of old roots and stems and leaves pulled from the ground and hurtled with enough force to slice through skin. She heard cries, but she had little time to think about it. She was using the soil itself, calling it to help her push upright and get to her feet while also creating a barrier around her body with mounds of thick dirt.

This lasted only a second when that same bind at her waist jerked again, dragging her further up, up, up into the air so she was not touching the ground. Without a direct touch of something of the earth, it would take longer for a barrier spell to form around her, longer for her to command roots and branches and other earthly things to do her will.

She felt a binding spell twine up and down her body, and even as she lashed at it with wind and leaves and twigs, even as she called to animals for help and could hear them scurrying forward, she could not stop its progress. She tried to remain free, desperate to fight those binds, when she heard something come towards her, hissing through the air at great speed. It slammed into her neck, encircling it and closing tight in a mere fraction of a second, so tight she thought it would start to choke her, but when she reached for it, she felt the smooth metal of the collar that was interrupted here and there by ancient Fae glyphs of power. Still suspended off the ground, she was now frozen in terror, trembling all over. Tears started to run down her face. Her magic was bottled inside her, screaming for release. Beyond that, she felt no other magic, nothing of the woods she loved so very much, and it was like a part of her had been ripped away.

She closed her eyes, tried to calm her breathing and stop her tears, and focus. He was here. Comus was the only one with the collar. Also likely the only one who could bind her that quickly, at least when he had the element of surprise in his favor. She could not reach out with her magic to sense him, but she strained to see and hear in the dark field around her as that invisible rope gently lowered her to the ground. It did her no good, a physical connection with the earth, as her magic was trapped inside. She was unable to call it forth or connect with it in any way. She heard a twig behind her snap a moment before she felt the heat of a body curving over her back.

A breathy whisper from wet lips creeped across her right ear. "Oh, my Lady. My precious sweetling. It is so good to see you."

All that followed was a flash of sharp pain at the back of her head and darkness.

CHAPTER 5

Nin slowly worked her way to consciousness, swimming into reality like she was surfacing from a deep dive into a murky lake. She could feel the effects, both physically and magically. The dull throb at the back of her skull and the memory of sharp pain told her she had been smacked, rough and hard, right at the base of her skull. The cloying smell of jasmine thick in the air around her, and the wavy feeling she had at the edges of consciousness, told her Comus had also used some magic to put her down, or at least keep her under for the time he wanted her out. She took stock of all of this with her eyes closed, not ready to let her captor know she was awake. She was being carted somewhere across a broad and bulky set of shoulders. This was definitely not Comus — while strong himself, he left the heavy lifting to others because he felt above such menial tasks. Not so above it all that he would not physically draw blood from her if he wanted to do so, but he left the lifting and carting and moving about to those he viewed as lesser, which was any other Fae in his presence.

She felt a brief moment of weightlessness and tried to brace but failed to mitigate the impact of her body slamming down on to cold stone. Her head cracked against the hard surface and she let out an involuntary gasp of pain, but she still did not open her eyes. She was working through pain, both old and new, so it was no longer a matter of hiding her consciousness from Comus. The sounds she made and the way her hand shot up to cradle her head made it perfectly clear she was awake.

"Imbecile!" she heard Comus shout, followed by the loud crack of a slap. "She is delicate and important. She is your better in all ways. Treat her as such."

She then felt his hands on her, a sadly familiar and exceedingly unwelcome feeling that made her skin turn clammy and her fight-or-flight responses scream inside her already ringing head. She tried to wrench free, but he grasped hard, and she finally opened her eyes to stare in hate up at this person she had once loved so much.

"There you are," he said with a smile. "I do love to see those beautiful hazel eyes looking up at me. I've missed you, sweetling." With that he raised her from the ground, took a firm grip of her arm causing another hiss of pain, and forced her to turn and walk with him.

She stared, narrow-eyed, at Comus, fear and anger warring inside her. She would be a fool to not fear him — as her current situation attested — but time away from him, new knowledge, and healing helped mitigate the fear. At this point, at least, anger won out.

She raked him over with a withering gaze, taking him in fully for the first time in a long time. He stood regal and proud, more than a hint of pompousness etched into the way he held his frame, cocked his head, refused to meet the eyes of the people around him. He was dressed in what she considered his uniform: a loose, crisp white toga, blood red sash, ropes of gold adornment, and a crown of gold-dipped laurel leaves at the top. It was a costume of sorts. In the past, he had worn this look most often, although he donned rich and intricately stitched robes on occasion. This, though, was his everyday wear, a nod to the tales humans had once told of his Fae mother and father, Circe and Bacchus. With a young woman's eyes and open heart she had fallen in love with this surface, finding it beautiful, especially with the touch of tragedy — the Fae orphan in all his splendor. It was intoxicating, for a time.

She could more objectively evaluate his overall appearance now, after so much time away, but being completely objective meant she could not call him a monster, at least not in reference to his look. Quite the opposite was true. He was masculine grace with a perfectly chiseled face featuring sharp cheekbones, a regal blade of a nose, and full, pouty lips. The sneer that so often stood there, and the calculating or cruel light in his eyes made him monstrous, but his beauty was still present.

He stood tall, well over six and a half feet, with broad shoulders and a muscled frame that was not bulging but still strong and fierce, like the human swimmers in their Olympics. All this was topped with a casual mop of golden waves, purposefully artless in its look but not in its execution. He was masculine beauty, noble and strong in physical appearance, and someone many lusted after or envied. She had, at one point, been so smitten and proud on his arm, confidently walking beside him and feeling pleasure in the fact he chose her to be by his side. That faded long ago, love and joy turned to fear and desperation. Now, anger burned brightest when Nin looked at him and remembered all he had done — to her, to her home, to her people.

At the moment, despite the pain and fear, she had one single thought. "What of the others?" she gritted out. Hating that she needed Comus for anything, let alone some form of assurance.

"Do you refer to your traitor family? Or that filthy human you associated with?" Comus asked.

All Nin did was nod. She did not trust herself to speak, her emotions too overwhelming and complex to do her thoughts and feelings justice.

"All still back in the human realm, I'm afraid. Your family is likely worried sick. The human, that woman who Borjigin was with for some inexplicable reason is cozy and oblivious in her beds at this very moment."

Her body folded closer to the floor, relief washing over her and relaxing her muscles. Of course she worried for her family, as their magic was likely what brought Comus to Wilde. However, she was most worried for Sabrina, who had no magic of her own to protect herself or fight of an attack from a Comus minion. Nin was lucky her friend had not drawn Comus' attention or ire. Mo, Serge, and Gin would relish a fight with this Fae. Sabrina would be unaware and unprepared. She needed to be protected.

Comus abruptly interrupted her moment of relief. "That human woman? The one with Gin? We used her human trickery to place you in the field because the scouts found her first. The told me of her and Gin. How she smelled of both your magics. It left me intrigued and more than a little disappointed in who you chose to associate with in my absence."

"She is no concern of yours. Just a silly human woman," Nin stated, trying to remain as nonchalant as possible.

"Oh, my Lady. You forget how well I know every single part of you. That protestation gives away so much. You also answered the signal for help from that treacherous human device too quickly to now act so unconcerned. Who is she to you?" Comus gave a wicked grin. Some may call it rakish. Nin knew it as manipulative and vile.

"It does not signify. She is there. We are here."

"I will find out all I wish to know about your time away from me, and much more. Be assured of this, Princess," Comus cooed in a sickeningly sweet tone. Nin stared hard, silently refusing to offer more.

When she wrenched her angry eyes away from this man she loathed, she finally registered where they were. They were outside the Throne Room of The Palace, the large, oval-shaped chamber where official business was conducted. She had been unceremoniously deposited in a heap at the foot of the large, arched brass doors that marked the formal entrance. Thoughts of others slipped into the background of her mind. In all likelihood, they were safe but worried for her at the moment. She, on the other hand, was now right outside the room that held the centerpiece of Comus' twisted Palace dynamics. Nin knew, without doubt, he brought her to the Throne Room to put on a good show for his perverted Court.

CHAPTER 6

She and Comus stepped through those massive wooden doors, walking the length of the room on the rich burgundy runner marking the official pathway from door to throne across the long expanse of cold, hard marble flooring. She stutter-stepped, dug her feet into the plush rug for a moment, but the grip on her arm tightened and she decided to amble along with her head high. She learned long ago to choose her battles with this Fae, and she thought a room full of his acolytes was not a place to successfully fight against him. Part of her mind screamed to rebel, to kick and fight with all of her power, but she rationally knew it would be a losing battle here and now. She would need to think, to plan, and strike when the blow would do the most damage to Comus.

The space around the runner was crowded with Comus hangers-on, a motley mix of fanatics, cruel minions ready to serve their own whims through Comus' own fearful and deplorable acts, and those too scared to do anything but stay and witness horror after horror visited on others. All were, of course, dressed for Court, a sea of gold brocade and velvet and silks in various shades. Comus liked a good-looking crowd for his shows, and this room did not disappoint.

She looked through them, seeing who remained from her time before and who may be new to the fold, elevated in status through acts that pleased the madman with a tight hold on her arm. She recognized most, and was not happy to see them, but it was heartening to know he acquired few new followers in the decade she was away. That spoke something to the lack of influence Comus wielded in wider Fae and sparked some hope, even if a small amount.

Nin stopped scanning the crowd when they reached the bottom stairs to the dais. Up twenty velveteen steps sat the single throne of Fae, the throne Comus profaned, the throne that should be reserved for the Mae Queen's return. Seeing it sent a pang through Nin's heart. The chair was a tall seat made from solid oak and inlay with a gold floral and leaf design along the arms and legs. Its carved back showed a sole Fae figure, The First Fae, the original woman of earth magic in the New Eve legend, surrounded by the Noble and Lesser Fae supposedly created from her after her birth. It towered eight feet above the seat, hovering high above for all to see, an artistic rendering of what was supposedly the start of Fae — the people and place — at a time before real memory or history. It was an origin story like many in the human realm she heard or read over the years.

The Noble Fae, as they were called, were made first, with the First Fae a woman directly birthed from the Great Mother – the earth and land in this legend. It was the reason Fae was matriarchal in structure. It was also the reason the Lesser Fae (a name Nin and others despised) were still discriminated against. The legend gave hope and inspired division, like most legends do. But it was still a lovely story in many respects, and one the Mae Queen was so fond of repeating in times of strife. She knew, from years of lectures, Comus took the story differently. For him it was a story of strength, superiority, dominance. A story he perverted for his own ends to empower those he found superior and crush those he found wanting. This, also, was an old tale in both realms, the way people used stories to manipulate and cause pain.

As he pulled her up the stairs, forcing her to follow his silent but determined demands, she saw the gold chain attached to the leg of the throne and bucked. Not again, she screamed inside her own mind. She would not again be chained to his side for the amusement or horror of the gathered crowd. She reared back as hard as she could, pulling her arm free and turning to race down the stairs. She got about two steps away when that same invisible rope from before pulled taut and made her stumble backward.

Comus walked up behind her, putting his arms around her at the waist and kissing her ear as he whispered, "There is nowhere for you to go, sweetling. Do not make me hurt you. You know where your place is. Take it." The last part he hissed, skipping from fake sweetness to harsh demand in an instant. He gripped the back of her neck and caressed the collar there. "Nothing you can do, my Nin. Your fate is sealed, and you are already tied to me by my magics. A physical chain means little given that." He pulled on the invisible rope, forcing her back, back, back, holding her in place with a grip on her neck as a servant scurried forward and clamped the golden shackle around Nin's ankle.

Tears filled her eyes. In her mind she could acknowledge it was but a symbol. Comus had her bound in many magical ways that were far more serious. However, symbols are important. They hold their own power over people. Having a physical chain on her again made her mind riot. However, after a moment, she caught herself. She walked across this room on her own without fight because it was wise to choose when and where she resisted. The chain may grate, but she told herself it was better to take this hit here and now and make a stronger hit herself when the time was right. Tears fell, and she did nothing to stop them or wipe them away, but she used her pain and frustration as a focal point. A deep breath in and out, a moment to let her mind clear, and Nin stood tall and straight in defiance, a woman forced into a position but one who refused to be bowed by it.

"Sit," Comus commanded, but Nin remained still, focused on reining in her temper at the moment. "Oh, I see you have picked up a number of nasty habits in your time away. Human willfulness has no place in my Palace. I will soon relieve you of that, pet. Now, sit." He flashed the wand at his side, slashing it toward Nin, driving blade-sharp pain through her knees, forcing her to physically bend and take a seat so she did not topple down the stairs. "Good. Good," Comus crooned at her, kneeling slightly to lift her chin and make her meet his eyes. "Will you make no sounds? No cries of pain or frustration? Not even a grand, misguided declaration at the sting?" he taunted.

Nin stared straight at him, unflinching and unblinking, refusing to open her mouth. Her words would come soon enough, and they would be blistering.

"As you wish. For the moment, at least. This will just be a quick show, my Lady, then we are off to more…private pursuits."

Nin's eyes widened at that and clawing fear ripped up her throat. Before she could catch herself, Comus saw the reaction dance plainly across her face and gave a dazzling smile — he loved to see fear and pain play across faces, especially her for some unknown reason.

"There we are," he whispered, and smacked a loud kiss on her cheek before rising and seating himself on the Throne.

Anger returned to Nin, mingling with her fear, making a hot, molten mix that fortified her. Her back snapped straight, she stared ahead and schooled her face into an impassive and aloof mask. She neatly folded her hands and feet before her, taking as dignified a seat as the circumstances allowed. Nin did not even wipe the lingering spit from Comus' kiss. She did not want to give him the satisfaction of knowing how it itched her skin, so she let it linger there with the residue of her tears for all to see.

With both seated in what Comus deemed their rightful places, a herald appeared at their side, blowing a curved horn a bit too loudly for the small echo chamber they were in, and began the usual recitation that marked the start of official business in the Court of Comus.

"Kneel before Comus, Prince of the Fae, Keeper of Ancient Magics, Ruler of All in the Realm. His reign shall be mighty, all-encompassing, and eternal. All hail Comus!"

Comus' courtiers knew their place; all in the Throne Room save Nin and Comus hit the marble simultaneously, an echo of bodies bending to the will of one Fae.

Comus nodded and gave a wave of his hand, signaling they could stand again and face him. "Yes. Very well. It is good to see all in attendance on this special day. The day when my beloved Nin, who was stolen from this very Palace ten years prior, has been lovingly recovered. She is whole and we will celebrate her return with a proper feast tomorrow eve." A cheer rose at this — the Comus crowd loved a feast — but he shushed them quickly. "Now we must name the conspirators who caused my love to be stripped from me, those who wished to weaken me with sadness over my loss. We name, as traitors of the state, Mosi of the Plains, Sergius the Whisperer, and Gin the Scholar. These Fae took my poor Nin as she was travelling with a tiny guard outside the Palace walls. They came like thieves and stole my beloved, never daring to confront me face-to-face, ever fearful of my immense power. They hid her away, in a dark and dangerous part of the human realm, keeping her from me and I from her, attempting to tear our love apart and defy fate. But, as we all know, my power has no match and fate cannot be escaped. She is returned to me, and I am thankful. The guards who allowed her to be taken were severely punished years ago. When Mosi of the Plains, Sergius the Whisperer, and Gin the Scholar are captured, they will be treated like the terrorists they are. My swift justice will rain down upon them."

The crowd cheered at the end of his ridiculous speech. Nin bristled at the lies, those told about her and the people she loved. She wondered at the hubris allowing Comus to ignore the blatantly obvious inconsistencies in his story. If he was so powerful, how could she be taken? How could she be from him for so long? How are Mo, Serge, and Gin still free? The cognitive dissonance boggled her mind. She also, for a moment, felt a pang of regret over the horrors faced by the guards she slipped in her escape a decade ago, but she shook that off quickly. She had killed a number of them when her wild magics rode her through her escape, and she learned to live with that long ago.

Comus' guards were cruel and fiercely loyal to him and him alone. She suffered much at their hands — there was no way to know what pure terror and pain they caused others not deemed necessary in the Comus Court. Nin did not wish pain or death on any being, but she also believed fate meted out its own forms of justice when it saw fit. She was not one to dwell on bad things falling upon bad people over much.

"While I immediately punished the majority of the Fae who helped those traitorous rogues steal away my Princess, two were kept sequestered, in the hopes they could offer more information to help in the return of my beloved." Comus looked down at Nin, a hint of concern and care masterfully portrayed on his face. A tiny shimmer of a tear hung at the rim of one eye. If he were human, and not completely bent on destruction, Nin thought for a fleeting moment, Comus would make a fine film star.

Those thoughts were immediately disturbed by the rattle and clank of chains on marble and flesh. A guard she remembered from her first captivity was escorted through the throng of the Court and shoved down on his knees at the bottom of the stairs so Comus could sneer down at him easily.

Nin thought back to this Fae and her times with him. Admittedly, he was less cruel than others. He never seemed to revel in the pain and horror of the Court. He was a guard, however, proven and tested again and again as a Fae who would follow Comus in all things. She had little sympathy for him in this new position, weighed down by steel chains made with just enough iron to dampen the magic and strength of any Fae. Pure iron was nearly impossible to find and wield in Fae and affected all Fae in one way or another — a real weakness humans folk tales revealed.

The imprisoned guard hovered there, on his knees, heaving great breaths from pain or exertion. Another guard came up from behind, holding a slim steel cage in his heavily gloved hand. It looked like a birdcage, with much less room. A tiny prison for the Wisp who sagged inside it, only held upright because his head and torso leaned heavily against the bars. The Wisp was so small, as all Wisps were, that she could not tell if she knew him or had ever seen him. Did not know if he was one of the many Lesser Fae forced to work the Palace under Comus or someone who had been captured after her escape, an unfortunate and innocent casualty of Comus' wrath. All she could tell from her perch is he was male, he was naked and shivering, and his body looked oddly colored and slightly swollen, likely covered with bruises from tortures and steel exposure.

It was improbable he worked the Palace prior to her escape — thinking back on it, she had never seen a Wisp in captivity. They were fierce warriors who resisted Comus at every turn, scrimmaging with his forces then quickly retreating back to their camps. They were Lesser Fae, so Comus viewed them as beneath him, of course. But the Wisps often drew his particular ire because they were a truly formidable foe. All the more reason to use one as a demonstration of his own cruel power.

Comus watched Nin from the corner of his eyes. She knew he hoped to get a reaction from her. This was all show, to intimidate and cow, and she sat straighter, hardened her face to stone, told herself she would not react. Would not give this maniac the satisfaction.

"If you do not recognize or remember, the Fae before you is Ragar. He served as a trusted Palace Guard at one time. It was clear, upon investigation, he and others conspired with outside forces to steal Princess Nin away from me, from her rightful place at my side. The other guards were swiftly dealt with, but Ragar remains. I hoped he would relent. Tell us more. But, alas, that was not so. He persisted in his evil, contrary ways, refusing to cooperate. Now, as my Nin is returned to me, I have no more use for him.”

Making sure he had Nin’s attention — knowing full well he already had the entire attention of his Court at his feet — Comus rose and glided down the steps, stopping a few paces from Ragar. He cocked his head, muttered under his breath, and began his awful spellwork.

“Rise,” he said, forcing Ragar up to his feet through compulsion. It was a handy piece of magic for one such as Comus, and a trick he often used. It showed his power as few could force another Fae to do something against their will. The steel helped in this instance, of course. It made the other Fae more open to magical command or suggestion. It was still impressive magic to behold, though dark and horrible. To take the will of another, disregard it, and shape it to your own was a stain on the soul, a black magic counter to all the natural rights of Fae in their realm.

Comus nodded to a guard, who slipped a long dagger into Ragar’s hand. Ragar blinked for a moment, amazed by this action, unsure of what was next. A lesson Nin learned long ago, one that everyone in the Comus Court should know, is that hesitation had a heavy price. Before he could turn that blade on another, at least attempt to escape, Comus waved the wand in his right hand, forcing Ragar's face to stare into his own. He was a hypnotist, mesmerizing the Fae in front of him the weaving of magic and words.

Again, he muttered a spell under his breath. Comus kept his eyes locked with Ragar and softly but clearly said, "Pierce yourself. Spill your insides on my floor." He then flicked his wand, adding to the compulsion spell the push and pull and force of strength, magical and physical, the wand produced.

You would think a gasp would go up. Nin wanted to give one. Others may have as well. It was better to stay stone-faced, immovable, stoic. Do not give anything away, she repeated to herself. It was another lesson of the Comus Court all should know by this point: do not let another in this place see hesitation or concern or fear on your face. It would always be used against you. Some did look away slyly. She'd learned long ago to cross her eyes a fraction. It was a small, barely noticeable action which made the world blur to a point she could endure. Others, however, nearly salivated, cruelty dripping from their grins and glinting from their eyes.

Nin forced herself to watch, to see again what she missed for a decade, to witness the pain suffered by those in Comus' Palace, by all of those in Fae, at the hand of this tyrant. She saw Ragar hesitate briefly, enough to know he was in there somewhere, fighting this. And that made it so much worse, really. Then, in a blink, the blade was turned inward, slammed into his stomach, and dug in deep. Ragar screamed, but did not stop, ripping the dagger across his torso, blood and viscera trailing in his wake. He left the knife embedded as he keened, tears streaming down his face. He sagged, then crumpled, only then breaking Comus' stare.

Comus looked down at the bloody and broken body of Ragar with no perceptible change in demeanor. Nin could not see his face, but she imagined a small, sad smile there. The sadness, of course, was an affectation. The smile would be truth. After a few beats, a pause created to force his audience to linger on the bloody scene before them, he motioned for a guard. He left a wake of blood and other bits as he pulled the body across the cold marble floor and out of sight.

Comus began to pace, giving Nin flashes of his profile. He looked at her now and then. She gave him nothing, masking the deep disgust and horror effectively. It was a mask she slipped on too easily for comfort, but it was necessary. Finally, Comus stopped, giving a hard glare to the Wisp still held in the cage. "That thing also helped the traitors. It was found lurking near where my Nin was taken. It is obviously weak and half-dead already. Such a creature is not worth my magic. Guard, rip it apart."

The guard holding the cage reached inside and clutched the Wisp in his fist. The man roused, attempted to fight, but before he could recover from the drain of the steel on his strength and magic, the guard tossed the tiny cage and grabbed his wings with his free hand. A cruel smile marked his lips as he pulled hard and quick, ripping those delicate but vital wings right off the Wisp's back.

He shrieked, loud and long, blood pouring from his wounds. The guard flung him to the ground and stomped his foot several times, smearing the Fae's small body into the hard stone beneath his boot. The screams died quickly, as did the Wisp, and Comus gave these actions barely a second glance, instead ascending the stairs with a smirk on his lips. Nin had flinched when the guard ripped the Wisp's wings, and Comus had obviously seen it. She couldn't help it. The Wisp did not deserve such callousness, such mistreatment based solely on who it was born to be.

"A good reminder, my Lady," he whispered so only she could hear. "It has been so long since you graced my Court with your presence, you may have forgotten our ways."

Nin boiled inside, raging at the cruelty and horror. Lesser Fae, bound and chained in magical and physical ways, were forced to mop up the blood as the Court paused. The gory red disappeared, flawless marble left in its wake, a cold slab marred only in memory. Yet memory was enough for Nin. She knew the death of the Wisp was now added to the long list of horrors she often saw when she closed her eyes at night.

CHAPTER 7

She scanned the crowd with her hard expression,
taking in all she could as Comus droned on and on at
his courtiers after the blood was wiped clean. They
stood at attention through his talk of how strong
Comus' love for Nin was, how happy Nin was to
return to him, how they would rule together, Nin
subservient at his side, for all eternity. It was a new
variation on an old rant, one she had heard often
enough before. One that held no truth, so was of little
importance. The lies of rulers are best countered with
concrete action. As she was in no position to fight,
she did her best to ignore him and, instead, took that

time to think through various escape plans and scenarios in her mind.

Last time, she managed to disengage the collar through a short-circuit of sorts. Her magic had started to build up inside rather than simply dissipate. This caused a surge that overwhelmed the collar and loosened it from her neck. It left her depleted physically but ruled by a wild form of magic she did not consciously control. It was unwieldy, but effective, and she had managed to both escape and cover her tracks. What she knew now, however, meant she could not simply escape and go on the run again. She must escape her collar but stand her ground here in the Palace. She had to save herself and fight for Fae, help her people throw off the yoke of tyrannical oppression and make sure Comus was no longer a threat.

After that, much would need to be decided about how Fae governance could avoid such as this in the future. That was a consideration for another, safer and brighter day. Now, the work of rebellion, of revolution and overthrow, was the order of the day, and a bit of Nin was happy to have a hand in taking down this man who had caused her so much direct fear and pain during their years together. Fate did what it did, and no outcome was certain for any Fae beyond the seers, but the idea of possibly being the cause of Comus' downfall brought a small grin to Nin's lips, though she hid it well.

After Comus bored of talking, he offered a dismissive wave of his hand and the herald again appeared from the darkened corners of the dais.

"Court business is now concluded for this day. All kneel as your Prince exits the Throne Room!"

As he boomed this, a servant silently released the golden chain from Nin's ankle and helped her rise, scampering back quickly when Comus walked forward. He smiled down at Nin and offered his arm. She took it with a suffering sigh but little overt complaint. Better to wait and see what was to come, as much more would be worth fighting over in the future. Of that she was certain.

"Smile, Princess. Show them how sweet you are," Comus encouraged as they started descending the stairs.

She ignored his comment as they strolled at a casual pace while all around knelt and diverted their eyes. Nin faced forward, counting her steps to help her remain calm and aloof they made their exit arm-in-arm. The large bronze doors slammed behind them with a loud clang of metal and Comus held firm to her arm, turning right and making his way down a maze of hallways that led to the family quarters of the Palace. Every step they took made Nin's heart sink further and further down in her chest. She dreaded where they were headed: the Royal Chambers.

The dark wooden doors, strong rectangles of thick oak reinforced with metal that could easily provide a barricade if clicked into place, swung open and Nin steeled herself like those doors. She stiffened her spine, determined to walk through that entrance with her head held high, not cowed or fearful as Comus expected.

The Royal Chambers were a quartet of connected rooms, each with a specific purpose. The central room was the bedchamber and everything else fed out of or into that spot, like blood pumping in and out of the heart. It was a dark burgundy and black room dripping in heavy velvets. It was designed for sleeping and sex, the comfort of each at the forefront in layout: a massive bed took up most of the square footage of the room. It was raised a few steps off the ground, serving as a platform and a staging point of sorts. A few deep settees lined the walls of the room, but the bed was the central point and that was how Comus liked it.

Off to the right of that room was a giant, decadent bathroom, all cool marble with a massive tub that was more like a wading pool. A line of sinks, bench-seating, and a sauna filled more space, with bathroom stalls tucked far away.

To the left was a dressing room which held rows and rows of clothes meticulously maintained by the valet. This old man, a relic from the Palace before Comus took over, was forced to sleep in a small recess, chained with an iron band encircling his wrist. He maintained all Comus' clothing, dressed him every morning, and undressed him every evening. The vast space had a few cushions and ottomans here and there to accommodate anyone Comus may favor at the moment so as to allow them the great honor of seeing him formally dress or undress, and Nin had been forced to see that ritual a time or two. However, this was a space usually only occupied by the old, abused servant and Comus.

A smaller chamber lay deep within that closet, a place for storing consort clothing. It was where Nin's garments were kept and taken care of by whatever favored maid Comus was having sex with at a particular point in time. This particular arrangement meant Nin's clothes were usually not well cared for at all. Not that it mattered to Nin when she had been forced to live there. Like all things, the clothes were procured for her without her input and were usually far too revealing and/or gaudy for her general taste. She'd had no choice in anything, including what she wore on a daily basis, and was ushered into the room every morning and evening, clothes placed on her or removed with so little care she had often felt like an ill-used rag doll.

The room they stepped into first, the one directly behind those imposing doors, was the antechamber — a small receiving room positioned as both a barrier to and waiting/lounging area before the massive bedroom. It held several high-backed chairs, a row of bookshelves filled by past inhabitants, and a large fireplace that often roared to life. The entire Palace was heated by an intricate steam system fed through the floors and walls. Radiators dotted those walls also, and were placed throughout The Palace to keep the old stone structure warm, so the fireplace was more aesthetic than strictly utilitarian. It was crackling now, filled with huge logs that likely took two servants to shove into the grating and arrange in a way that would allow them to burn at an even and steady pace.

The guard of six who had flanked Comus and Nin as they traveled down the halls broke off at this point. Two stayed outside the suite doors, two posted directly inside those same doors, and two moved to stand at attention outside the open bedroom doors. Comus did not swerve towards those doors, but instead directed them both toward the chairs and lounges surrounding that roaring fire.

Nin let out a huff of air she did not realize she had been holding for quite some time. Comus chuckled at this, a smug look on his face. "Don't worry, sweetling. We will be there soon enough," he answered lecherously to the unspoken fear he'd witnessed. "For now, we must chat, you and I." He forced her down into one of the large wing-backs close to the sweltering fire and took the seat opposite her. He flounced for a minute, arranging himself in the chair, then leaned back and steepled his hands together before resting them under his chin. "My Nin. How have you been?"

"Fuck you," she spat back.

He clicked his tongue at her, "Not a very lady-like response, Princess. I was polite. I can move on from that quite easily if that is what you choose. So, let us try again. How have you been, my Lady?"

"Much better without you in my life, thank you for asking," she replied with mock sweetness in her voice.

"That wounds, love. I have missed you so. Have you not missed me? There was a time when you would cry at my leaving for mere days, when you begged to not be away from me for any period of time, even a single hour."

"That time has long passed, as has the love that caused those sentiments then. You killed that, as you well know."

"Oh, I don't know. You must love me still, Nin. Why run and not fight? Why not come to attack? You are very powerful. Well, without that collar you are very powerful. I feel there may still be something in that cold heart of yours left for me and our time before."

"I had my reasons for hiding, but love was not one of them. If I could, I would carve out your heart right now and revel in the blood spilled by my hand." She rose at this, heat and hate flowing through her body, her magic rippling under her skin, bristling for an outlet that was now blocked. Four guards took a step forward and Comus waved them away with a shake of his head and a sneer her way.

"No need to worry about our Nin, men. There is little she can do with that lovely piece of metal magic adorning her neck. Oh, but I see she wishes she could. Part of me was longing to find a spark of love or longing still in your eyes. I hoped time had softened your view of me. Yet…" Comus cocked his head, a wicked gleam in his eyes, "I'm also liking the challenge you present. It is a lovely opportunity to break you, bend you to my will for a second time."

"You never broke me, Comus," Nin hissed back, before calmly seating herself again and staring hard at the man opposite her. "You hurt me, yes. Made me beg and weep, true. You gave me plenty of physical and emotional pain for years, but that is all. I was never broken, just slightly cracked. What creature is not left a bit cracked and damaged in their time?"

Comus heaved out a sigh, placed his arms on his chair to hoist himself up, and said, "Well, sweetling, we will see about breaking you fully, then.

In the end, you will be my creature, wholly and completely, and none — not you or your family or that ridiculous rebellion the attempt to ferment — will be able to stop it. I will have your love, I will have your will, and I will have your power. There will be none who would dare stand against me. I will reign for eternity with a docile Princess of the Green at my side.”

“I escaped once. I will do it again. When I do so this time, I will end you before I leave these grounds. You will not be able to hurt me or the rest of Fae ever again.”

“Hurt them how, exactly? Take their magics, perhaps?” With that he laughed. “Oh, for Gin’s intelligence, they are so very easy to fool. Everyone is. I never took a Fae’s magic. You will be the first and only. You can be the only, based on what I have at my disposal. The rest, just trickery and performance I allowed to trickle out of the Court I control. All of it intended to do exactly what it did — get that silly rebellion and your family concerned enough to finally reach out to you. I knew you were well hidden from me and mine. I tried for long years to track you down myself, but not a trace of you existed, at least not one I could follow. However, you

354

are a sad creature of habit, too easily manipulated by ideas of love and loyalty. I knew I could not reach you, but I was certain you left a door open for your family in some way. I knew all I needed to do was plant the right gossip, stoke vicious rumors, get them to a point when they felt they had to go to you, and follow in their wake. They led me right to you, or at least your general area in the human world. The smell of humans was overpowering and sickening, but I caught traces of you outside your wards. Again, I had no real need to worry. Your pathetic sympathies for that human brought you right to where I waited. If only your oh-so powerful and intelligent family had taken the time to investigate me instead, you could still be in your tiny, warded woods out in the human realm."

Nin gritted her teeth and seethed. She raged at his words and the sad truth of them, even if there was little she would change about her feelings or actions despite the way Comus manipulated her and others. There was nothing for it now, it had come to pass, so she calmed her emotions. He was cunning, that was certain. It was one thing she had to admit about Comus. It did you no good to underestimate your enemies.

"Now, sweetling, I have some private meetings to attend. I will not be seeking your lovely company just yet. I find I do not have a taste for you. You smell too much like human for my liking," he said with a crinkle of his nose. "You will be chained in the Royal Bedchamber. I will not cage you this time unless you provoke me, so do not provoke me. Do what you will with the short leash you are given. Know these men present will guard you unto death. They saw what I did to those who allowed you to escape before. They will fight hard to save themselves from a similar fate."

He wandered to her chair, looked down at her with a condescending shake of the head, and moved to stroke her cheek. Nin ripped her head away and hissed at him like a cat ready to pounce. "Oh, love. You will be mine again, in all ways, in all things. You will come to beg, to plead, and to call me your loving Prince, your everything, your King. Until then, sweetling." In a flash he bent forward and placed a hard, bruising kiss on Nin's lips. She tried to wrench away, but he clasped her head in his hands and kept her in a tight grip, squeezing her to the point of pain while keeping her head locked in place. He ended the kiss, and she was thankful it ended quickly even though she saw the triumph in his eyes.

He turned and exited without a backward glance. Nin was carted roughly out of the chair and thrown into the Royal Bedchamber where she was shackled to the wall with yet another golden chain. The guards left, posting outside the door, and Nin lay down on a settee, curling into herself while facing the wall. She gave herself the time and space to weep silently, for what was past and what was to come. It was not a weak cry, because crying is not weakness, but release. It was a good, strong choice for that moment, to vent the complexity of emotions swimming inside her. After that cathartic cry, however, she wiped her face clean and started plotting once again.

CHAPTER 8

A decade ago she fled, wild with relief that she managed her escape and not quite sure how exactly it happened. Her only thoughts were freedom and safety, both for herself and for Fae overall. Once again, she had to escape, but she needed a plan. She knew she must turn her mind to the past she tried so hard to block out so she could consider how her escape happened then, how she could potentially replicate the events now on a shorter timeline, and how she could defeat Comus in the process.

Her mind raced with possibilities, probabilities, and connections. It seemed obvious, to her at least, she was the one who must bring down the would-be Prince. She alone had the power to match his own, and if she did it immediately after getting the blasted collar off her neck, she would have access, surprise, and, possibly, a boost in her already formidable power. Surprise and distraction had worked for Comus in the human realm — his planning and speed at getting the collar back on Nin while she was alone and thinking of other things was what allowed him to take her this second time. She doubted, in a fair fight, he was her equal in power, but she was not fully certain in this, so she would not fight fair.

Nin knew she needed to think like Comus in some ways, use every advantage she could wrench from him. He was a formidable opponent, and she recognized this. However, she believed she was not a Fae to trifle. She had also used her decade away wisely in case she faced him again. She honed her own internal understanding of her magic, learning to block the outside world through both Fae and human forms of meditation, so if she ever confronted Comus, she would be as prepared as possible for the fight.

A soft sadness filled her, but she willed it away. Sabrina would occasionally meditate with her or join her in yoga. It was often not productive but always enjoyable. Sabrina liked to laugh and joke and she rarely held still. Always full of energy and action in both her body and mind. With a small shake of her head, Nin acknowledged she missed her friend. It would be disastrous if Sabrina were here now, in Comus' Court, but that did not stop the ache of loss or the wish for comfort from a kind woman she loved after the terrible events she was forced to watch. She felt the same way about her family as a captive to Comus, then in hiding in the human realm. It was a familiar yet deep well of longing and loss, persistent even in its frequency. All Nin could do was give herself the space, however briefly, to feel it. A stream close to her cottage in Wilde came to mind, a steady trickle she lay beside in her imagination, placing leaf after leaf in the water to represent thoughts and feelings as they occurred to her. Recognizing the emotion and idea was the best practice. Nin then let it float away, a single point in a stream of complex thoughts and feelings she attempted to let pass by to both consider and clear her head.

She used these practices to center herself, move with purpose through her mind, and pull up memories she had of her original escape. They were hard to pull apart and put back together in a logical order. Part of that was the intense emotion that went with these memories. Nin knew emotions were both real and necessary. Some like to believe logic and emotions are divorced, or should be. That logic is better, more objective, and therefore more true in some scientific sense. Nin knew that was a bit of foolish thinking. Emotions drive both Fae and humans. It is impossible to disconnect logic from emotions — in a balanced, fair, and thoughtful mind they work together. The trick is to understand the origins of both, to be able to work through them, not deny one side. Denial of emotions is just bias masked as objectivity.

At the same time, logical formulation, inductive and deductive reasoning, work within each individual's own value system and knowledge base, meaning what people think of as logic can never actually be objective. We all learn and grow and think in context — that context often mandates how and why we think in certain ways. Logical thinking is never free from bias or created within some untouched vacuum, but a person can work to recognize how bias comes through in their thinking, how it affects their thinking, so they can be more objective. The myth of pure logical objectivity and the devaluing of emotion is a tool used in both realms to create hierarchy and assign a higher value to certain groups of people for purely subjective, and often nefarious, ends. More often than not, that myth was employed against women, Fae or human.

She had to use all this to help her address her very real, very pressing concerns of the moment. Nin would not forget those emotions she felt when she escaped. They had a hand in what happened. Those emotions were strong, and they colored everything in her memories. She had to be able to work through those emotions now and think about what they meant, how they helped and hurt, and how they could be useful in the future. At that time, fear was the driving force. It meant she felt as if she operated on impulse, but that wasn't necessarily true. Her fear, for herself and others, drove her to think quickly based on her previous knowledge. It meant split-second decisions were made, but those decisions were not necessarily illogical because they happened quickly or were based in a driving fear. Nin remembered she had been testing herself in the month or so before she escaped. She noticed the collar weakening, felt her magic begin to swell inside of her rather than dissipating through disuse week by week.

Nin knew magic was like any form of energy in the universe; it never disappeared, it just dispersed into something else. The genius of the collar (and Nin did have to admit Comus was a genius for developing such a diabolical and effective device) was that it trapped the energy of magic inside an individual until it leaked out in non-threatening forms. It leached from the body in other ways that the collared could not harness or control. Nin had seen this happen. Her cage, when she had one, had to be replaced periodically because the waves of invisible magic warped and changed it over time, infusing it with an unwieldy power that such an object should never hold. It was the same for anything Nin had around her often: it had to be changed or replaced because the magic that leaked from her skin contaminated it in some way. Or, it just made it a magical object that could be effectively wielded against her captor if she was able to use it enough, learn how it functioned in a real way.

For years, with that collar around her neck, Nin would feel her magic slowly drained away from her. It might build a little, but for the most part the collar kept her from using what was inside and kept those levels fairly low through some type of leaching effect that dispersed her magic outside herself.

In the weeks before her escape, she noticed that changed. The thing Nin had not understood was if it was she or the collar that changed, and that was important. If it had been a collar malfunction, without more knowledge and time, she had little hope of overcoming that powerfully magical object quickly. However, she could feel her power building inside her now, a soft murmur that in a few days would become a roar for release. That was good. It was about her last time and she had overcome the collar. It could now be intentionally done.

She had gone to great lengths to hone her power while hiding in the human realm, to know her magic in more thoughtful and intimate ways, so she was confident she was up to the task. However, she had no knowledge of Comus' plan. Like most villains in human movies, he was prone to bragging, revealing the ingenuity of his plan at the end so it could be appreciated. He liked appreciation in all forms like any good narcissist. When would he tell her? Not too soon, because sadly he was as cunning as he was egotistical. He was also sadistic in many ways, savoring psychological and physical pain in others in equal measure. She couldn't fully trust what he said because he could be playing her mind or using actual facts to hurt her. It was a tossup.

No, she had no real way of knowing Comus' immediate plans or trusting anything she overheard in the Palace because he was no longer lax in her presence as he was so long ago. His slip, allowing her to know what he planned before he could execute that plan, was something he would learn from and not repeat. He would be mindful and fully alert, especially now that he had apparently acquired everything necessary to permanently drain her magic and take it into himself. Her only way forward was escape before that happened, and she needed to be prepared to take every opportunity presented to make that happen.

Right then, there was little she could learn, chained up and alone in that bedroom. She had to start somewhere though, do something, so she felt a bit more control. She closed her eyes and called up her power, forcing it to test and push the boundaries made by the collar. It felt odd, like trying to pull on a constricting pair of tights. The feet and legs of her magic could push and strain against the confines, but not rip or break it. Not yet at least. She concentrated for a solid thirty minutes, breaking out in a sweat as she focused on her magic, her body, and the thing that now confined her. She stopped after a time, feeling a bit ragged, and wiped the sweat from her brow. It would take time, yes, but not years. Mere days if the level of magic she felt now continued to grow and not dissipate to objects outside of her. Then she would break through the power of the collar and her magic would rain down in the Palace, right onto Comus.

Fear was the driving force of her last escape. A surge to protect, and a hint of vengeance, were what would course through Nin when she broke free this time, and all of that would be directed right at the man who now called himself a prince without ever rightfully earning that title, not the way Nin earned the title Princess. Those memories were bittersweet, but fortifying, reminding her what she had been and giving her confidence in what she now was. Tired, she thought back to her early years in this place.

CHAPTER 9

Nin kept pushing the magical restraint of the collar, letting herself rest between bouts so as not to overextend herself. She had been at it for a few hours when the bedchamber doors flew open and Comus strode in, head held straight and regal as he made his way toward her settee. She sat up straight, wanting to meet him eye-to-eye, showing no hesitancy, putting on her own regal look and adding a bit more to it, shifting her head with a bit of a tilt, turning her eyes just so, so that even though he literally looked down at her from where he stood, she gave the appearance of looking down her own nose at him. It was a look she learned early in her training with the Mae Queen, a joke between them she had never thought to use seriously. She thought she would have no reason to condescend, but here she was, doing whatever she could to get under Comus' skin. That look definitely did it. He sucked his teeth in annoyance while glaring down at her.

Of course he was intimidating to Nin. Very much so, and especially to Nin. This was a man she had loved. A man who used that love, perverted it into years of emotional and physical pain all in the name of power, and who even now was ready to bring her realm, and all the people and things and ideals she held dear, to ruin in order to be the one being at the top of a smoldering heap if it came down to that. His power was great, his ambition and ruthlessness greater, and she was at his mercy until she could once again free her magics, so she was scared. She would be a fool not to be terrified, but courage comes not from a lack of fear. Courage requires facing fear and moving forward despite it, maybe even because of it.

That was a lesson she learned from her years in the human realm, a sentiment shared by soldiers and scholars alike, and one she took in like a healing balm while there. It helped her forgive herself for her fear, see it as useful, and move past it, so now, even as she feared for herself and all she loved, she could look down at Comus with disdain and not tremble before him.

That was something Comus very much disliked. He enjoyed the terror of others, almost as if he savored fear and panic, feeding on it. It could even be that his magic required it. His power, without additions and objects and whatnot, was very much grounded in manipulation and emotion, so fear might be central to that. It pained Nin to make the comparison, but it was helpful for her to think through: Comus and Sergius were similar in their magics and what that meant for the people they eventually grew into. Their attitudes towards pleasure, their ability to charm, the use and focus of emotion in their magic. It all connected in a way.

However, there was a crucial difference. Serge, while occasionally oblivious and even sometimes selfish, was not amoral. He had limits and ethical lines he did not cross. He saw the value in things like love and family and community. Serge chased fun and pleasure often, sometimes at the expense of other things, which Nin could not say was heroic. Sometimes it was not even ethically sound behavior. Serge was a hard person to love, a Fae who could easily be dismissed as frivolous and callous from the outside. Yet, Serge would lay his life down for Nin, for Mo, for Gin, for their mother. He served the Mae Queen loyally all his life. He would not knowingly hurt another even if he was flippant and insensitive at times. He absolutely did not find pleasure in suffering and had, throughout a life filled with certain selfish impulses, managed to remain dedicated to ensuring the health and happiness of his family and his Queen.

Comus, on the other hand, appeared to have no limits and lacked the ability to perceive value in things outside of himself. He relished terror and tyranny, saw it as the natural order of his world, and worked to make the realm into his reality, everyone and everything in it be damned. He had no grounding outside himself, nothing that tethered him to a value, nothing that he loved, even if he feigned love for Nin for so long he might believe that lie himself — that he had always loved her and did still. She could not tell if he believed any of his lies or committed solely to the focused performance and maintenance of these deceptions. Neither was a good option, so Nin knew it mattered little. In the end, he was a monster, peddling lies and fear to gain as much power as possible, intentionally mangling anyone or anything in his way. Sadly, none of this was obvious when they first met.

Nin could still remember it vividly. It was seared into her head, the day she met Comus at Court, the first time he looked at her. It was so different from how any had looked at her before then, so different from the way he looked at her now. She trained with the Mae Queen for long years before she was officially presented as a courtier. Then, it was more years before she was bestowed the title of Princess of the Green. However, the title was a foregone conclusion. Once she became part of the Mae Queen's Court, all knew what her place was, what her powers meant for her future position in the realm. She was born with these powers, but her training and her survival meant she earned her position. She would be the first Princess in several centuries, the first to hold a place beside the Mae Queen and, if the worst happened, take up the throne to lead the Fae. It was a heady mix for a young adult woman coming into her own in all things. Her power, her position, her time away from family, her proximity to power made her both hesitant and arrogant. She held herself apart because of both reasons. She's had little experience with men beyond anonymous and hasty fumbling or short courtships that quickly fizzled and died.

Part of this was her attitude, she had to admit that now. Part of it was the tendency of most others to treat her differently. A big part of it was a general masculine courtier aversion to anything or anyone that might be perceived as more powerful than themselves. It was a lonely and boring life, but one she expected, one she was raised for by her mentor. It was the same for the Mae Queen, she could see that clearly. Because of this, on the first night she spotted Comus in the Throne Room, regal and proud and staring straight at her with blazing interest, it caught her off guard.

They locked eyes across the swell of Fae courtiers, and Nin's body had felt pinned in place. Her eyes roamed, however, taking in all his masculine beauty and grace as he swept across that floor, avoiding or ignoring others. She seemed to be his sole focus, the only thing he saw. When he stepped up to her, his flowing white robes pristine and a speckle of gold dust on his cheeks highlighting his facial structure and vivid eyes, her breath caught. He said nothing at first, just kept his eyes on her as he grabbed her hand without permission and brought it to his lips. The back of her hand flared with heat as he placed a lingering kiss there.

Not bothering to drop her hand, his mouth still grazed her when he muttered, "My Lady, I would have your name if you would give me such an honor."

Nin was a mess at that point. The heat of his eyes and his lips made her flushed and a bit dizzy. Him acting like he did not already know who, and what, she was, sealed the deal. She was already tired of people assuming, a clean slate with a man with no preconceived notions about her was what she desired most in a potential partner.

Her voice was barely above a whisper when she replied, "Nin of the Valleys." It was a wonder he heard her at all in the noise from the courtiers' festivities around them. That had fallen away for Nin, and Comus seemed oblivious to it all.

"Nin. Fitting. You are but pure grace and beauty, my Lady. Please, allow me to present myself. I am Comus of the Isles, and I am now, and forever shall be, at your service." He dropped her hand to give her a low bow and Nin blushed deeply at the gallantry. Even in the Fae court these over-the-top declarations did not often happen on first meeting.

She looked for her voice, locked on it through the haze of lust that felt like the budding of something more, and managed to clear her throat. "Oh, please, Comus, sir. Do rise. No need for bows."

"All men should bow to you, my Lady. I am happy to do so now, to stay bowed at your feet, if you would give me more words from your lovely lips."

She was flustered now, unsure how to proceed, too green with men but too assured in her powers to think overly much about it. "That is all very well, but do rise. I wish to speak to you face-to-face."

At that Comus slowly pulled himself up to his full height, catching and keeping her eyes once again. "As you wish, my Lady."

He stared like a man unable to move, to breathe, to blink in fear of losing what was before him if he looked away for a moment. To be the focus of that intense and beautiful stare was too much for Nin. She needed an escape but did not want to leave him. The first strains of a song she enjoyed started and she steeled herself to ask with fake confidence, "Would you dance with me sir?"

Comus smiled slyly, took her hand, and without a word, led her to the dance floor at the end of the room. He engulfed her in his arms, held her tight, and deeply inhaled her scent, seeming to savor every second of these actions, causing her body to heat and her heart to flutter.

"Ah, my Lady. You smell so sweet. Look so lovely. Tonight is a night I will forever cherish for having the chance to hold you in my arms."

If he had not been holding her tight, she may have buckled from the weakness in her knees. The dance started, he twirled her around the floor while whispering in her ear, and with every step she became more and more infatuated with him.

Years later she knew it had all been a lie. He knew exactly who and what she was that night. Gleefully recounted to others in his Court how easily the young and powerful Princess of the Green was seduced. How quickly he got into her bed and her heart. How loving she had always been. It was a sore spot for having been both a beautiful memory and a point of pain. It was proof of Comus' duplicity, her naivety, the world that was and what Fae became, all rolled into one glittering lie of a night. It stung, but the sting had soothed with time in the human realm. Now when she thought of it, she looked at the memory for what it was — proof of Comus' cold and predatory nature, his use of a young girl barely out in society for his own ends, and the strength she had to let go of those fairy tale notions of love and heal from the abuses he heaped on to her for years.

CHAPTER 10

The Nin of the past was a tool for Comus. In the
present, she knew the Nin he stared down at was a
thing he wished to conquer once again. He thought
the Princess of the Green's abilities the only match he
had to his own magic and the powerful magical
objects he wielded. He did not fully understand the
extent of her powers, or how she worked to build
them in the human realm. If he did, she would be
under, unconscious until the moment when he
drained her. His hubris, the downfall of all the old
Greeks in the human stories, did not allow him to see

the level of power she could summon was far more than he could ever fully comprehend.

The Mae Queen had told her this long ago, a warning and a nod to responsibility Nin had brushed aside in her youth. Now she knew firsthand, and that assurance in her power, even as she was not fully sure in herself, would likely save her and all of Fae. In this moment, however, there was little she could do but wait, let her power unfurl even while bound, and strike when the time was right. She only hoped she had the time to get free and the fortitude to survive Comus long enough to see him fall.

The self-styled Prince squinted down at her, anger rising at the defiance in her eyes. He was so used to deference at this point that any questioning seemed aggressive to him in general, but what Nin offered in her eyes would be downright blasphemous to him. His temper visibly simmered, he tensed, and the four guards behind him, stationed by the chamber door, started to move forward, very attuned to what their ruler was feeling in a given moment. They were anticipatory even, both of what Comus desired and how those desires fed into their own dark needs to power and pain and authority.

However, Nin was not a plaything for them to trash, as Comus had so kindly conveyed when she first returned to the Palace, so he raised a quick hand and slashed it down at his side, causing them to stop in their tracks. "Leave. Us," he gritted out, and the guards bowed and shuffled backwards, closing the door as they exited.

Nin thought that was irrational, leaving himself completely alone with her. He had done it often in the past, but knowing she escaped once should have changed that behavior. Hubris again, and a boon for Nin. Getting the collar off was one thing, access and surprise were also essential elements to the plan she was forming in her mind. If Comus treated her like he did in the past, if he did not fully learn all his lessons or completely comprehend the power she had, all the better for her and Fae.

Comus waited a beat after the guards retreated and seemed to deflate a little. He heaved his shoulders and let out a tired sigh, rubbing a hand over his face then looking at Nin with a sad grin. "It has been a trying day, has it not?" he asked, using his body to crowd Nin in, to push her over against the raised arm of the settee so he could slide in beside her. Appearing for all intents and purposes to be letting his guard down, he hung his head, forearms to his knees, then peeked over at Nin through a mop of beautifully messy golden curls. "I was too hard with you earlier. I am sorry for that. You were gone so long, and I was worried for you all that time. When I found you I reacted too harshly." He moved closer to her still, running a hand along her back, trailing strong slender fingers across her shoulders in a way that was well practiced. She had once loved him to touch her in that way. Now it made her skin crawl and her back stiff with tension. "You ran, my Lady. That ripped me apart. All I did after was because you ran from me, from my love."

Nin stared straight ahead and did not acknowledge a word Comus said. He was using a hushed tone, congenial and encouraging, and she knew exactly what he was doing. He was foolishly hoping to get them back to the honeymoon phase — an abuse concept she learned when reading about domestic violence in the human realm. It fit Comus perfectly. When he felt he had gone too far, or when he thought to get her on his side to make something he wanted easier, he coddled. He apologized. He wooed and vowed and expressed all the love and sorrow for past crimes that he could in an effort to get

Nin cooperating. He hadn't done it in a very long time, though. Captives did not need to be coddled to get what one wanted from them. Now, he thought he could go back, play on Nin's past misguided love for him. It was actually astonishing that he thought this particular psychological tactic would work on Nin, but it also revealed he still needed something from her. Something was required that could not be physically forced. There was no other explanation for this ruse.

"Get off me," Nin spat out.

"But, lovely…"

"No. Stop. Whatever this is, do not attempt it again. I know what you are, what you want, and have known this for a very long time. This is an act for a purpose. It is better you reveal that purpose."

"No more love for your Prince?"

Nin let out a raspy, mirthless laugh. It was so forceful it made Comus lean away from her a fraction, a move that showed either surprise that his play did not work or a small amount of fear of Nin or what she could do. Nin thought it was likely the first and hoped it was not the second. She wanted him to underestimate her.

"The honeymoon was over for us a long, long time ago. The love for my Prince died a thousand deaths before tonight, before I even escaped The Palace, and you were the executioner of every single one of those deaths. You revealed in killing my love. It was hard. Every physical, psychological, and emotional blow hurt. However, I am scarred over. Here I am now, so very glad you left all those marks as constant proof of what your so-called love can do."

"Well," Comus said nonchalantly, "you cannot say I did not attempt to accomplish my aims in a much more enjoyable manner." With that he pushed Nin off the settee with surprising speed.

She was not expecting a direct physical attack, but she should have been. She cursed herself in her mind as the wind got knocked from her lungs when she landed hard on the cold stone floor. She should have expected it. In Comus' Palace, one must always be ready. In the time it took you to get ready, you could be bleeding on the floor. At least Nin wasn't bleeding just yet. Comus slid on top of her like the snake he was, rubbing against her body, grinding her roughly into the floor as she struggled to regain her breath. He licked her neck and reared up, a look of disgust on his face. "Blah, you still taste of human. So sad. I wanted to play a little more tonight. I have missed the feel of you squirming beneath me."

Nin was frozen for a minute, flashes of past assaults running through her head, incapacitating her.

"I want nothing from you like this. Soon, though, you will be my docile old Nin. Even better as you will be drained and the collar will no longer be necessary. It will be you and me and all the delicious things I will do to you. You'll scream that you love me again, when we are alone and where all can hear, and the Prince and Princess will become the King and Consort. You will stand, quiet and supportive, at my side as I rule."

"Why?" Nin croaked out. It was a question that haunted her, one she pondered again and again since she was first captured by Comus. Why her? Why did he do this to her specifically, other than her position? Or was it just because she was the Princess of the Green?

Comus chuckled. Nin knew he saw a flash of pain in her eyes, something else he craved from her, but she could not help it. Answers, reasons, whys and hows ran through her head constantly. She needed Comus gone for good, she needed herself and

Fae free of him, but part of her also wanted answers for all the pain he had caused her before he was permanently removed from her life. "Why choose to take and torment me? Why not kill me and be done with it? Why all of this pain directed at me?"

"Because you are my Lady," he answered in a tone that said he thought the answer obvious. He gazed down at her with those piercing blue eyes and said with bold vehemence, "I will do what I wish with you and your power because you are mine and only mine. I love you."

"You love nothing but yourself and power!" Nin charged, screwing her courage in place and pulling on her rage to help get her through.

"That does wound, love, but no matter. I will prove all to you. It is me for you, and only me for you, just as it is me for Fae and only me for Fae, for eternity. All will be as it should be soon." He smacked a loud kiss in her cheek and quickly wiped his mouth. Jumping up from her, he strode towards the giant bed. "It is now time to sleep. Busy days ahead. You will not sleep with me tonight, of course. That human stench still clings. It must have seeped into your pores."

He disappeared from her view in the wide expanse of the bed and Nin pulled herself up to rest on the settee once again. She rolled onto her back and looked blankly at the ceiling as Comus, somewhere in the room, quickly used magic to extinguish the lanterns and plunge the room into darkness. Questions still hovered, and likely always would for Nin. However, in life, some questions were never answered. In this time and place, it was out of Nin's control. All she could do was take a deep but shaky breath and silently push her building reserve of magic against the confines of the collar while Comus drifted to sleep mere feet away.

CHAPTER II

Nin never thought she'd be able to sleep in the Palace again. Or, more aptly, she didn't even consider the idea of sleep once she had woken from her ambush in the human realm and found herself back in that place. Her body had other plans. She pushed herself, maybe a little too hard, in trying to breach the magical field of the collar. After several long attempts interspersed with a few short breaks between, Nin took what she thought would be another ten-minute respite, but, instead, drifted off to sleep. It was a deep sleep, one she was able to consciously recognize because she was quite obviously dreaming.

In that moment she was back in the safety of her cottage, snug on her couch with a quilt thrown over her legs and a hot mug of tea between her hands. All that was standard, things she could see doing in her day-to-day in the human realm, nothing that would make it seem unusual. The thing that made her realize it was a dream was the presence of the Mae Queen, who sat in Nin's glider chair, swaying gently back and forth while loudly munching her way through a sleeve of Thin Mints.

"My. These are divine," the Queen exclaimed. "I really should have gone to the human realm more often. Or, at the very least, had a Fae bring me back food on occasion."

Nin just stared for a beat before hurriedly putting her cup down and jumping up defensively from her comfy position. She looked left to right, trying to determine what this was. Was it a dream or some new trick from Comus?

As she worried and fretted, the Queen began to wave her hand at Nin. "Oh, do sit down, child. You are safe here. For now, at least. This is no trick conjured by that vile creature. You are not here in your human place, not really. Neither am I. We are just…in a space where you could find comfort."

Nin looked askance at the version of the Mae Queen before her. She sat with the same air as her Queen, wearing the Mae Queen's favorite dress. She was also barefoot. That detail made Nin relax slightly. The Maw Queen never went around barefoot, but she actually longed to do so. She was barefoot around few people, but when alone with those few, she always pulled her shoes off quickly. Nin happened to be one of those few people. One of only a handful that would actually know this about the Queen of Fae.

"This is a dream? You are not real?" Nin asked, easing back onto the couch while still remaining a little on guard.

"I am real, in a way. This is a dream. Of a sort," the Queen replied cryptically.

"And you are you, the Mae Queen?"

"As me as I can be."

At that last quip, said with a very distinct lilt and tilt of the head often used when teaching or teasing, Nin was finally, fully assured this was her Queen. She deflated a bit and tears started to gather in her eyes. "My Queen…I…well…you…" she stammered, unable to settle on a particular thing to say because there was just so much to say about what had been, what was, what could be, and how Nin and so many others missed her. She finally settled on, "Where are you? Where were you?" That last question came out a bit harsh, just shy of accusatory. So much had happened and Fae had needed its Queen. Nin had needed her mentor.

"I'm here, as you can clearly see. Where I have been is a little complicated."

"Are you dead?"

"Not in one important sense, to you at least, but nor am I alive. I am, that is enough for you to know now. I have been waiting to speak with you for some time, my child. I need not be the focus. What is occurring with you, what you may do or become, is of much more importance."

"What do you mean?"

The Queen set down the cookies and rose, regal and tall and sure in herself as she had always been. She glided with purpose, a walking embodiment of royal will and force, and eased down beside Nin. She took her hand, staring at it for a moment before coming to look directly into Nin's wet eyes. "I am so sorry, child. I knew what Comus was in many ways, but not in all ways. I should have done more to protect you from him."

"No. No. That was never your fault. You gave me warnings. Plenty of them. I was in love, or at least thought I was in love, and nothing could change my mind about him. You gave no direct orders, and even if you had, I may not have listened at that point. He had me ensnared. I made my choices and I lived with them. Owning that is part of both forgiving myself and knowing I can move forward with my life."

"So wise for someone so young. You always were, my Princess." On a sigh she turned away briefly but refocused. "What you are, what I now am, that is all that allows such talks to occur. This may be the only time. I may come again. I cannot tell for certain. I also cannot offer you many direct answers. It is not the way of things in this inbetween place."

Nin nodded, "I am no seer, but tell me what you will."

"Much lies ahead for you, for your family, for Fae. You will need courage and strength and fortitude to endure. You will also need to trust others to help along the way, as what can be is not possible through your actions alone. There are no guarantees. What I can tell you is you must practice patience. Your magic is formidable. Do not squander it now, depleting it when it is not necessary to do so, pushing it beyond its limits when you will soon need to be at full strength."

"Do you mean with the collar? Pushing at those bounds?" The Queen nodded slightly. "I cannot rest quietly, my Queen. Comus is a direct danger to Fae and to me. To not fight feels too much like giving up. I may be a Princess, and I was weak at one time, but I have never needed saving like in the tales the humans favor so much."

"Now you do. You need to be saved. You need to allow that to happen so other things can come into play, so your own magic can be saved and repurposed, not pushed past its limits. Wait and gather strength for future fights. To do this is not to give up, child. It is learning when to wait to fight another day."

"But…" Nin attempted to interject.

The Queen wagged a finger at her. "This is as it should be, Princess. Listen to your teacher, if not your Queen. You do value teachers so much. Gin. Your human, Sabrina."

"How do you know of Sabrina?" Nin asked with a hard edge to her voice. Any Fae knowing of her human friend felt like a risk. The Mae Queen was good and true and a thoughtful monarch, but like all monarchs, could be capricious. Even in the Mae Queen's Court, humans did not often linger. The Queen never discriminated against humans, but she also never outright protected them, either. It made Nin nervous, Sabrina's name on the Mae Queen's lips, even if it was in a dream state.

"So fierce, Princess," the Queen replied. "You have no need to worry, as I am only in this place, at this time. Even if that were not so, your love for her is clear. You will fight for this one, and her for you. As it should be. Both doing what you must, in your own way."

"How is Sabrina any part of this? She is in the human realm."

The Queen shrugged and was about to say more when she jerked her head slightly. It was as if she heard something in the distance, calling her. She offered a sad smile to Nin. "So much of your future, and the future of those you love, must pass as it will, to ensure Fae survives and, hopefully, thrives. I can do nothing to stop what is now set in motion. However, know this. If I could take your pain, I would, child. I loved you as if you were of my own flesh." At that she lifted a hand to gently stroke Nin's cheek. Nin closed her eyes for a second, happy at that touch, a touch she hadn't felt for long years.

Soft as a whisper along the skin, it passed, and Nin knew before she opened her eyes that the Mae Queen was gone. She let out a shaky breath, fell back into her couch cushions, and let sleep once again bring darkness down on her. When she awoke on the settee in the Royal Bedchamber, it was like mere seconds had passed, but she had no real concept of dream time or space or how it worked. All she knew was she felt honor and sadness warring inside her as tears slid down her face.

She could not actually see across the room. The Bedchamber was still shrouded in darkness as the soft snores of Comus ripped through the silence. She ignored all this, instead focusing on a place she knew was directly opposite from her — the Dressing Chamber.

* * *

She had many memories of her Queen. Some were harsh and filled with twinges of pain — learning complex magic can be physically demanding. Some included long discussions of Earth magics, what it was and how it could be properly harnessed by Nin in the future. She also remembered seeing her Queen rule while she was her student, and after when she was a member of the Court and Council. The Mae Queen was not perfect. She could be quick to anger, prone to favoritism, stubborn, and oftentimes too haughty. However, she was fair-minded, willing to learn, and above all, cared for the common good of all of Fae. She was the first on the field in any battle, the first to sacrifice when it was needed to help the realm, the first to pull back or charge ahead, all for her realm and her people. She was a good leader, and Nin had the privilege of seeing her lead. She cherished these memories, all of the lessons the Queen taught her, through both actual instruction and example.

Her most cherished memory of her Queen took place in that Dressing Room. For many years, while caged and degraded in a variety of ways, she blocked out that memory, the ache of it and what was and what would never be again too much to take at that time. Now, it roared through her mind, a bittersweet reminder when she needed it the most.

All Fae had a responsibility to their magics and to help newer generations learn and harness their magics. Most often, teachers like Gin helped hone skills in young Fae and, when they reached teenage years, they then went to mentor with a Fae they knew who had similar magics. It was an apprenticeship and independent study rolled together. Nin's schooling had been different. She was the first Fae born with Earth magic for millennia, and Earth magic was the sole province of the Mae Queen.

The Queen was the only Fae who knew the intricacies and methods of this form of magic, so the Queen was the only one who could mentor her. She was a demanding but fair teacher, just as she was a demanding but fair ruler, and Nin both respected and loved her. But the Queen, like most rulers, was a bit remote, standing just a little removed from all others. It was caused by a combination of things — the weight of rule, the need to guard oneself at all times, the feeling of being pulled in all directions at once, the need to protect yourself both physically and emotionally from those that may use you or just need you too much. Nin had felt it acutely while she was mentored by the Queen.

Being able to properly wield Earth magics made a Fae powerful, but also put them in line to rule themselves. Since before record, the rulers of Fae were women who wielded earth magics, so not only did Nin need to learn how to use her gifts, but she also needed to learn what it was to be a leader in Fae Court. It was a great deal for a young, often shy, girl to take on, a lot of expectations and responsibility weighed on her shoulders from the moment she realized she was different than other Fae she knew, before and after coming to The Palace. Having the Queen at a distance, unsure of her place within the Queen's world, made Nin nervous. Those nerves ramped up when she neared the time for her formal Court presentation at sixteen. She was taught by the Queen for nearly three years at that point, worked well with her and respected her. Loved her even, but ultimately felt unsure of her place with the Queen and the world of The Fae Court.

However, one evening about three weeks before her formal presentation at Court, a guard came to fetch her in her quarters to attend the Queen in her Dressing Room. She'd spent time in the antechamber before but had never seen beyond the lounge area. Nin was ushered through the Royal Bedchamber so quickly the bedroom itself was a bit of a blur in her memory and brought directly to the Dressing Room. There, rows and rows of royal dresses and fighting

clothes and everything in-between was pristinely
preserved and on display. The silks looked like liquid
given momentary form, gleaming with a high gloss.
The scent of leathers filled her nose. It was opulence
and abundance. Nin drank it all in, staring in awe at
the sheer amount of options before her, a bit envious,
but in a way that lacked true force or spite. At that
moment she thought it would be good to be Queen.

At the back, seated to the side of a panel of
curved mirrors, was the Queen. Standing by a
pedestal was the Queen's personal designer, a woman
renowned throughout the land for creating every
stitch of clothing the Queen wore. The Queen
beckoned Nin forward and gestured to the pedestal.
"Up," she said, and Nin followed directions, used to
taking a lead from her Queen even when she
remained unsure or unaware of what was happening.

The designer pulled and pushed her,
prodded and draped, taking a mind-boggling amount
of exceedingly exact measurements. She and the
Queen discussed colors, fabrics, styles, and Nin just
stood, still uncertain of what, if anything, she should
say in all these conversations. Finally, the designer
bowed and exited. The Queen glided towards Nin,
who still stood frozen on that pedestal. "We have

reviewed the formalities and expectations of the
Court. We have also stressed preparation and
intention in all our lessons, magical and political.
You are young, but it is time to learn that for a
woman in power in the Fae Court, what you wear —
even if it is not combat clothing — is always armor,
designed to project and protect. However, that does
not mean we cannot enjoy the luxury and security of
that armor. It is best for you, who will come to be a
leader of the courtiers and The Council in a few short
years, to have proper armaments from the start."

The Queen hesitated a moment and seemed
almost unsure. It was startling for Nin, to see her
mentor, her Queen, look at her in a moment of
vulnerability and doubt. The Queen seemed to make
her mind up and stepped closer to Nin, looking at her
with a sincere smile. "You, young lady, are all a
mentor could ask for in a student, all a Queen could
ask for in a loyal and true subject. You are smart,
kind, inquisitive, and responsible. You care for others
above yourself. You should be prepared for what is to
come, because The Fae Court is not always as kind
and considerate as you are. Before you were thrown
among that throng, I wanted to give you something to

make you happy. Enjoy this time, my child, and learn to find private joys where you can."

At that she reached up to gently stroke Nin's cheek. Nin remained rigid. It was the first time the Queen touched her with something resembling affection. It was also the first time the Queen called her child rather than by her name. Nin's heart nearly burst with love and pride in that moment and it must have shone in her eyes.

The Queen nodded at her, affection clear across her face, but she abruptly turned away, back toward a corner of the room to examine some dress hanging there. "You may now go, Nin. Your new Court attire will arrive within the week."

Nin scurried away, knowing she was dismissed, happy about so much in that moment, but also tucking away all the Queen said. It was both an experience and a lesson, a feeling and knowledge, and although she was young, Nin knew it marked a turning point in her life and her relationship with the Mae Queen.

The dresses came and they were marvelous. It was a staggering number of silks and satins and organzas mirroring the Queen's style, though made to better fit Nin's age and form. The dresses also continued to come, well into her youth and up until she was old enough to hire and pay her own seamstress and elevate another designer for having dressed the Princess of the Green. Yet, the dresses were not the issue. The brush of the cheek, the name of child, the care and love the Queen expressed for the first time in that very private moment, which was a rare occurrence to have with a ruler, was what sat in Nin's heart and mind. It grew and cemented there although it was only the first of many times the Queen did this after her Court presentation. She did not show it often, but she was affectionate with her student after that night, up until she disappeared so many years ago.

Yes, Nin missed a great deal about having the Mae Queen as ruler. She wished for her power and guidance and fierce fighting ability to stave off Comus' takeover of Fae. But she also wished for the brush of a cheek, a nickname to be heard once again, a care she felt in her heart to reignite when the Mae Queen returned. In the here and now, Nin wept, because her dream confirmed the Mae Queen was somehow completely lost to Fae, and the loss of a just and fair ruler is a blow for any realm. She also wept for what she lost personally, the woman who called her child with affection, who taught her so much, and who let her know without so many words that she was loved.

She was not without a mother, as Sabrina was, and her love and loyalty to Inanna was ferocious because she was the best of mothers. However, she lost a woman who was like a mother to her, and the tears she shed were delayed grieving for a hole she felt, but had never named, for many, many years.

CHAPTER 12

Her second day of captivity began in a fairly
uneventful manner, which did not bode well. The
Palace under Comus was not a safe place for anyone
other than Comus, so easy mornings felt like being in
the eye of a storm. Nin lay in darkness for a long
while dreading whatever was to come that day. She
also adhered to what the Mae Queen asked of her —
she no longer pushed at her bounds but allowed her
magic to preserve and well inside herself. It grated,
both because of the magical backup and the idea of
doing nothing, but she knew it was important to do
this even if she did not understand exactly why it was

important. This means she sat in the dark for long hours, waiting.

Comus was a late sleeper. When he did finally awaken, he ignored Nin, going about his normal morning business as if she were not there. In reality, he very well may have forgotten in the haze of waking because he did a double take when he passed her after exiting the bathroom. It would have been funny to Nin if it did not also mean she had snagged his attention, which she absolutely did not want.

"Sleep well, love?" he purred, grinning and stretching up, showing off the toned and golden body that hid so much malice. He scratched himself low on his stomach when he noticed that Nin stared at the sliver of taut abs peaking from beneath his silken sleep shirt. She knew he assumed her look was one of appreciation, but it was more in wonder. How could a person so beautiful be so vile? It baffled her at times, but also pointed to a solid fact that, although cliche, was true in both Fae and the human realm: do not judge a book by its cover.

He winked at her and slid closer. "Sadly, I have plans for both of us today that do not involve acting on that look. I will say I am glad to see it."

Nin did not bother correcting him, as he would take it however he wished regardless of what she told him about meaning or intention. If it was another small act or idea that made Comus less hesitant or guarded around her, made him think he had her where he wanted her, then all the better for what was to come. Although, with a sigh and a slump, she remembered she had little hand in what was to come. No more testing the collar. No more actively attempting escape.

Comus again took this physical sign in a very different direction and chuckled. "My Lady has seemed to miss at least one part of me. Fear not.

We will reunite properly very soon. We must first finish business, then it is all pleasure. This body will be yours again, and all of you will be mine." He blew a kiss her way while she stared back at him blankly and then strutted to the Dressing Room to prepare for whatever plans he alluded to just then.

She knew not what was to come, but she was now certain what he wished to do with her, on many levels, would happen soon. Either today or tomorrow likely. She itched to stretch her magic, test the limits of the collar once again. It burned and churned inside her, swelling. It wasn't demanding release yet, but that would be soon, and if it happened without intention and thoughtful control on her end, the magic would be wild and unruly, as it was at her first escape. She didn't want that, for herself or anyone who was near her.

Comus dressed and sauntered out toward Nin. He had swagger, as the humans would say. A particular roll of the hip, hitch of the step, tilt of the head, lop of the arm, that made his walk look simultaneously effortless, careless, and seductive. He had a way of staring at a person, a gaze so intense and focused that it made you feel like the only person in the room even if you were in a crowd. It had all been heady and sexy and intense when Nin was younger, but that charm wore off long ago. While she could objectively admit Comus was a beautiful package, that package was filled with vile things. She not only wanted nothing to do with this smirking man in front of her, she actively wished to harm him — for Fae and for herself. It was a simmering rage, but it was there, and Comus stopped short when he saw her reaction to him.

"Come now, my Lady. I thought this all over."

"Only you could be so arrogant, so blind to past and present, to think a little flesh would tempt me to forget everything," she snapped back.

"Oh, but sweetling, flesh can do so much. With a look, a touch, I can do so much. You are here now, fully in my power. More so than you know. Soon, completely at my mercy. Why not let this flesh give you pleasure? It would serve you well."

Nin shook her head, "You and your flesh serve no one save yourself. I want none of it. You disgust me."

Like a flash he was on her again, pushing her back against the wall, pinning her down on the settee with the hard weight of his body. His eyes were like blue stones, flawless but hard and inanimate. It was chilling. He roughly shoved his arm into her throat, the rough cord of his muscle making it difficult for her to breath. In a low growl he said, "You should remember where you are, who I am. Soon, you will not forget this. You will be mine completely and you will beg for a look or a touch." He knifed off Nin and turned away for a moment. When he rounded toward her again, his saccharine smile was in place. "Gooday, my Lady," he said, before he blew a kiss and breezed out the doors.

Nin sat on the settee alone for hours, nothing to do but think through past and present and future concerns. She knew what Comus wanted — her and her magic. She knew he at least thought he had a way to take her magic, effectively leaving her powerless and, in his mind, docile and subservient. All this, however, was for the wider aim of power, the complete and utter control of Fae and all in it. She wasn't fooled into thinking that was the end goal. Yet, it did not account for why he had not done more to Nin. The hints he gave about her taste and smell made that point and highlighted another reason why Comus needed to be stopped.

When he was a small child, humans killed his mother and father because they used their magics to abuse and capture. The more wicked stories of Circe and Bacchus were true, as were the bloody tales of their fates in the human realm. The human race did not have magic, but they did have numbers and weapons and intelligence. That could all be a match for Fae powers in particular ways. Comus was orphaned by humans, and even if he was a horrible Fae and his parents might rightfully have deserved their comeuppance, that fact was sad. However, his orphan status had either broken something in him or highlighted something that was already there in his personality. It made him a sociopath bent on power.

It also made him hate all things human as much as he craved power. The two emotions in many ways tangled together into a form of Noble Fae prejudice and supremacy. He had hidden it well for many centuries, but he became vocal about this hatred as soon as he took The Palace. He had not yet made the leap from hatred to war, but she saw it coming. If Comus took Fae, it was only a matter of time before he marched on the human realm, revealing magic to all, and attempting to wrench control and power of the entire human world for himself. It was madness for a variety of reasons logistical, theoretical, and ethical, but she could see him attempting it and killing any human who crossed his path or even acted like they could stop him. It would be a Fae and human bloodbath and Comus would not care about the mass of casualties that would fall on both sides. He would be after more power, more pain to feed his hate, more lackeys to bow before him and stroke his ego.

Nin and her love had not been enough in the past, his control of The Palace and many in Fae was not enough for him now. Whatever that was inside him, driving him, was insatiable. Nin knew this. All of Fae must be his, then all of the human realm, and when he was alone on the hot ash heap of whatever was left of the two worlds he burned, he would still be unhappy with what he had. That was the thing people like Comus never realized: power, influence, control were all fleeting and held little actual solace or comfort for anyone who actively sought them.

All of this meant Nin had to eventually have a final confrontation with Comus, to the death if need be, to keep herself, her family, Sabrina, all of Fae, even all of humanity, safe. That was a great deal in terms of expectations, so she had to keep those thoughts at bay, keep all that awful weight off of her shoulders. Step-by-step was the only way forward, which meant she needed to know whatever she could about Comus' powers and plans while in the Palace and she needed to escape Comus before he hurt her or managed to take her magic (if such a thing was even possible).

The Queen squashed her escape plans during their dream visit and she had to trust that someone would come for her in time. Best to not even dwell on that. This left knowledge. She needed to get as much information as possible, retain all she saw and heard, in the hopes it would be useful after she escaped this second captivity. She already knew a great deal about Comus as a person and his overall plans/schemes. Now she needed details. How would it unfold? When? Who was helping? How would they help? All the who, what, when, where, and how of it needed to be discovered. The why could come later, and with much thought. The data, though, needed to be collected. She would wait, watch, and listen carefully. If her time was not to be spent actively escaping, it would be spent actively collecting all the information she could.

* * *

Morning eventually bled into afternoon, but as she was trapped alone in a windowless room, Nin only guessed this because guards had brought her both a small breakfast and lunch at appropriate intervals. Both anxious and bored, Nin was pleased when two guards entered the room and walked toward her. Instead of trays, they carried heavy shackles, so Nin knew she was about to be escorted somewhere. One of the guards gestured and grunted at her, indicating she should rise. She recognized him immediately. He was the guard who killed the Wisp. Even though she needed to leave the room to learn more about current Comus plans, she did not want to go easily for this Fae. She employed that same look she gave Comus, the regal stare learned from the Queen, and sniffed at the bulky man before her.

"And why, exactly, am I being forced around in chains? I think I would rather stay here today than be bound and dragged."

The Wisp killer grunted at her, gave a leering smile and reached forward lightning quick, grabbing her by her hair and wrenching her up off the settee by her roots. She winced but managed not to cry out as she stretched up on her tiptoes to alleviate some of the pressure. The tall man nearly dangled her in front of his face. "Comus has commanded you attend his Council meeting, so you shall attend. Princess." He added her title on a sneer and released her to fall hard on the floor.

Her thud upon landing did not quite drown out the snicker from the other guard in the room. That man, a bit shorter and less muscular but just as hateful in the eyes, bent down to slap the cuffs on her hands and feet quickly. He closed them tight around her, looking her right in the eye as he did so, practically daring her to say something. Or maybe just hoping to see the pain in her eyes there. She gave him neither, just a dispassionate look as he completed his task. It was smaller in scale, they had less reach, but these men obviously liked pain and power as much as Comus. He was smart to surround himself with such guards in this Palace, but it would do him a disservice later. Those who followed for the wrong reasons abandoned on a whim.

When the first guard stooped to grab her arm in an effort to pull her off the floor, she scooted out of the way and gracefully rose on her own, keeping her head high and her back straight as she stared down the two men who not only did what they were told, but obviously found some measure of pleasure in hurting Nin. She ran a hand over her hair and down her soiled jeans and shirt, acting as if she was making herself presentable. She then turned sharply and started out the door on her own, leaving the guards with no choice but to follow behind her swift pace.

"I know the way to the Council Chamber. I have been a member of Fae Court for decades. I was a leader in The Council of the Mae Queen. I do not need to be led there like a lost lamb." The men allowed her this, whether from shock or indifference, but it gave her a measure of solace to make her way around the Palace rather than being carted like a prisoner. These men, Comus, this Court — all of them favored and feared power. Nin used it now and filed all this away as more data, more people who would need to be dealt with, more information that would require action when she took down the supposed Prince.

CHAPTER 13

She breezed into the Council Chamber, gliding past the guards as if she attended these meetings regularly and it was of no real concern to her. Thanks to the Mae Queen, she learned long ago that projection and confidence were invaluable in Fae politics. She used that lesson now even as a captive. Many at the Palace remembered her previous life in Comus' Palace, the humiliations she endured, her pain and suffering. She wanted to replace those ideas with a different image. She would show them she was an assured and confident Fae who escaped and thrived in the human realm. It made others a little less ready to challenge her when she lacked the magical ability to protect herself. It also annoyed Comus, so there were many benefits.

Nin was not prepared for memories to hit her so hard in this place, but it seemed her second captivity was marked by a series of remembrances and reactions. The Council Chamber was a large room a short walk from the Throne Room. When the Mae Queen ruled, a large round wooden table was the focal point for Council meetings. It was where all sat to discuss whatever matters were pressing for the Queen, Court, and all of Fae. The table was always a thing of beauty, intricately carved with moments of Fae history, highlighting famous deeds and achievements of Noble and Lesser Fae. However, there was not just one table. There were twelve old tables in all. The table occupied by the Council changed every few decades. However, when one was in use, the rest were not hidden away. They remained on display in the Council Chamber, hung securely on the high walls so that any Fae in the Palace could view them at their leisure and contemplate Fae history and achievements. All of those tables now sat propped against a far wall, dark drapes covering each as if to hide or ignore the past. Comus had done this soon after his coup.

He'd also restructured the rest of the room like a miniature version of the Throne Room. He sat in the center in an elevated wooden chair. It was a smaller version of the Mae Queen's throne and had its own carvings. These depicted the life of Comus, what he saw as his great deeds, told from his perspective. There was a romanticized version of his parents, his upbringing as an orphan, his knowledge and power in magic, his leadership as a courtier, his overthrow of the Mae Queen's Council and taking of the Palace, and his rule. It was all pretty lies hiding the blood spilled and pain caused over centuries. It was not history, but mythmaking in its worst form.

Because there was no longer a table in the room, The Council members, lackeys all, were splayed out around him, two to each side. Their chairs were turned toward Comus and tilted inward so they could not easily talk with each other, or others present in the room, but could easily grovel directly to their so-called Prince. Comus had taken the past away, quite literally, and left no room for discussion, rebuke, or questioning. There were no nods toward egalitarianism in this space. Comus had covered that up, believing he and his power deserved all attention, concern, and deference.

Everything disgusted Nin in this Palace, but what Comus had done to the Council Chamber rankled a great deal at the moment. The anger and disdain were not comfortable feelings, but they did help, providing more fire behind her projected assurance. She pulled herself up even straighter, tightened her outward armor, now more prepared for whatever battle of wills would come.

Comus looked delighted to see Nin strolling into the room rather than being dragged by the guards. He even felt his lofty chair to greet her. Nin met him with a cold stare. "Love, you have come to join us. So very good of you to do so. I know the affairs of state are tedious and may be too much for you right now, but as some of this concerns you in direct and indirect ways, I felt it best you be here." He grabbed her hand and kissed it, lingering and tightening his grip when she tried to pull away. Nin flashed a harsh smile when she pulled free and dropped into a mocking curtsy.

"As I had little choice in the matter, I can take little credit for attending," she stated as sweetly as she could. Comus ignored that verbal jab and turned back to the Fae gathered. He pulled her closer, pushing her against his side to make her face the Council. She squirmed at his touch, but the bite of pain from his fingers digging into her upper arm meant she did not struggle violently. It was not the time or place for a physical altercation. She was outnumbered, without her magics, and Comus would happily hurt her if she gave him a direct challenge. She stiffened, made her body hard to control, forced Comus to exert strength to get her where he wanted her. It was not direct confrontation, but it was resistance.

"Nin, you have been gone long, but not too long that you will not recognize the dignitaries in this room. They are all valued Council Members who offer advice when I am in need."

This was not true, of course. The Council in Comus' Palace was a farce. It did no actual governing, offered no advice outside of what Comus wished to hear. He would never allow his rule to be questioned in any way, and he saw any type of differing opinion or idea as a challenge. He trusted only his own ideas and his own council. The men here — and they were all Fae men — nodded at the false words of their Prince, pretending their voices mattered. Comus was right in one way, however. Nin knew all of these men. They had groveled for power or proximity to power when the Queen ruled and quickly changed sides when Comus took the Palace. They were fickle Fae pretending to be leaders, unconcerned with anything or anyone outside of themselves. They were the perfect match for Comus needs.

"Come, my Lady. We must begin."

As in the Throne Room, Nin took a seat on the floor beside the chair of Comus. She was not offered her own chair or position and no one batted an eye at this arrangement, but she was also not chained. This was a small mercy, but one much appreciated. The meeting started with Comus droning on about his successful military mission to the human realm, his rescue of Nin, and his return here. The rest of the council gave appropriate praise where it was required and commended Comus on his bravery and military prowess. One chirped, "A successful mission to the human realm bodes well for future plans, Prince. It was clever of you to plan such an exposition and prove the power you could wield there."

Comus nodded and preened in turn, taking in the false praise as his due. Next, Comus asserted taxes would be levied once again to pay for Palace needs — which for Comus meant more luxury and parties and over-abundance. All agreed, saying more funding was a dire need that must be met for the good of Fae when all present knew it helped only those in the Palace. Fae had always paid taxes and tithes to ensure basic services the Palace provided for all. Comus' Palace did not do this, only taking and never giving. It was not need, but greed. And it was not only taxes.

The same cycle continued for at least thirty minutes. Comus would present a horrible idea sure to do harm to the realm in one way or another and the Council would not only acquiesce, but praise him for his sound judgment and leadership. It would be laughable if Nin was not so disgusted by what was happening to the Fae based on these council chamber discussions.

Nin, however, perked up when a council member brought up preparations for some type of chair and Comus nearly jumped from his seat. The so-called Prince shook with rage. "That is not to be discussed now," he hissed.

The man who spoke of it paled and trembled, and the guards closed in ranks, flanking the Councilman in a way that boded ill. It was obviously information Nin would later find useful, so she tucked it away to ponder later. She did not have time to consider it now, as Comus was now intent on offering an example.

Comus crooked his fingers and the guards seized the Councilman, who slumped forward and offered no resistance. The guards posted him in front of Comus, who looked thoughtful for a moment. "That mouth of yours," he stated, "seems to need something to occupy it so it does not give voice to things you can barely comprehend. You now have a choice."

Comus reached hands into his robe. One pulled out his wand. The other offered his cup. It was his mother's chalice, the very same Circe used to bend humans to her will long ago. Her son found it after her death, hidden away somewhere deep and dark. He hid its discovery until he took over the Palace, offering the brightly shining golden goblet to Fae he wished to gain a more permanent control over or punish for some reason or another once he had his Court in place. It did not come out often but was used enough for everyone in the room to know what its appearance meant. The Councilman, now faced with these objects of power, trembled at what was extended his way.

"You may choose my wand, and the quick compulsion spell that will accompany it. Your death will be swift with this choice. Or, you may choose the chalice, and give yourself over to me completely. You will be changed. I will use a bit of my mother's old draught, as you have greatly displeased me. But, you will likely live to serve me long after you drink it down."

The Councilman hesitated, not answering until he was roughly elbowed by a guard. Then, he nodded toward the cup, choosing subservience. This did not surprise Nin. Any Councilman working for Comus would surely choose that path — they already had without the imminent threat of death hanging over their heads.

Comus leaned deep, pressed the golden lip of the chalice to the trembling lips of the Councilman, and tipped it forward. The Fae swallowed deep, taking what was given even as he sweated with fear. A gasp passed his lips, Comus pulled back, and the Councilman's hands reached to claw at the sides of his throat. Small lines formed there. Three slashes split each side, quivering and pulsing. His skin slid away, not falling or rotting, but inverting, turning inside out. One second it was flesh, the next it was iridescent scales. Eyes wide, Nin finally realized what he was becoming: a fish.

Years ago, during her first captivity, Comus confessed that the brilliance of his mother's potion was not that it turned human men to pigs, but that it brought out something in an individual based on who they were or how they behaved, choosing an animal they connected with on some level in the moment. For whatever reason, this Councilman was like a fish, so a fish he became. The problem was, he sprouted gills and appeared to no longer be able to breathe air.

The guards, partially in disgust and partially because of the writhing of the Fae, dropped their hold on his body. He flopped on the ground, fishy Fae eyes wide, searching for aid from those in the room. Comus was fascinated by this turn of events, staring down at the fish-Fae with open wonder and a hint of glee. Every other Fae in the room held an impartial mask in place. The other Council Members likely feared similar fates. Nin wanted to give no hint of alarm away, even as she screamed internally at the horror in front of her.

The flopping slowed to a twitch, and often long minutes stopped all together. He had suffocated. Comus gave a wry smile and quipped "A very rare turn of events, indeed. A treat, even. Some men are more fish than mammals, it would appear. A poor choice for him, a fascinating study for those blessed to watch the power and will of my magics."

After the Councilman's body was whisked away, Comus turned to her with a saccharine smile. She would obviously need to give what came next her full attention. "Finally, we must discuss what is to be done about The Falls."

Nin paled at this, though she schooled her face and remained as stoic as possible. She knew little of The Falls beyond the fact it was where her family hid and the rebellion plotted. It was where she would likely go when she escaped/was rescued, but she had never been there. She was a captive to Comus when it was created and fled to the human realm when she escaped.

Baron of the Mine, an old and withered Fae who had drooled after Nin at one point before she began dating Comus, looked at her with a smug expression as he began to tell his Prince what was known of this place. "Dear, sire. It has been discovered there are several layers of protection in the area itself that will take time to review. The good news is that we now know where it is located — the jungle region of Qat."

"Of this we are certain?"

"Yes, sire. Our infiltrator can say little and cannot directly lead us there, but we have discovered ways to extract certain information from them. It is a long, painful process, but they are eager to serve you, Prince Comus."

"Very well. I would wish to know more, Baron."

"Yes, sire. Certainly, sire. We will have all their secrets in time."

"Time continues to slip by and we have little to show for it, Baron. They are a terrorist plague on our Fae," Comus boomed, "and must be stopped. This brings us to my lovely Nin, who was taken and held by her family in the human realm. The same family that now rules The Falls with an iron fist. They are tyrants and must be stopped, but they are also dear to my Lady. What would you have me do, Princess?"

Nin knew this was a trap. He would offer no mercy to her family if they were found. He loathed Mo and Serge because they defied him and acted against him. He hated her mother and Gin because he saw their power as a threat. All would meet bloody ends by his hands if captured, no matter what she pleaded. He would execute them in the name of justice, railing about tyranny and treason while he stripped Fae with these very tools every single day.

She blinked up at him, rusty at the political game but sadly still knowledgeable enough about Comus to read what she should say. However, she just couldn't give him what he really required: the pleading he expected or the full acquiescence he wanted.

"Why not duel them all one by one, my Prince? Surely your power and might would be too formidable for them to overcome. Then all of Fae would be able to see what you are worth."

Comus' eyes narrowed and the Council members held their collective breaths.

"Perhaps, my Princess, if they are captured alive. I do not see that. They will fight and likely die in battle. They know, if they are taken, they will have to face me. They fear this. It is why they hide and plan covert attacks, never directly attacking me or this Palace. They know in their hearts they cannot win against me. They will die at the hands of my mighty military because they are cowards who will not face me directly."

"Will you not ride to battle against them yourself, meet them face-to-face on the battlefield with honor, as the Mae Queen did before you?" That was a touch too far and Nin knew it when his slap cracked hard across her cheek.

"Do not test me, Nin. I do what is best for Fae, in all things, not what will please my own vanity and bloodlust, as the Mae Queen once did. I am now decided. All associated with The Falls are to be killed on sight by any loyal and true Fae. If I find someone has not confronted them, not fought them as they should, those Fae will be executed. As of now it is illegal to see a rebellious Fae and do nothing. I will have my realm fight for me and for what is right. Meeting adjourned."

The Council members mumbled and bowed and praised as they exited, and soon enough only Comus and Nin were left in the room. He sat, chin in hand, looking down at Nin quizzically. "Why must you do such things, my Lady? Why must you try me so and make me cause you pain?" He pulled himself up, brushed out his robes, and stepped off the chair, leaving Nin behind. Over his shoulder he called for the guards to take her back to the bedchamber. "And dear Princess," Comus paused to throw back at her with a grin, "late in the night I have such a treat to share with you. I am all anticipation for what is to come for us."

Nin's insides revolted at this promise, not wanting to guess what it meant for her as she watched Comus proudly walk out the Council Chamber doors.

CHAPTER 14

Nin had no idea what time it was. She figured it was night, given the combination of laughter and tears she heard in the halls. It likely led all the way to the Throne Room, which was the central location for decadence here. In the Palace of Comus, night had little to do with sleep. Nin was no prude, few in Fae were, and she enjoyed parties and feasts and balls as well as any Fae did. They were known for it in the human realm after all, and that was for good reason. For the Fae, wine and spirits often flowed, dancing into the night was nothing out of the ordinary, and laughter rang out loud and often in their realm.

However, it was all within their own particular idea of moderation. This was not a human standard of withholding or denying, but a definite understanding that a good party, as fun as they were, had times, places, and limits. Those limits were exploded in the Court of Comus. There was taking without giving or inclusion, torment masked as games, and consent in all ways was too often ignored. Nin had spent years as both a witness and, if Comus was in a certain mood to make an example of her, a victim to parties such as this and wanted no part in it now.

The current revelries were loud, which is what woke her. She must have dozed, but she did not remember falling asleep after being escorted back to the Royal Bedchamber. And she could have sworn she was left locked to the settee as she had been before. Now she was in the seating area of the antechamber in front of a large, crackling fire. She was still chained, but not to a wall. Her hands and feet were bound and she was curled up on the plush carpet. Comus must have moved her and used magic to do so. There was no way she would have naturally slept through such maneuverings, not in this place.

Comus himself sat, smiling, staring down at her from his perch in one of the large armchairs.

"Good!" he practically shouted, clapping his hands together in delight. "You are finally awake. I thought my spell too much for you when it took so long for you to rise from slumber, but it is not so. I am so happy for it. Big things are happening now, and we must have you with us for them. All must be in its place, including you, my Lady."

Nin sneered in return, sitting upright and taking a moment to wipe the sleep away from her eyes and face as best she could with bound hands. She felt and heard the stomp of guards close at her back and knew they closed in to control her should her movements appear too threatening, despite the collar.

She did take a moment to look around her, to position the others in the room for future reference, and that was when she noticed a chair. Calling it a chair seemed too simple a description. It was huge, dwarfing all the other seating in the room by a few feet, looking like a random dining room chair placed in the middle of a nursery school playroom. It was also clearly metal, and based on the waves that pulsed off of it, she suspected the metal was pure iron. Steel was used sparingly, to detain and drain, and there were iron bars in The Hold, but pure iron in this quantity was practically unheard of in Fae. It must have taken a great deal of effort to construct and move that thing into the Palace.

The human realm told tales of the Fae's hatred for iron. Hatred was not exactly true, but it was not far off. Iron was the one metal from the human realm that did not occur naturally in Fae. The Fae themselves had no iron in their blood, as humans did, and no iron ore was within the ground of Fae. The human realm was the sole province of iron. As such, most Fae were slightly allergic to it, almost like lactose intolerance in human regions where cows are not used for their milk. Some reacted more violently than others. Reactions ranged from a slight itch from prolonged exposure to violent illness if in the presence of iron for mere moments.

Because she was an earth wielder, her magics tied tightly to the earth of Fae, she should be weakened greatly by iron. It was known to be the Mae Queen's one weakness. However, Nin always exhibited a fairly mild reaction to it. Even that had lessened with exposure with those long years hiding in the human realm. Now, she was fine. She could feel it was iron, as all Fae could sense its wrongness to them and their natural realm, but it did not chafe. At least, it did not chafe her. Right then she noticed a guard swaying, trying to keep his feet as his face turned green. He was about to go down — not a solid choice of guards with this iron in the room.

She also noticed the physical space reacting to the object. The room itself shimmered and felt a bit fuzzy. It was hard to pinpoint exactly what was wrong, but the Fae Palace was inextricably connected to the land, the earth of Fae, much like Nin herself was. Anything not of that earth was bothersome to this place. The Palace itself wanted to reject this intrusion. This was why it had to have taken much time and magic to get this chair here, in the heart of the Palace. The walls, the floors, the physical space itself would have ways of trying to fight off iron. None of this meant good things for her, obviously.

"Yes, yes. I see you've noticed my newest contraption. I have been eager to use it for so very long, but it took much planning. First, getting it constructed. Then all the magic I had to pour into it over time to give it intention and function. Then getting it here! That alone was quite the ordeal. If it was for any other purpose, I would have let go of my plan, but as this is so important to our future, my Lady, I had to persevere." He stopped by the chair, lifted a hand to it, and patted it quickly. He winced slightly when he did, clearly affected by the touch of iron in his own way, swiftly turning his head away and wiping his hands as if they had been sullied.

That gave Nin a smile.

Comus narrowed his eyes on her. "Smile as you wish, sweetling. This is a special gift for you. It is my own magical creation, culled from ancient accounts that swore it could not be fully constructed, much less utilized to its ultimate potential. We shall show them, yes? We will show all what my magic can achieve, even before I acquire yours. For this, my dear Lady, is the chair designed to strip you of your magic."

"No," she whispered, backing away from the thing in horror. Comus smiled widely as she scurried away.

"Oh, yes. I will not bore you with the specifics, but for years I studied to perfect the theoretical understanding of such an object so it could be forged. It took many Fae many years to make even after my knowledge made this possible. Scores died in the process, but those lives were sacrificed in glorious service. Now it is here, in position, drawing on tension from The Palace and all the residual magic inside. From my understanding, it will only be useful once. We shall test that at a later date, but it is no matter. Even if it is so, in your case, once is enough."

"I don't understand how such a thing can even be brought into existence in Fae. It is antithetical to all magics, a thing against nature."

"Does it matter? I have no time to explain to your feeble mind the ways in which I have manipulated the very foundations of magic. Suffice to say, it will take yours, store it inside itself, and transfer it to me. You will be without your magics and I will not only be Prince, I will be King of Fae once I acquire earth magics and connect myself to our land. No one will be able to match the combined power of word and earth, and we shall rule together."

"Fool, you haven't thought this through. You attempt to toss aside nature, go against the Great Mother. There will be consequences for these actions which you will never be prepared to pay."

In a flash, Comus was there, yanking Nin up painfully by her hair as he leaned down to spit out at her through gritted teeth, "You will not be so flippant

when we are finished here. I have thought of nothing
for decades at this point." He softened then, easing
his grip and bringing his other hand to her head to pet
her condescendingly. "I had heard of you for years,
of course. Whispers of the power and force of the
young girl who would surely become the first
Princess of the Green in centuries. I knew I needed to
get to you then, but what I did not know was how you
would make me feel until I laid eyes on you. The first
time I saw you across the Throne Room, a vision in
yellow silk and organza, laughing with the Queen's
top advisers, I knew you would be mine. All of you.
And you shall, my Lady. You shall. I will have your
body, your mind, and your magics."

"You cannot touch the power of my mind or
my magics. Both will forever elude you, no matter
what occurs this night. Who and what I am is not
something a Fae like you can understand, much less
grasp and hold. I am earth, I am a direct daughter of
the Great Mother, and your magics may bind me for a
time, but they can never truly take that from me.
Mark me now — this will fail and you will die
screaming." Nin heaved this out hotly, unconcerned
with consequences. She had been so very afraid
before of the possibility of this, but now, staring it in

the face, she felt at peace. She did not know exactly what was to come, but down to her very marrow she felt Comus' plans would not work. She may die. That was still true. But she felt assured that he would fail regardless.

At that venom openly shot his way, he dropped her and turned. When he came back, he offered her his magical cup, something he had never before done. Again, resolutely, he plainly stated, "You shall be mine."

Nin turned away from the offered cup. "Never," she spit out, swiping quickly at it. Comus jerked it back in time and gave a little scolding shake of the finger her way.

"Oh, sweetling. Do not fret. This potion will not change your form. I like it far too much to allow such a thing. It will bind you to my will more firmly. That is all."

"I will never drink from that accursed thing," Nin bit out.

"I feel you will change your mind soon enough. As the chair drains your magic, your will and your power will soon follow. Then you will drink and be mine. Sadly, I am afraid our talks must end for now. The chair requires time to do its work properly and we waste valuable minutes with your meager protestations."

Comus ordered to pull her to her feet as he took several large steps back and raised his wand. The guards quickly grabbed hold, surrounding her and propping her between them. "Situate her in front of the chair."

When they were placed, Nin felt the hum of magic there, a dull pulse that wafted from the iron. It was not a pleasant sensation, and she started to struggle, doing what she could to try to break free, even if only for a moment.

"Hold her tight," Comus barked. With the flick of his wrist and a tug from the back of her neck by the guard positioned there, the collar fell free. Instantaneously, Nin rose in the air from the surge of her magic, and from her fingertips it poured over the three guards, each now cemented to the floor, which was actually no longer stone, but large living vines that curled and crushed and choked the men who had bound her.

She turned to Comus, full hate and magic crackling in her eyes, just as he shouted something and she was forced back by a stream from his wand. She'd also gotten a shot in, or her magic had without conscious thought from her. Comus now sailed across the room, hitting the far wall with a thud. He was instantly entombed in earth that burst forth from the ground where he landed, encasing him in a thick clay that could bind and suffocate. Other guards she had not seen now raced to him, pulling chunks of clay away from their leader as quickly as possible. It was a minute of tension before his frantic breaths were heard and he and his wand were fished from the earthen tomb Nin's magic had created.

Nin, however, could do nothing else, intentional or unintentional. Comus had prepared well, and his spell had knocked her directly into the iron chair. She slumped there, straps having formed the moment her body hit the seat, tying her tightly across her lap, her chest, each wrist, each ankle, holding her steady to the cold metal. She tried to usher her magic, direct the pent-up force to escape, but the chair seemed to grip that as well, wrangling it within its own magic, swallowing it down like a great whale. Her magic roared inside her in response but still swirled down, disappearing not into the air, or into herself, but into the chair. It was an odd sensation.

She felt her magic tingling, tasted and smelled it, but the moment it pulsed forward, ready to be used, it was trapped, ensnared just as she was, tied to this infernal contraption. It was even more infuriating than the collar. It did not hold in, it took — and she had a lot of magic to take. The feelings of impotence and rage that welled up in that moment were too much for her. She let out a scream, primal and loud, that reverberated through the castle, even silencing the mad partying outside the Royal Chamber for a moment. It caused the very air in the Palace to crackle, almost as if the place desperately wanted to bend to her will. But that damn chair kept the air whole and intact, and Comus, brushing clumps of clay from his hair, was only momentarily startled. Seeing her held, unable to use magic, frustrated and tearful, his anger at her attack dissipated, replaced by a leering smile.

"You will pay, in a number of ways, for the reckless and unwarranted attack that resulted in the murder of these men."

Nin looked down and indeed saw all three guards who held her were dead, crushed or choked by the vines that had reared up to save her. She should feel bad for this, and a part of her cringed at the sight before her, but it was just at seeing the physical evidence. She doubted she would feel remorse later. Those that aligned with Comus deserved little mercy, especially those who would willingly participate in an activity so against Fae nature.

"No," Nin gasped out, fighting for breath for some reason, as if she had just run a marathon. "It is you who will pay for your insolence and your affront to the very nature of Fae itself. You are tainted to the core, Comus. Not a drop of good remains in you, if there ever was any to begin with. You are a scourge on our realm, something which desecrates the land and the people in it." Her anger gave her steam, but also gave her clarity. This land was connected to her through her magic, and her magic called her to protect and save and rule. She was the one who would see this sordid stain on Fae history cleared for herself and the people she would lead. And she would lead them. She had hesitated long enough. She fully accepted what her future held because of her magic, even as she felt a nagging doubt in her personal abilities in the back of her mind and mustered the strength assurance gave her to issue what sounded very much like a royal proclamation.

"Listen carefully, Comus, and know your fate. I will be the last face you see. I will wipe you and all traces of you from my realm."

Comus was taken aback for a moment by the force of her words, the will shimmering in her eyes, but he brushed it aside quickly. "Bah. Mere moral babble, my Lady. Your tune will change soon enough, with more time in the chair. Until then, sweetling, think of me fondly." He kissed her hard on the mouth, biting down on her lip and drawing blood. She ripped her head away as fast as she could, but Comus was left smug and smiling. "I must change and go join Court festivities. We have much to celebrate."

Nin watched him walk away from her without a backwards glance and her eyes shot daggers at his back, trying to wield her magic and feeling it being siphoned as she did so. It created an odd sensation of swelling and loss that made her exhausted in short order. She eventually slumped back in the chair, leaning her head back and gazing at cracks in the ceiling she must have made at some point in her brief magical freedom, for wildflowers now grew there. A tear slid from her eye and a sigh escaped her lips. All she could do was hope her dream of the Queen was correct. She needed help and she needed it to come for her soon.

CHAPTER 15

Nin's head listed to the side. She barely had the energy to right it again, but she tried. That was all she could do for now — try. Try to keep faith in the Mae Queen of her dream. Try to believe her family would come for her soon. Try to hold on as long as she could. She was stuck in the infernal iron chair, it's power pulsing through and around her, draining her. She felt like a battery, slowly leaking energy until she ran out. She could not let that happen, though there was little she could physically do to stop it. She had to try to survive with magic intact somehow. At times it felt easier to die than to live, but much depended on her life and she had come to value it herself. She would not resign herself to this fate Comus wished to hoist on her and all of Fae in the bargain. That was not who she was — both because of her status in Fae and her very nature. She may have forgotten for a time, lost in her emotional and physical pain, which she understood as necessary even if she felt guilt over the leaving. However, her time away helped her heal and connect more clearly to her magics. Her second captivity had not broken her but spurred her to accept her connection to all of Fae and her the importance of her magics in Fae leadership. Her magics were needed to make Fae heal in certain ways, to unite Fae now that the Mae Queen revealed to her what all in Fae feared. If there was no Mae Queen to follow, the Fae would follow her magics, if not her. They would trust in her magics, as she did, and she believed, though hesitant in herself, those magics would see them all through.

She was Princess of the Green. She had earned that title partially with birth, but she had endured, kept her magic, survived all tests and trials and tribulation when other past Princesses had not. She had to soldier on, lie back and think of Fae as she gritted, tight-mouthed and stiff-lipped, and retain as much of her magics as possible to help her and her people in the future.

Comus left hours ago, but she doubted he would return any time soon. The sounds of the party spilling out from the Throne Room still hit her ears, which meant he and his Court were obviously lost in their revelry — overindulgence marked with cruelty traits that would ensure the festivities did not stop until Comus wanted them to end and he had a high threshold for these things.

She sat still in the chair, having stopped struggling long ago. She found that the more she tried to use her magic, the quicker it was drained, the flow of an open faucet circling and disappearing down the drain. If she held back, kept rein on her magics, the chair had to seep in and take, and taking magic was no easy process. Beyond the horrors of doing it to a Fae, one reason it had never been successfully attempted in Fae history was because it was damn hard. But, she must grudgingly admit, Comus had found a way. If she conserved, it would take a long while to completely drain her. She may not last that long in the chair itself, without rest or water or food, if she held out and refused such things. Then a sacrifice could save Fae after all. As it was, Nin could only sit and wait, tired but unable to actually rest, exhausted physically and emotionally with no outlet or respite.

There was still time for help to come. She knew help was out there, somewhere. That Fae and fate were somehow working in her favor. Her family, the Falls, the Fae Council — all were making plans for her rescue. The Mae Queen said as much, that she needed to trust in such things, but that was a tough thing for Nin to fully do. Trusting was hard when the man you once loved had done so much to you, this last incident only being the most heinous and destructive in a long line of heinous and destructive acts. It was not impossible, however. Her brief chats with Mo, Serge, and Gin and thoughts of Sabrina and her mother and father all buoyed her. She had experienced true loyalty, love, and care in her life, she just needed to focus on those moments rather than the betrayal of a fleeting yet false love. These joyful memories would keep her focused, restore her faith.

She heard a sharp crack, like stone splitting, and screams ripped through the Palace. This was nothing new for Comus' Court, she had heard many screams here before. She herself had screamed long and loud earlier that night. These screams seemed different somehow. They were also followed by a jostling and frantic bustle of a mass exit and entrance. First, the yelling ebbed and flowed as what sounded like hundreds of people pounded down marble hallways in a hurry. Then, the steady march of heavy steps on stone. It was the exit of the Court and the entrance of soldiers, but Nin had no way of knowing why or who or how. She only heard more splitting cracks, the clang of metal on metal, and the grunts of fighting growing louder and more frantic.

She eventually perked up at this. It was a battle, to be sure, not some cruelty perpetrated by Comus. This was the sound of soldiers fighting each other, not harming courtiers for amusements. Wisps! She heard the shrill battle cries of wisps zooming through the Palace hallways. Then she heard a voice that felt like a splash of cold water on her face — a loud bark of a command so familiar it filled her with both joy and pain, wrenching her heart with hope and love and fear for Mosi, as he was here, in the realm of Comus, so close to her and therefore in so much danger.

She tried to yell out, but her voice was reduced to a low rasp from her earlier scream. She cleared her throat, swallowed a few times, and tried once again. "Mosi. Mosi! MOSI!"

"NIN!" she heard, a frantic scream from her beautiful Serge, echoing down the hallway, calling for her. She yelled in reply and knew then the Mae Queen was right. She would be saved. Others would help her. Although she could do little to ensure this outcome, she struggled in her seat as if she could free herself at this last moment, making the rescue a bit easier on her siblings. She froze, ceasing her efforts, when the doors to the Royal Chambers flew open on a bang and Comus thundered into the room.

"Bar it. Now!" Comus ordered on a high pitch yell. He came to Nin, cup in hand, ignoring the way his skin sizzled and crackled as he leaned against the magical iron force of the chair. "Drink this." He had desperation in his eyes, and although she had spent hours in worry and pain and fear, Nin gave a beaming smile.

"I think not," she replied firmly.

He muttered to himself, "I need more time," then came back to her, trying honesty for once. "I cannot force you to drink, you must do it by choice, of your own free will, for the magic to take hold. It will help restore your power and energy."

Nin doubted the last bit. It felt tacked on to encourage her. But all his years of impossible choices for other Fae now made sense. It fed into his sick desires to make someone choose such a fate, but it was also apparently tangled up in the power of the chalice itself.

As for Nin, she just gave a shrug, happy to resist. "A pity, that. For someone so good at forcing others to do things, you now have no way to use force when you need it most. Ironic, really."

"Damn you, and your brothers. They will pay with this with their lives. If you do not drink this before they enter this room, I will slay them both in front of your eyes."

"You can surely try, Comus, but I doubt you will find it such an easy task."

"Would you risk the lives of your two brothers rather than simply drink?" Comus was incredulous.

"Yes. As I know they would want. It is for Fae, but also for them. I trust they will succeed in their battle. I hope one day they give me the same trust."

Comus, frustrated and with no recourse, backhanded Nin, cutting her lip so that the taste of blood was sharp on her tongue. Her head banged against the chair, which caused a physical and magical jarring that clamored around inside her head. No matter, that. She was about free. Comus was almost finished.

"Very well. A poor choice for us both. Nin, you will die here, with nothing to save you. If I cannot have you and your magic, no one will."

Nin braced, thinking this meant Comus was about to land a killing blow in some way, physically or magically, but he simply bent forward, a wan smile on his lips, and kissed her on cheek. "No more from me, my Lady. The chair will do its work, and if I can, I'll come back and collect the magic once it has drained you of life. Because it will. The chair will continue its process, without my magical touch, until it drains all from you. If you had chosen me, if you had sipped from my chalice, your magic would be gone but your life would remain. Now, you will have neither, and I will get back to this chair to release the drained magic and make it my own." He stroked her cheek as she turned her head sharply away from him. "I love you," he said, standing and stepping away from her.

"Yourself and power are all you know of love," she spat back, not allowing that lie to be the last words spoken between them.

Comus was about to reply when the door blew open, causing him to stumble back from the force of the blast. When the rubble stopped falling, there stood her brothers. Mo, tall and proud and sweaty with a fierce and determined look on his face, stared with hard, hate-filled eyes at Comus. Serge held one arm at an odd angle as blood trickled down, but he managed to make his signature smirk drip with disdain. Comus, cup oddly aloft as if to create a shield, was forced back yet again by a magical blow created when Mo smacked his shield and spear together with a loud clang. The chalice fell to the floor.

Before it could be scooped back up, Mosi forced it high up into the air and out of Comus' reach, muttering words under his breath, focusing all of his immense metal magics on the cup. It quivered violently then shattered into a thousand glittery shards, gold falling like confetti around the room. Comus screamed, rage pulsing from him.

"That was my mother's," he ground out at Mo.

"Now it is but pretty metal scrap," Mo replied before lifting his shield to land another magical blow. Before he could complete his attack, Comus lashed out with his wand, hitting Mo with an invisible blow that knocked him to the floor. By the time he regained his feet, Comus was on top of him, turning his wand into a long, sharp wooden sword. He raised it high to hack into her oldest brother and Nin's breath caught, but Mo easily stopped the downward blow with his spear, deflecting it to roll away and rise.

"I have longed for this," Mo declared through gritted teeth. He started raining blows down on Comus, who deflected with his sword. Each hit caused sparks of magic to fly, bathing both men in golden light as they tried to kill each other.

At the same time, Serge stepped forward to engage Comus, but the two guards who had attempted to keep the door bar had recovered enough to round on him, tackling him to the ground. Serge disappeared in a tangle of metal armor, limbs, and grunts, rolling on the floor. Nin saw him rear up and headbutt one guard as if he were a soccer hooligan, making the other Fae fall back from the pile in a daze.

Nin noticed he was the Wisp-killing guard, the same who man-handled her before The Council Meeting, and she felt petty satisfaction in watching his pain.

Serge managed to get the upper hand, pinning the second guard to the ground. He even threw out a quip like he wasn't in the heat of battle. "This is not the usual way I roll around with a man, but I do aim to please."

Nin chuckled at that but winced a little when she watched him pull the other Fae's head up, up, up, and slam it back down on the hard, cold stone with a crushing crack.

Serge was stooped to rise when the first guard regained his bearings and attacked him from behind, managing to ensnare him in a wrestling hold that put his arm at an odd angle. A hard, loud snap sounded, followed by a howl of pain and rage from Serge. He shrieked out a Faeish spell in a seething tone and the guard stopped, momentarily transfixed by the surge of word magic her brother used.

Nin was quite impressed with her brother's skill in that moment — compelling another Fae to obey on command was a rare feat. Yet, it felt too close to Comus' power, which she'd recently seen on full display. It caused a shiver to crawl up her spine as she watched Serge righted himself and pull a blade from the guard's belt as the Fae shook himself from his stupor. The guard skimmed his fist across Serge's jaw, but the blow lacked force on contact because right as he pulled back to land it, Serge pushed up with the dagger and buried it to the hilt in the Fae's stomach. They were still for a moment, as if locked in an embrace, and the guard fell from her brother, leaving blood in his wake. Serge stared for a beat at his bloodied hands and breathed deep, but shook it off quickly to go aid his brother.

Mo and Comus were still locked in battle, trading blow-for-blow, with neither gaining too much ground. But Nin saw the sweat drenching Comus' face, knew he was not used to a challenge such as this, and felt he would be the first to waver. When Serge pulled up next to his brother, bloodied dagger in hand, Comus' eyes widened a fraction. He muttered a curse and pushed a harsh breath outward as he flicked his sword back into a wand. He used a quick spell to hurl a couch at her brothers, who both dove out of the way to avoid the hit. When they came back to their feet, Comus stood, looking much less concerned than before.

He twirled his wand in front of his body and soft puffs of smoke began to encircle him. The spells Mo and Serge both sent his way did not penetrate his smoke screen. Comus began to fade where he stood, disappearing in mere moments. Right before he was completely gone, when he was just a hollow imprint, he turned to Nin, blew a kiss, and ended with one final parting shot, "May your last moments be peaceful, my Lady." Then, a candle flame flickering right before it blew, he blinked out, disappearing from all view.

CHAPTER   16

"What the hell was that smoke thing?" Serge grunted with a hint of pain in his voice.

Mo grumbled a reply, still staring at the spot where Comus stood only seconds ago.

Gin appeared at the door then, frantically searching the area. They visibly relaxed when they saw Nin, Mo, and Serge present, but then stood confused. "Where is Comus? This is the place he retreated. He should be here."

"He's up in smoke," Serge said in a bit of a hysterical giggle. Gin would not know that reference and sure enough they just stared blankly at their cousin. Nin barely got it. She made a mental note to discuss the human realm with Serge more. Seems he spent a lot more time there than anyone knew.

"Gin, he put up some form of magical shield then faded away."

"I do not understand. No one can simply disappear. Please describe it to me more fully."

"He was solid one second, hazy the next, and completely gone within mere moments. We could do nothing to stop him."

"Did you get his objects of power?"

Pointing to the shards of gold on the ground, Mo said, "His cup is there, broken by my metal magics. His wand was what allowed him to escape, so no, we did not retrieve or neutralize that object."

"As we tried to convince everyone at the Council, this was foretold in Milton."

Nin knew of Milton, only because of Sabrina rambling about him on occasion, and thought it odd Gin would bring that human writer up here and now, but it slipped from her mind quickly. There were things of more importance to consider.

Nin's heart hurt looking at this scene, so very indicative of all the people she loved who were there, all who they were on display in the rubble of a battle they bravely fought to free her. "They tried, Gin, but it could not be helped. They did everything they could," Nin said, looking at her brothers with such love.

"It's okay. We're a little banged up. So are you. But we're here and we're taking you away. Somewhere safe and far from where Comus could ever reach you again" Serge urged as he stepped closer to her.

"I am afraid that will not be immediately possible," Nin sighed.

"What is this, now?" Mo asked. "We will help you move forward in any way. Heal in any way. And fully protect you from Comus."

"I am stuck in this chair as it slowly drains my magic. Comus claimed it would also drain my life away if he himself did not free me. Whether that is true or not remains to be seen." She was not gone, yet, but Comus believed there was no way to save her, and it was a possibility, or at least more likely, given the fact that Comus was the only Fae who understood the magical workings of the chair.

"What? No. That's ridiculous," Serge scoffed, stepping up and reaching toward her with his uninjured arm. As soon as his hand grazed the metal, he hissed in pain and snapped his arm back, looking at an angry red welt that now rose on the spot where his skin contacted the metal.

"It is iron, forged and dipped in magics we know nothing of. It may take hours or days to understand its workings, but I am stuck, and unless I am somehow freed, the chair will continue to drain me."

Mo and Serge started yelling in turn, at her, at each other, at themselves. This was the part where blaming themselves occurred, but she wanted no hand in placing any amount of blame where it did not belong. Instead, she looked towards Gin, who moved to the large, blank expanse of wall next to the fireplace. The fire there still raged, and beside it, it seemed her cousin was drawing something with a piece of stone. It was, oddly, a very narrow and crudely-shaped rectangle with a circle placed about waist-height on Gin's right.

"What are you doing?" Nin asked, more to talk about something other than her tenuous situation, if only for a second.

"Drawing a door, obviously."

"That is supposed to be a door?"

Gin huffed at her. "I am no artist, but this is very clearly a door. See?" And with that, they grasped the circle, which had popped out in three dimensions in a wink. The door did as well, creaking as they pulled it open and stuck their head in the frame. "You are needed, my friend."

Nin heard running steps and, to her amazement, saw Sabrina barreling toward her. She started crying. Nin thought her friend, her sister, was left behind in the human realm. Here Sabrina was, in Fae, for some reason. When she reached Nin, she hugged her tight, her own tears wetting Nin's shirt. Sabrina may not be magical, but she was human — the iron did nothing to her. She could touch and hug and hold her friend, and Nin, who had been holding herself up for so long in this place, sagged against her in relief.

Pulling away to stare at Nin from arm's length, Sabrina wiped her eyes and said "God, it's so good to see you, lady. I've been worried sick. Fae has been so weird, and I've been re-reading Milton, which is this whole thing, and your mother has been great, but Michel was so not feeling me and was rather rude. I…I've just missed you and worried sick over you for the past few days and so much has happened that it really does feel like I haven't seen you in ages. But you look solid. Tired and done with bullshit, for sure, but solid."

"Oh, Sabrina. I do not understand how or why you are here, but I am so happy to see you."

"You better be. I crossed realms for you, girl."

Nin laughed, overjoyed to hear her friend's voice and humor. "Alas, I forgot to greet you properly, as you know I love to do. This chair seems to have also made me lose my manners. I do hope I lose no more, but…" She trailed off, feeling defeated. She knew not how to free herself, and began to doubt anyone else could figure it out in time. She was away from Comus, who had fled, but she was still trapped by him, and it was starting to creep into her mind that her ordeal was not over.

"Oh, that? No big. I take it Comus escaped with the wand and now you're stuck in this chair with no way to get out?" Dumbfounded that Sabrina knew all this, Nin nodded. "Whelp, as we thought, Gin. Milton was right and it's time for me to come into play after all." With that, she fished a vial from her jeans pockets, gave a lopsided grin, and declared

"Who's ready for the laying of hands, from a goddess no less?"

Nin had no idea what was happening, but she laughed, because this, too, was so very Sabrina, and it made her heart happy. It made her trust, just for a moment, someone had some answers that could help. If Sabrina was in Fae, using magical doorways and staring down the Fae Council-head, then Nin's salvation was not completely out of the question.

Gin broke in then, eagerly reaching Sabrina's side and exclaiming "You figured it out, the 'drops' from Milton? You have it?"

"Yes. Yes. Yes. Unlike what some might have believed," and here Sabrina quickly cut eyes to a stoic Mo, standing across the room and silently watching all of this unfold, "I do have my uses. And my strengths. As you said, Gin, I just needed some alone time to think and remember." Turning her full attention to Nin, Sabrina walked to her friend and laid a hand on her arm.

Nin had no idea what was going on, but had faith in her friend, who stooped down and offered her a rushed explanation to help ease her mind. "I know you're confused, lady. Of course you are. Long story short: there's an old play I knew from grad school that somehow lays out all that has happened here in the last few days. It's eerily accurate. Gin and I used this to help guide the battle, to come up with some protections for people, and to discover this." Here, she flashed a vial at Nin, whose dawning recognition of the object itself did not really seem to help her confusion. She'd given that to Sabrina as a gift long ago, a small bit of her Gran's dandelion wine mixed with a little magic. Sabrina now shook it gently in front of Nin's face and spoke in a voice quiet but fierce. "I know you remember this night, this wine, what you gave me. This will help. Promise."

"But how? Why?" Nin knew nothing of this magic, had to idea what a human play had to do with her situation.

"No idea, lovely. I just know it will." It was unknown to all, but confidence shined off her friend, and Nin leaned back, prepared to try whatever Sabrina had to offer.

"What is it?" Gin asked.

"It's a present Nin gave me a while back, a bit of my grandmother's wine mixed with a bit of Nin's magic. Or, at least, I now assume that."

Nin nodded, letting her know her thought process had been correct.

"I think it's symbolic, my past and present and Nin's magic mixed together, a tangible symbol of love and care for each other, for family. I cannot say why it will work, but I know it will. I believe it must. And, oddly, intention is very important in this place, with all of your magic. I think the intent behind each step in the creation of this — the wine itself, the exchange we had together, the love and remembrance Nin offered when she made the vial. It's too perfect, too serendipitous not to work."

Gin nodded, eager eyes turned to Nin. Nin dipped her head in acquiescence. She knew nothing of the play or why something of Sabrina's would be so important to her now, in Fae, but she would let her friend try to help and bring her own intention to bear as she did. Sabrina took a deep breath, cracked open the vial, and started placing droplets on her fingers and, oddly, started speaking in rhyme.

"Brightest Lady look on me,

Thus I sprinkle on thy brest

Drops that from my fountain pure,

I have kept of pretious cure,

Thrice upon thy finger tips,

Thrice upon thy rubied lip,

Next this marble venom'd seat

Smear'd with gumms of glutenous heat,

I touch with chaste palms moist and cold,

Now the spell hath lost his hold"

When Sabrina finished, hands flat against the seat of the iron chair on the outside of each of her legs, Nin heard a loud popping sound, like a tether breaking, and for a brief second she felt relief as the draining sensation from the chair ended. She grinned, but then the world spun as a tangle of pain and power surging through her body.

Sabrina, still hovering with a hand on the iron chair, was thrown across the room. Nin lifted into the air, suspended there as all the magic that had been siphoned from her body reentered it in a flash. Tendrils of that magic leached out, but after focusing her mind, Nin took hold of it all, pulling it all back in with the force of her intention and the connection she had to those special earth magics. Reigning in her powers helped push the pain away, made her mind ease from the internal panic of possibly losing her connection to magic and earth. Her magics roared for full release, but she controlled them now and slowly lowered herself to the ground.

Mo knelt by Sabrina, who looked dazed but uninjured. Gin acted as if they would reach out for

Nin, and she stopped them. "No, Gin. Please. I am trying to control this, but it is hard to do so. Give me a moment before you come near."

Knowing she had physical space and was in a room filled with people who would always respect that helped her focus more intently. She closed her eyes, gave deep, measured breaths, calmed her mind as best she could. When the pain began to dissipate, her body loosened its tension, and she knew she was fine. She had control. Nin shook out her arms and legs, testing and stretching. She was fine. Better than fine, energized and filled with power. All would be well.

As long as Sabrina was fine, that is. Nin whipped around to check on her friend, who gave her a small smile. "Are you okay?" Nin croaked out, hesitant to go near for fear of hurting her again.

"Just peachy," Sabrina replied, although the bite of sarcasm was clear. She held her hand at her back awkwardly, a sign of pain.

"I am so sorry, my friend. If I could…"

"Nope. Stop. This is not your fault. None of this is your fault. I'm fine. I'm up and moving. You're free. We're all good."

"All good?" Nin asked, still hesitant. Her very existence in Sabrina's life had obviously caused a great deal of pain and danger and anxiety.

"All good, sister." Sabrina walked over, stretching out a hand to Nin. She grabbed hold, happy to feel that touch, the love that was in such a connection. She also noticed Mo shifted slightly, as if ready to pounce if needed. He had an eye toward Sabrina, assessing the situation with her as his focus. That was interesting indeed, and something Nin would want to know more about — though getting that information from her brother or her friend would not be easy.

She shook off her pain and her doubt like an old, worn coat and addressed the room at large. "Come now. We must meet and plan. Comus has fled, but he will not stop. He must be dealt with as soon as possible." There were nods and mumbles and curses from the room, but all filed in a ragged line behind her. She led them from the room, as she would now lead them in all things. First, to assess the Palace and what the battle had accomplished. Then, the hard work of putting Fae back to rights.

EPILOGUE

Mo and his men had made quick work of rounding up all the Comus lackeys still in and around the Palace. The wisps, who were seriously badass, offered a lot of assistance on this front. Allera especially was very happy to help bind and bring forward traitors. The visual juxtaposition could be seen as funny at first — a few small flying people making a large Fae march, bound, to the Palace dungeons. The hard scowls on the faces of the wisps, and the horror stories she heard about what Comus and his Court did to certain wisps they found, made it no joke. They were bloody and fierce, filled with a righteous vengeance Sabrina understood on some level, but it still made her uncomfortable.

The Fae she knew, the people she considered her circle, awaited discussions with The Council, who had moved from their place in The Falls to the original Council Chamber to ease the transition from a Comus-ruled Fae. There were many questions left unanswered. Comus was still out there, having not yet been captured by Mo, but the anger in his face whenever Comus was mentioned and Nin's cold stare made Sabrina feel that Comus' days as a free Fae were numbered.

They didn't talk about Comus much in front of her friend unless she brought it up. Nin relayed her experiences in the Palace with Comus quickly and succinctly: how she had been captured, what the rank and rule of the Palace under Comus was like, and what Comus' plans were, or as much as she was able to discover in the few days she was captive to the madman. She was physically fine. She was also often quiet and contemplative, which was to be expected. Sabrina could not imagine the complex emotions that rolled through her friend while she battled for her life and her realm against a man who she had once loved but had turned into her most hateful abuser. It was supremely shitty, and she was giving Nin the time and space to process a little on her own while reminding her in little ways that she was there for her, ready to lend an ear whenever Nin needed to tell her the truth about what happened. She had told the facts, yes, but not how she had endured, how she had felt and still felt, and that was important to her healing as well.

The chair was the big Palace mystery now. It still stood in the antechamber of the Royal Chambers. No one was staying there at this point, so they saw no reason to try to move what was a serious and highly dangerous magical object until they learned more. Nin shared all she learned about it from Comus and described, in detail, how it felt being drained by that thing. It made Sabrina shudder and she shed more than a few tears for her friend after hearing that particular story.

Gin and a few other scholars were tasked with studying it. They asked Sabrina to come along once, to see what she observed and felt from the chair. They said all data helped, and as she was the only human available, she was also the only being who could potentially touch the chair without sustaining major damage. She told them about a shock she felt from the chair when she freed Nin, but she left out the odd phantom tingle that occasionally still pulsed from her palm up to her heart, the static that seemed to crackle under her skin, the hum in the back of her head. She was already the odd man out, a human in Fae.

She gave her brief, and admittedly withholding, recitation of events and sensations to Gin and the other researchers there, intentionally leaving out a lot. Like how she felt an odd, warm pulse from the chair whenever she prodded here and there to help the scholars test function and activity. There was no flare in the other symptoms, so she figured they would ease on their own. The less they studied that thing, the sooner it was out of commission, the better, and her adding additional mysteries wouldn't move the process along at all. She hated the contraption on her friend's behalf, but she knew scholars, whether they were Fae or human, and that chair would be around a while for study and observation if they had a choice in the matter. Even though she thought of herself as a human scholar, her curiosity extended only so far, and that thing had done serious damage to Nin. She'd be happy to make it disappear, but no one knew exactly how to do that, or if more magic was still stored in it.

Too many questions open ended, too many unknown variables to just take a blowtorch to the damn thing, although Sabrina had a very satisfying dream of doing just that. She'd also had fabulous *Flashdance* hair while sporting the helmet and wielding that blowtorch, but that was neither here nor there.

Mo and his men were trying to bring order and justice to Fae. Gin and the scholars were trying to study the chair. Nin was emotionally recuperating and quietly planning, although Sabrina wasn't yet let in on those plans. Serge, who had one broken arm and nasty burn on his hand from the chair, was physically recuperating.

Serge lounged, with only a few winces of pain, in a bed right outside Nin's private room. He was acting as a quasi-guard, although others were posted a little further down to back him up if necessary. He smirked and flirted with most anyone who walked by, but as there were not many in The Palace right now, he amused himself mostly by shouting ridiculous jokes at his sister in an effort to make her laugh. He'd gotten a few out of her at times, and they were like rays of sunshine for Sabrina. So she worked like Serge, telling stories of funny times past and offering jokes to help her friend in this way.

Sabrina thought it was really the only reason she was still here. She didn't think anyone could technically ask her to leave — she was Nin's in this realm, to do with as she pleased, even if Nin did not view it that way. The task that brought her to Fae was over, or at least she thought it was, so she was surprised and a little hesitant when she was summoned to appear before the Council. She had, of course, seen a lot of Inanna in the past few days. She was a good mother who stood by her daughter and son as they healed in different ways. She was also a mother who had missed her daughter, so she had various reasons not to leave Nin's side.

However, Sabrina had no reason to see the rest of the Council. She didn't look forward to any discussion with Michel, for sure, but she was also a little miffed at the rest of them in general. All had voted against her at their last meeting, siding with Mo and his rush to get into battle. It wasn't exactly the wrong choice, given the available information they had at the time, but Sabrina still held a bit of anger over it. She was a lady who could hold a grudge, and she wasn't ready to let go of that grudge just yet. She'd go in there with her head held high, ready to give all of them an unpleasant piece of her mind.

When she entered, she saw the whole gang assembled. Inanna was there, smiling at her. She had taken a moment to pull Sabrina aside and thank her profusely for saving her daughter. It made Sabrina a bit uncomfortable, but also felt good. Sabrina assured her she understood why Inanna did what she did. Of all the Council, she did not blame her, she had just wanted her daughter back as quickly as possible. She smiled and nodded to Inanna, again seated at the far left, and then quickly sliced her eyes over the rest of the Council, not here to put up with any of their shit. She folded her arms across her chest, leaned her weight on one foot, and put the most bored look she could muster on her face. She offered no bows and no greetings, just a look she knew could freeze hot coffee.

Michel puffed up, ready to demand the formalities, when Jane, of all people, stopped him. "Hush, you," she shooed. "No need for you to open your mouth right now. As we discussed, I will handle this."

Jane rose, clothed in her full Elizabethan garb that dripped velvet and gold brocade. She walked briskly towards Sabrina and dropped into a deep bow. "We, the Fae Council, wish to formally thank you, Sabrina of Nin, for your courageous action. Your efforts led to the freeing of our dear Princess of the Green and helped restore order to our entire realm. We had long been held at the whim of the evil Comus. Now, we will be able to slowly rebuild. Thanks, in large part, to your efforts. You study, loyalty, and perseverance are to be commended. And, it must be added, you are the first human to go to such lengths to help the Fae realm. You put yourself in grave danger, heeded your own council, trusted your instincts and knowledge, and they did not lead you astray. For all of this, you will be celebrated."

The Council and all Fae in attendance began to applaud. Inanna and Sten both beamed at her, Sten clapping so hard it sounded like he could break his own hand. Jane blushed prettily and gave a quick squeeze of Sabrina's hand before beginning a quick clap. Dre still looked bored — what else could be expected — but his eyes revealed a bit more respect when he nodded towards Sabrina while clapping slowly and lazily. Michel looked pained, but he still offered a few claps.

"As payment…"

"Oh, I don't need payment," Sabrina put in. "It's nice to hear a thank you, but I did it all for Nin. I'd do it all for Nin again. In a heartbeat. I don't need a reward for that or anything."

"See, she's fine," Michel quickly added. "No need to continue."

"Enough, Michel. You were outvoted, even before the Princess of the Green gave her full support of this measure. It will be as the rest of the Council and the Princess wishes," Dre interjected. "Jane, please do continue. No need to drag this out."

"Quite right," she quipped. "The Council has decided, and as such, will not be deterred, by anyone, even you, Sabrina." Jane then shoved a hand into a massive pleat in her gown which now appeared to also be a pocket, though that wasn't very Elizabethan, and pulled out a gold chain with a large pendant swinging from it. The pendant, round and weighty, depicted a hand holding a quill over a scroll. It was beautifully crafted, intricately rendered so that it looked like a piece of art hanging from a small chain.

Sabrina was mesmerized by it for a moment, but then Jane continued. "This, Sabrina of Nin, is the scholar's medallion, bestowed on those Fae who have proven themselves masters of magical study. Because your efforts were based in your reading and interpretation, as well as your direct actions, you earned this change in title, and all the benefits it bestows. With this medallion, you are given the rank of Fae scholar, a sign you are a true teacher and researcher in our realm."

"What?" Sabrina was a bit dumbfounded and uncertain of what this meant. She felt someone by her side and started a little when she noticed Nin there. She definitely had not been there moments before, Sabrina didn't even think she'd been in the room, but now she smiled at her. "This means you will have a new formal title. It also means you have freedom to study and learn all you wish about Fae, to come and go as you please, even without me. You are of my heart, always, but you are now no longer Sabrina of Nin."

"Kneel a bit, dear," Jane commanded. Sabrina was stunned by this honor. She had spent years in her own realm studying, researching, and teaching. Few recognized that as a real achievement, or if they did, it had fleeting meaning for them. It was different here. Study got you rank.

Sabrina, not knowing what to do other than what she was told, knelt down a little before Jane, who dropped the chain around her neck. "Rise, and be Sabrina, Scholar of the Palace, and live to enjoy all the rights such a title grants."

She felt the weight of the gold hit her chest with a thump and brought a hand up to feel the lines of that beautiful hand. She turned, a bit dazed, to Nin, smiled broadly at her friend, happiness and a hint of pride clearly on her face.

"Do I have to start wearing robes?" Sabrina asked, a note of sadness in her voice. Michel huffed, clearly offended, and stated "The robes of scholars are an honor," while Nin let out a crack of a laugh.

"No," Nin replied. "You can still wear your jeans, though a gown may be in order every now and then."

"Gowns? Like ball gowns?" Sabrina gasped. "I've never had a gown. A prom dress, yes, but that doesn't count. Can we go gown shopping around here somewhere?"

Nin chuckled, looped her arm with her
friend, and said, "I'll have my seamstress come and
we will make a day of it. You'll need your own
courtly armor soon enough."

"I'm staying?"

Nin now looked a bit hesitant. "I do not wish
to presume, but I must admit, I feel I need you with
me still. Do you mind staying in Fae for now?"

"Yes. For you, of course. I'm in no rush to
get back to my trailer."

Nin patted her on the hand in
acknowledgment and thanks. There was no need for
her to say it, Sabrina felt it. Nin let go of her arm and
moved away so others could come speak with her.
There was more clapping, more congratulations,
more well wishes. Sabrina was left both anxious
about all this attention and joyous at the true
recognition of her talent and efforts. She'd surely
learn later what "rights" she now had, but now, to
feel and smile and breathe a bit easier was enough.

After most had drifted away, Mo stepped
close to her side.

"There was much occurring in the moment,
so I was remiss in saying this then. What you did in

the Royal Chamber for Nin was extraordinary. I have never witnessed a human perform such magic."

"I don't have magic," Sabrina declared, shaking her head at the absurd thought as she absentmindedly rubbed at her hands and ignored the hum in her ears.

"You may think that, and it may be different than the overt magics we so often witness in Fae, but it was magical nonetheless. A true wonder to behold. I underestimated you, Sabrina, and for that I do apologize. As for my sister, I am forever in your debt for freeing her from that contraption."

Sabrina shrugged off Mo's words. It was all she could do. She'd never taken compliments or gratitude well.

Mo, however, was not appeased with this response. "Sabrina, hear me," he said, looking her directly in the eyes so as to completely capture her gaze. "You have done great service to Nin and all of Fae. It is right and just for you to be celebrated for that."

Sabrina, unable to fully accept these things without a lot of awkward fumbling, nodded in agreement in the hopes that it would make Mo stop. "I understand you, Mo. And thank you for those words and for acknowledging my contributions. But, really, Nin is my sister — not by blood, but by bond. I'd save her in any way I could, all day every day, if need be."

"I do believe you would … and could," Mo said, staring intently, before giving a smirk that rivaled Serge's. He grabbed her hand in a flash, twisted it around and pulled it up to his lovely, lush lips, and planted a heated kiss on the inside of her wrist. It felt raw and oddly intimate in this crowded place, so Sabrina blushed and pulled her hand away. She fidgeted, as the tingle in her skin cranked higher and the hum in her head thumped to the rapid fire beat of her heart.

She turned, looking for Nin, who watched them from across the Council Chamber with a grin on her face. Sabrina shrugged at her friend, but moved her way, gravitating to the place where she was sure she belonged.

Book II of The Comus Duology

The Queen and The Scholar

Release Date: May 20th, 2022

WANT MORE?

Enjoy *Sabrina and The Lady*? You can make sure you don't miss out on the final installment of *The Comus Duology, The Queen and The Scholar*, by pre-ordering it now for Kindle via Amazon.

Want to learn why/how Sabrina came to have a bit of Nin's magic in a bottle? Or want to read a copy of John Milton's *Comus* with an amusing and informative introduction from the author of *Sabrina and the Lady*? Join Sonya Lawson's newsletter for access to these free texts and so much more. Just visit www.sonyalawson.com and sign up today.

Acknowledgements

First off, I have to thank my husband, Ario. His love and support made all this possible. Khalii dooset daaram. Also, my family, especially Dad and Shannon, have always had my back. Love you, and thanks for the decades of unwavering support.

On a very practical note, this book wouldn't be what it is without a whole team backing me up. When I was first drafting, a number of people read very early chapters, and their feedback was exceptionally helpful. So, big thanks go to Curtis, Johnny, and Tammi for reading and offering feedback. My beta, Ellie, gave excellent advice. My team at Partners in Crimes books did everything from editing to formatting to cover design and marketing and promo things, so they are true rock stars. My ARC readers were so helpful and gave excellent last-minute feedback and pointers. The entire (huge) network at 20Booksto50K (on Facebook) and 20BooksVegas2021 Writer's Conference gave me so much practical advice about indie publishing. I would not be in print now without their knowledge, sharing, and encouragement. If you're an indie writer, or are considering self-publishing, immediately check them out.

During the writing of this book, and years ago in what feels like another life, I spent a lot of time thinking about John Milton and his Lady. I have my dissertation advisor to thank for that. Once again, Katharine, you helped me get a book done, whether you realize it or not.

Last, but definitely not least, this book is dedicated to my friends, so I need to name a few sets here. This book is all about friendship and wouldn't be what it is if I didn't have the best, most loyal ride-or-die friends out there. This is to you —HCHS crew, LWC girls, UL and Miami grad group, CBs, and my Cbus fam. I know I'm exceptionally lucky the list of amazing friends I've had in life is too long to put individual names down here. Know you have my love and my time, whenever and however you need them, always.

ABOUT THE AUTHOR

Sonya Lawson is a recovering academic. She has published several essays in academic journals and collections but is now focused on writing in a wide variety of fantasy genres. Her most recent fiction work appears in the *42 Anthology, 666: Dark Drabbles,* and *Dark Magic: Dark Fantasy Drabbles of Magic and Lore.* While she will always be a rural Kentuckian at heart, she currently lives in the Pacific Northwest. Her days are filled with writing, editing, reading, walking old forests, and watching sitcoms or horror films with her partner. You can follow her occasional ramblings on various social media platforms listed below. You can also find more information about current projects and upcoming releases at www.sonyalawson.com. You can also follow her across social media.

TikTok, Instagram, & Facebook
@sonyalawsonwrites

Twitter
@sonyawazhere